No Man's Land Series Book 1

SKY ON FIRE

A heartbreaking and unforgettable WWII novel
of love, war, and enduring hope

C. K. McADAM

For my mother ...

Chapter 1

August 1942

Wallhausen, Germany

Gisela Fahnrich opened her eyes, unsure what had awoken her. A turn of her head toward the other side of the bed confirmed she was alone, like most mornings. She sat up and swung her legs over the side of the box bed that had always reminded her of two side-by-side coffins that had been pushed together. Gisela shared the bed with her sister, Irmtraud. The impression of her sister's body was still visible on the sheet on the other side of the bed. Irmtraud was an early riser and tended to be up before Gisela was awake.

Gisela felt the pleasant, slight coolness of the wooden floor seep through her bare soles as she went to the window to draw back the curtains. The morning sunlight flooded the room, and specs of dust danced around her head. Involuntarily, she held her breath as if not to breathe them in on her way to the commode that held a wash basin and crockery pitcher that had once belonged to her grandmother.

When her grandmother had died, Gisela and her sister had moved into her bedroom and slept in the very bed where she had succumbed after a devastating hip injury sustained in a fall. Generations of her family had inhabited this bedroom, which was located on the first floor near the front door. Her grandmother was not the only one who had died in this room. With several generations under one roof and most bedrooms on the second floor, this room was typically occupied by the oldest family members in the house. Consequently, quite a few had taken their last breath in that very bed. Now, with only two generations in the house, Gisela's and Irmtraud's father had assigned them the bedroom, much to the distress of Irmtraud, who claimed she felt the spirits of their ancestors who had died here. While Gisela agreed that their new bedroom felt different from any other room in the house and she hoped that didn't mean she and her sister would die next, she felt comforted by the wooden cross and the brass-framed picture of Jesus on the wall, as well as the wooden figurine of an angel that watched over her from the nightstand.

Studying her reflection in the vanity mirror, Gisela admired her long, wheat-blond hair, which was often complimented and made her look so much like her mother, Paulina. Only, she had never known her mother, or rather, she could not remember her. Their mother had died shortly after giving birth to Irmtraud. When people spoke of Paulina, it was her beauty and elegance that were praised. When Gisela passed her mother's portrait in the hallway and stopped to study it, she could only agree.

In the framed photo that had begun to yellow at the corners, her mother wore a stately dress with a lacy high-neck collar and a brooch adorning the hollow of her neck. Her light hair was coiffed into a beautiful updo, and the slightest of smiles played around her lips. To Gisela, she looked like a lady, and she secretly liked it when people compared her to her mother. It meant she, too, was beautiful. Gisela had realized a long time ago that people often treated her differently because of her looks. She understood that their admiration and desire to please her were an advantage and, when necessary, she never hesitated to use it to get her way.

With the well-trained movements of the experienced, Gisela quickly twisted her long hair into braids and let them fall behind her shoulders. But then she shook her head. It wouldn't do. They made her look like a child. After all, she was nearly eighteen, almost an adult. She took some bobby pins, stuck them between her lips, and, ignoring the metallic taste, wrapped the braids around her head, pinning them down tightly. She dipped her fingers in the pitcher to wet them and slick back the baby hair around her hairline. Then, with a nod at the image looking back at her, she took the ewer and proceeded to pour water into the enamel wash basin to splash her face. It felt as refreshing as she had hoped. After dabbing herself dry with a small towel, she gave the image in the mirror another approving nod and proceeded to change out of her long, sleeveless white nightgown into the light blue summer dress that complemented her skin and grey eyes.

Gisela could hear the distant chugging of a train, which told her it was nearly time for breakfast. Her mama would have a slice of dark bread with butter and jam waiting in the kitchen. She would offer Gisela a cup of fresh milk, but today Gisela would decline. She wanted a cup of coffee and hoped her father wouldn't be present when she asked for it. She was almost an adult, but he still treated her like a child. And coffee had become a luxurious rarity in recent months. Her mama, who was also Gisela and Irmtraud's aunt, their mother's younger sister, would indulge her and give her the coffee if she asked for it.

His wife had only been dead a year when their father married their aunt, Maria. Unlike Gisela's beautiful and graceful mother, Paulina, her sister, Maria, had broad shoulders and rough hands formed by house and garden work. She was a kind, quiet woman who never complained. She wore her hair in a severe bun at the nape of her neck, making her misleadingly look like a strict school headmistress. To Gisela, the tight bun looked like a permanent headache. Not once had Gisela seen her wear her hair down. Their aunt, Maria, was the only mother Gisela and Irmtraud knew, and they loved her. To them, she was 'Mama.'

The door burst open, and Gisela jerked around.

"What is taking you so long?" Irmtraud rushed in, completely out of breath, her braided pigtails dancing wildly on her shoulders. Her forehead was glistening from perspiration, and a few flyaways of her dusty brown hair stuck to her temples.

"It's barely eight. Why are you running around this early in the morning?" Gisela replied, trying to keep the annoyance out of her voice. Her sister was two years younger and had not been blessed with the same beauty. Irmtraud made up for it with a zest for life that was challenging at the best of times and exhausting to live with.

"Because you need to come. Quick! A plane just crashed. In the meadows by the river. You know ... by the old oak ... where the storks feed," Irmtraud said between ragged breaths. Her hazel eyes were wide with excitement. Gisela breathed out slowly as if it would help calm her sister down. She knew Irmtraud could get excited easily, over lesser things than a crashed aeroplane.

"Come on," Irmtraud started to pull her along. Gisela gave in and let her. She now realized what had awoken her earlier, a very loud but distant thud, like a great oak felled in a quiet forest. These kinds of sounds were all too familiar now. After all, Germany was at war. It had started almost three years ago, and while they hadn't seen any fighting, the racket of passing columns of tanks, planes overhead, and battalions of marching soldiers had become a weekly occurrence.

Their village of Wallhausen was located along both the main railroad tracks and the autobahn that Hitler's Reich Labor Service units had built to move his armies. The government work service had been created to reduce unemployment and instill a sense of national duty among young men who served in the organization. Gisela knew all about it because she had overheard her oldest brother, Heinrich, speak with their father often and proudly of the honor of having been enlisted. She had also observed that her father usually only responded to her brother's enthusiasm with grunts. While the talk of war and the cacophony and spectacle of the military campaigns had terrified her in the beginning, Gisela had gotten used to it all now, except for the fact that she missed her older brothers. All three had gone off to either fight in Hitler's war or serve the Führer in another capacity. She hadn't seen them in months. All the young men in Wallhausen had been drafted.

Gisela's brothers remembered their dead mother well. When Gisela was younger, she would often pester them with questions about Paulina. Heinrich, who had enthusiastically joined the Wehrmacht after his Reich Labor Service and was named after their father, was stationed in Italy now. That's all she had been told. Gisela didn't know her oldest brother too well. Growing up, Heinrich had shown no interest in her and had usually ignored her very existence. Waldemar, her second and favorite brother, was serving in France and often sent her lovely postcards from there. He loved horses and books, and Gisela had always been drawn to him because of his gentle nature. Karl, the youngest of the three, was closest to her in age and looks, but not height. He was so tall that she barely reached his chest. Growing up, Karl had seized every opportunity to taunt her, chase her around, or pull her pigtails. Gisela knew he was stationed somewhere in Bavaria, but he never spoke of what he did there. His uniform was different from Heinrich's and Waldemar's. Karl's was black and rather menacing. When she had pointed that out to him, he had laughed before leaning in and whispering conspiratorily in her ear that it was necessary to look menacing when protecting the Führer. Karl, too, knew how to use his charms and good looks to his advantage, even more so than she did.

Irmtraud pulled Gisela down the long dark hallway, past their mother's photograph and the kitchen, and out the back door of the house. All too keenly aware of the empty pit in her stomach, Gisela wanted to protest. But she let her curiosity win out over the mouthwatering thoughts of breakfast. Outside, the brick-laid courtyard between the house and the big building that housed their family's carpentry business with its workshops, machines, and an office, lay quiet in the early morning sun. It was Saturday, so the usual screeching of table saws and hammering was absent. Gisela enjoyed being greeted with only the tweeting of a couple of sparrows that nested in the eaves of the roof. Grass was springing from the cracks between the bricks. Gisela hated that it always seemed to find a way through. She had declared it her mortal enemy years ago because she and Irmtraud had to weed it every few weeks. It was their job, and it would take days.

They headed toward the shed where her father's black Opel P4 was parked. He rarely used it. The painter's cloth draped over it was covered in fine sawdust that always found its way out of the workshop, even when all the windows and doors were closed. Her mother's old bike was leaning against the wall right next to the car. It had a tall, black, worn frame like the old iron gate of a forgotten palace. As far as Gisela knew, the bike had been around since the Great War. She pretended it was the inheritance her mother had left her and Irmtraud. They treated it as such, since they were the only ones who ever used it. Mama never touched it, and her father never moved it. Although it was too tall for them, Gisela and Irmtraud rode the bike whenever they needed to get around the village and the surrounding area. Neither of them could sit on the seat and reach the pedals, so they rode standing up. They could have adjusted the height of the saddle; their father had offered to do so on more than one occasion. But Irmtraud and Gisela had always refused, as if changing the height of the saddle would further erase the memory of their mother. Gisela wished to be as tall and erect as her mother had been. She hoped and prayed that she wasn't done growing, and that one day she would be able to sit on the saddle of her mother's and reach the pedals.

Now, Gisela gripped the handlebars with both hands while Irmtraud climbed on the rack behind her. As Gisela pushed off, the bike swayed precariously from one side to another. She felt Irmtraud's nails digging into her sides. Putting her full weight into each pedal, Gisela sent them rattling off down the road.

Irmtraud was reminding her where the plane had crashed, but Gisela knew the spot well. Everyone in their village and any of the surrounding villages knew where the ancient storm-beaten oak stood. Many legends had been told and recorded about the things that had happened at and around the old tree. Mama used to tell them at night when they were younger, and there was an old dusty book with a torn cover that held a collection of the stories. It sat on a wall shelf in their bedroom, but neither Gisela nor Irmtraud had ever touched it. They had preferred their mama's recounting of the stories. Her husky voice was like the hushed whisper of leaves stirred by a gentle night breeze. It had always put them to sleep, so they had to beg her to retell the same story the next night to find out the ending.

And now an aeroplane had crashed near the place of lore and legend, the pilot unbeknownst to him becoming legend himself. At the thought of the downed plane, Gisela pedaled harder. Passing other villagers heading in the same direction, she swerved around them, ignoring the chattering of her teeth as the thin bike tires tried to find a grip on the slick cobblestone.

Once they left the village behind and the cobblestone had turned into a dirt road, Gisela found a steady rhythm, although her legs were burning from the extra weight of Irmtraud. They crossed the bridge that spanned the river, which snaked along their village. Ahead of them lay the meadows of the wetlands bordering Wallhausen. The river flooded in early spring, and the greenest, fattest grass sprang forth for the rest of the season and the summer. Storks who wintered in Africa returned every early spring to feed in these lush floodplain meadows until fall came. This natural flood protection prevented Wallhausen from being overtaken by the waters when the river swelled precariously. For centuries, their village and the surrounding communities had relied on these fertile plains for agriculture and grazing cattle. In the midst of it all stood the old oak, a sentinel of the forgotten woods that had surrounded it in ancient times, its gnarled branches still reaching out as if to guard the secrets and legends that whispered through generations of villagers and passerby.

They smelled the smoke before they saw it. When the wreckage came into view, Gisela wondered if they would come upon the dead body of the pilot. She had seen the bodies of the dead. Against her will. Her grandmother's. Her great-aunt's. Her uncle's. Her father's only brother. Like most families in her village, hers too believed that the living needed and deserved the opportunity to bid farewell to the deceased at their home in the days after their departure.

Her grandmother had been the first corpse she had ever seen. At first glimpse, she had looked as if she was just asleep in the bed that Gisela and Irmtraud now shared. Friends and family who passed by the foot of it had obstructed Gisela's view for the most part, but when everyone had left at the end of the day and Gisela had stepped up to the bed to get a closer look, she had shrunk back in horror. Her grandmother had looked like a wax figure, her skin an odd and unfamiliar shade of grey with a sickly greenish tint. Gisela had decided that night that this was no longer her grandmother and had promised herself that it would be the first and last time she ever looked at a dead person. When her uncle and great-aunt died the next year, a few months apart, she had refused to pay her respects. But at each passing, her father and mama had ignored her protests. Together with her family, she had to stand at the foot of their beds and swallow down her discomfort and disgust.

Gisela shook her head at the grizzly images in her head and gulped air to clear them. Her gaze fastened on the column of black billowing smoke that rose from the wreckage. She stopped pedaling, and they got off the bike. Gisela pushed it on for a while in the long grass, but it was just too difficult, so she let it fall into the thick green without her eyes leaving the mangled metal ahead of them.

"Told you so," Irmtraud said as she followed Gisela to the smoldering wreckage where a few villagers had already gathered, Gisela's best friend, Gudrun, and her mother among them. It was not an everyday sight, and most of them had never seen a plane, or what was left of it, up close.

Gisela and Irmtraud pushed their way to where Gudrun was standing, ignoring the grumbled complaints.

"Isn't this a sight?" Gudrun greeted her. Grinning, she motioned to a tall man who was explaining to a wide-eyed boy in front of him that the plane was a Messerschmitt. The pilot, Gisela thought in relief, and studied his appearance before her eyes fell on the mangled mess of metal.

"Who were you fighting?" The boy asked.

A hushed silence fell over the group of onlookers that had swelled into a small crowd. Everyone leaned in to hear the pilot's story.

"All night, we were fighting off Royal Air Force bombers heading for Kassel. They have gunners on board, and one of the tommies got me in the tail and I went spinning," the pilot said in a strong Bavarian dialect Gisela remembered from a trip to the Alps her family had taken years ago. The boy was gaping, awestruck.

To Gisela, the man looked too young to be a pilot. A smudge of blood and dirt grazed his right cheek, and his flight suit bore an angry triangular rip at the shoulder. His light brown hair, which he must have slicked back before taking off, was dirty and fell into his tanned face, making his teeth look incredibly white. He was handsome. Gisela reminded herself not to stare.

As the pilot tousled the boy's hair, Gisela noticed a bloodstained cloth wrapped around his other hand, which he held pressed against his torso. Besides the injured hand, she couldn't detect any other injuries, a miracle considering the mangled plane. Then her eyes fell on a pile of billowing silk near the old oak. The pilot's parachute, some of it entangled in the ghostly, gnarled branches of the tree.

The young man looked around, scanning the villagers' faces. His eyes found Gudrun, then flicked to her. Gisela thought his gaze lingered, and she felt herself blush. Then he turned to an old man to her right. "Is there a telephone in this town?"

Irmtraud elbowed Gisela in the side.

"We have a telephone," Gisela choked out.

His eyes flew back to her. Thanks to the successful carpentry business he had inherited, their father had acquired a black bakelite rotary phone, which had been sitting ever since, mostly unused on the desk in his office. Gisela and Irmtraud had been forbidden to touch it. Once, when she had been sent to fetch her father from his office but had not found him there, Gisela had dared to lift the handset to her ear. But when she heard someone come into the workshop, she had dropped it back in an instant.

Now, the pilot came over to her, urgency in his step. "Can you take me to it?" he asked. " I need to inform my superiors."

Gisela nodded. She searched for Irmtraud's hand, grabbed it tightly, and was relieved when Irmtraud squeezed back.

"What's your name, girl?" the pilot asked.

"Gisela," she said, clearing her throat, which suddenly felt tight.

"I'm her sister, Irmtraud," Irmtraud said eagerly, cutting in front of Gisela, who couldn't help but roll her eyes.

The pilot nodded kindly at them, but then his face grew hard. "Please," he said. "Lead the way."

Gisela turned around to find herself facing Gudrun, whose mouth was curved into a smile. Gisela thought she detected a flicker of admiration in her friend's eyes. She stepped around Gudrun and her mother, the pilot and Irmtraud following her. With a murmuring hum, the crowd parted like the Red Sea to let them pass.

Gisela, Irmtraud, and the pilot stalked through the thick, long grass, lifting their legs higher than usual like storks wading through water. Gisela stopped where she had abandoned her mother's bike and picked it up. She pushed it along with Irmtraud by her side, and the pilot following. They walked in silence for a while. Gisela could feel his eyes on her back. She felt a shudder and was surprised by the butterflies in her stomach. When they had crossed the bridge, the pilot appeared by her side.

"I'm Erich. Unteroffizier Erich Schmidt," he said, not looking at her. Gisela glanced at him curiously out of the corner of her eye. His stern, businesslike demeanor disguised his youth, as did the worry that lined his face.

"How did you survive the crash?" Irmtraud asked excitedly. Gisela shot her a warning look. But as usual, Irmtraud ignored her.

"I parachuted out just in the nick of time," Erich answered with a slightly amused look on his face. "We were defending Kassel in a bombing raid. The tommies were raining hell down –"

"But that's quite a bit away. Like at least 70 kilometers, no?" Gisela interrupted him.

"Yes, you're right. I got hit in the tail by the gunners in one of the bombers I tried to down before it could reach Kassel. I wanted to make it back to the airfield ten kilometers from here. But obviously, it wasn't meant to be. I saw the meadows surrounding your village and thought I could land safely, but when I saw that humongous oak, I decided it was best to eject."

Irmtraud gaped at him, her eyes wide with a mixture of fear and excitement. Gisela thought it best to bring her back to the present. Her sister didn't need to hear any more about bombing raids and crashed planes.

"It is a bit of a walk," she said. "We live on the other side of the village. My father's telephone is in his office—" Gisela bit her lip, embarrassed that she was rambling. Irmtraud smirked. Gisela ignored her and focused on the houses of Wallhausen that appeared ahead of them.

The pilot followed her eyes. "We'll have to hurry, then," he said and picked up the pace so that Gisela and Irmtraud had to do the same. "We are expecting more bombing raids. I need to get back to the airfield as soon as possible. If there's another raid, I need to be up there."

He studied the pale blue summer sky, void of any clouds. Gisela followed his gaze but had to squint at the brightness. She looked down at her hands resting on the bike handle and found it odd that she felt a tremor, considering they had not yet reached the cobblestone-paved road.

A distant murmur like that of a river began to fill the air. But they had crossed the bridge already. The tumbling water was out of earshot. Did she imagine it? As the murmur grew into a low growl, much like the rumbling of a distant lightning storm, Erich jerked around in the direction of the noise. His face darkened as he scanned the sky. They followed his gaze, but there was nothing there. Then the whole earth began to vibrate. An unrelenting hum made Gisela's ears throb, and the bright morning sky drew dark as she watched dozens upon dozens of heavy bombers swarm like locusts, blotting out the morning sun.

"Down!" Erich yelled and yanked Gisela's arm, so she lost hold of the bike, which crashed to the ground. He pulled her and Irmtraud to a group of bushes nearby, his hands on their backs, pressing them down into the dirt.

The smell of earth and grass engulfed Gisela. She caught a glimpse of Irmtraud breathing shakily next to her, Erich's bandaged hand still resting on her back. He then scooted his body on top of them both, his weight almost crushing her. She managed to take some shallow breaths while trying to unpin her hands to cover her ears. But she was unable to muffle the roaring of the planes overhead. Just as she wondered if the bombers even had any interest in targeting them at all, gunfire erupted in the sky above.

"Get those bastards," Erich growled.

Curiosity won out. Gisela wiggled herself free enough that she could catch a glimpse of the sky.

"Stay down," Erich hissed.

Overhead, she saw a much smaller aircraft bearing the black cross-circle and attack one of the large bombers like a mother sparrow defending her nest and young against a hawk. Gunfire ripped the sky as the fighter plane attacked, then dove away only to come back from another direction. The bomber answered with its own gunfire. More fighter jets appeared, and Gisela heard Erich grunt in satisfaction. She wondered if they were safe now and could get up. Her body ached from being pressed into the ground. But just as she moved to free herself completely, gunfire sprayed the ground next to them, some of it hitting her mother's bike, then bouncing off in all directions.

One of the bullets whizzed past them with the hiss of an angry tea kettle. It took Gisela a moment to realize it was Irmtraud's scream that was penetrating her hands, still clamped over her ears. Then she felt Erich's body on top of hers go stiff, and suddenly, limp.

The angry droning had faded slowly. Now, it was completely silent. Nothing moved. There was no sound above or around them. No birds tweeted overhead. No crickets were chirping in the grass. The familiar hum of nature in summer had been hushed into silence. But even in the quiet, the air still seemed to carry the echoes of the bombers' relentless roar. The sound, now a ghost, lingered in Gisela's ears much like the smell of metal and smoke did in her nose. But another unfamiliar smell joined them, one which she could not place. It crawled up her nostrils and stirred the acid in her stomach.

Gisela swallowed down the bile and opened her eyes. The sky above had returned to its innocent pale blue. She felt Irmtraud shift next to her, waking from her shock-frozen state. "Are you hurt?"

"I don't think so." Irmtraud's voice had an unfamiliar hoarseness to it.

"Erich?" Gisela pushed at his body, which seemed heavier than ever. There was no response. She pushed harder to free herself and managed to push him off them. He rolled to the side, and she saw him stare back at her with vacant eyes. "Erich?" She asked.

"Is he ... is he dead?" Irmtraud sputtered. She had managed to get up. Her dress was grass-stained and torn at the hem. One of her pigtails had come undone. Her right knee was bloodied, and her face was smudged with dirt. For a moment, Gisela wondered if she was in the same state, then she turned her attention to Erich, trying to see if he was indeed dead.

His expression hadn't changed. Reluctantly, she scooted closer to him and put her trembling hand over his heart. She was surprised to find it pulsing strongly against her palm and breathed a sigh of relief. With some reluctance, she looked him over to see why he was unconscious and found him bleeding from the neck where a bullet had grazed him. But the wound seemed superficial and didn't explain the fact that he was unconscious. Then Gisela noticed the rip in one of his pant legs. There was a hole in his thigh. Blood was seeping out to the rhythm of his pulsing heart.

"Bike home, Irmtraud!" Gisela shouted. "Get father! Have him bring the car. Quick!" She yelled at her sister. But Irmtraud was only staring at Erich, not moving. "Go! Now!" Gisela urged. "He's going to bleed to death if you don't hurry! Pedal like the devil is after you!"

Irmtraud's eyes flicked to her, then to the bike. She ran to it, lifted it, climbed on, and pedaled away like a fury. Gisela was relieved to see the tires had not been hit. She stared after Irmtraud for a moment, then turned back to Erich to inspect the wound in his thigh more closely.

A wave of nausea washed over her, and she tasted bile again. With steady deep breaths, she tried hard to keep the rising nausea at bay. After a moment, Gisela recovered and pressed her hand on the wound. She had nothing to stop the flow of blood.

Erich started groaning. She felt relief wash over her. He lifted his head, his face twisted in pain. With his bandaged hand, he reached for his thigh.

"My sister has gone for help," Gisela tried to reassure him, but Erich's eyes rolled back in his head, and he collapsed back into the grass.

With her elbow, Gisela pushed down the door handle while balancing a tray with tea, slices of bread, and cheese. She and Irmtraud had given up their bedroom for Erich until a Wehrmacht ambulance could take him to a military hospital. Her father had been able to stop the bleeding. Fortunately, it had been a clear through shot that didn't require the removal of a bullet and had missed major arteries.

Erich greeted Gisela with a big smile as she came in. She knew it wasn't just gratitude for the supper she brought him. She had been tasked with looking after him, and they had grown close over the last few days. She couldn't help but smile in return, glad she had taken the time to fix her hair before bringing him his supper.

Her eyes fell on his bandaged leg as she set the tray down next to him. Her mother, together with Irmtraud, was changing the bandages daily. Gisela hadn't been able to bring herself to do it. Witnessing his pain was intolerable. She much preferred to bring him food and occupy his time. She wasn't cut out for wound care or any other things a nurse would do.

"Are you ready for your supper?" she asked, adjusting the pillow behind his back.

He caught her by the arm. "I've been looking forward to you spending the evening with me again."

His broad smile made her blush, and she couldn't help laughing. "You saw me a mere two hours ago. And I spent most of the morning with you," she said in playful protest while pouring his tea from the small teapot.

"Will you read to me again tonight?" He asked between bites of bread and cheese, his eyes blue as a lake on a bright summer's day, and wide with unabashed expectation.

She smiled at his boyishness and nodded with a small laugh. "What would you like me to read to you tonight?"

"How about some Rilke?"

"Poetry?" She looked at him. "No legends?"

"Tonight, I feel like poetry," he said, making a grand gesture with his arm.

"I don't believe we own a book with his verses," Gisela said, her face contorted in playful dismay. She thought it best not to mention the Rilke poem she'd had to memorize in school a few years back, in case he asked her to recite it. She couldn't even remember its title. Something about a panther in a zoo.

"Well, if you don't have a book, I will recite some of his poems for you," Erich said. Gisela stared at him in disbelief. He laughed at her reaction. "What... you don't think a pilot reads poetry? Or is it that you didn't think me capable of memorizing verses? Believe it or not, I have read a lot of his poems and memorized some of them. I think Rilke a great genius."

Erich took a sip of the tea, then cleared his throat. He sat up straighter as he haltingly began to recite but soon fell into a confident rhythm.

"When my soul touches yours a great chord sings!
How shall I tune it then to other things?
O! That some spot in darkness could be found
That does not vibrate when'er your depth sound.
But everything that touches you and me
Welds us as played strings sound one melody.
Where is the instrument whence the sounds flow?
And whose the master-hand that holds the bow?
O! Sweet song—"

Gisela watched his lips, mesmerized, then she caught the meaning of his words and felt herself blush. She and Erich had grown close over the last few days. They had shared much time together, and she had enjoyed reading to him whenever he had asked her. He could very well have read for himself, but he seemed to enjoy her company.

Gisela felt his hand on hers, and a small shiver went up her spine. The intensity she saw in his gaze made her swallow. He looked at her expectantly. She pulled her hand away and applauded playfully. "You surprise me, Erich."

"Did you like it?"

"Very much so," she said shyly.

His hand searched again for hers and found it. He squeezed it lightly. "On to your stories now?" He asked with a twinkle in his eye.

"As you wish." She laughed and got up to get the book of legends she had read from last night. Gisela felt his eyes on her as she walked over to the nightstand on the other side of the bed, where she had placed the old book with its ripped cover next to the wooden angel who was now watching over Erich.

Gisela had assumed the angel had been carved by her father or grandfather until one day, her brother Waldemar had revealed that it actually had been fashioned by her mama.

"Your father told me that the ambulance will be here tomorrow," Erich said, interrupting her thoughts.

She didn't look at him but reached for the book, trying to still her hand that slightly trembled now from the news she had known would eventually come. Erich cleared his throat, his voice much lower and more serious than usual. "May I write to you, Gisela?" He asked. "When I'm gone?"

Gisela's heart leapt in her chest as she walked back to his side of the bed and sat down, crossing her legs and resting the book in her lap. "I would very much like that, Erich," she said, smiling shyly at him. Gisela knew she had never been in love before, but she guessed that what she was feeling was probably coming close to it.

"Then it's settled," Erich said and leaned back on his pillow, looking satisfied as Gisela opened the book and began to read where she had left off yesterday. "You truly are the most beautiful girl I have ever seen," he said, interrupting her.

As Erich's eyes lingered on her, Gisela saw something in them that reminded her of the way people had spoken in adoration of her mother's beauty.

"I think you haven't met many girls, Unteroffizier Schmidt," Gisela teased with a light laugh. She cleared her throat and returned to where she had left off reading, growing serious again. But in her chest, something unfamiliar stirred, a flutter that had nothing to do with pride or arrogance, and everything to do with being seen.

Chapter 2

December 1942

Obersalzberg, Bavaria, Germany

Karl tried to keep his eyes open. He never thought one could be this tired and fall asleep while standing up. He could tell by the faint tolling of church bells from the town below that his eight-hour night shift was coming to an end. Now he just needed to wait to be relieved of his post. He had spent the last two hours standing watch at the *Torhaus*. It was freezing, but even the cold couldn't keep him awake and alert. He cast his eyes around, looking at the beautiful snow-covered mountainside dipped in the golden morning light, and wiggled his numb toes and fingers. He yawned involuntarily. His eyes flicked to Wilhelm, the other guard, and the first friend he had made in the SS *Leibstandarte* at the Führer's headquarters at *Obersalzberg*. But Wilhelm hadn't noticed his yawn, seemingly struggling to stay awake himself. He was leaning heavily on his rifle, and his head was resting against the folded-up, furred collar of his heavy SS uniform winter coat as if it were a pillow.

The sound of boots crushing snow reached Karl. Wilhelm had heard them, too. Immediately, they straightened up, standing at attention once again. Karl smiled to himself in satisfaction. He was finally being relieved of his duty. His mind drifted for a moment, picturing the SS guards' barrack not far from the *Berghof*, Hitler's residence, where his bed and a warm breakfast awaited him. He'd fill his belly quickly and then sleep. The thought of a hot meal and stretching out his legs under a warm blanket to thaw his frozen body made him moan with pleasure. He quickly cleared his throat when he noticed that Wilhelm was studying him with raised brows.

Two guards appeared in front of them, dressed in their fur-lined coats, gators covering their ears, necks, and chins underneath steel helmets. Rifles hung from their shoulders. The four men saluted each other and accompanied their 'Heil Hitler' with a click of their boots. The guards' salutes were more energetic than Karl's and Wilhelm's. Karl's jerky movements made him realize how stiff his limbs were in the early morning freeze. He slowly moved out of his position so the first SS guard, a burly man from Hamburg Karl had seen around but had never spoken to, could relieve him. But to Karl's surprise, the guard did not take his place. Karl looked down at the black-gloved hand on his arm and then at the guard who had placed it there.

The man from Hamburg smirked at him. "No breakfast for you just yet," he said. "You are to report to the Berghof immediately. Out the back." Karl exchanged a look with Wilhelm. "Both of you," the man added.

Wilhelm immediately saluted. Karl followed suit with some reluctance. Muttering under his breath, he trailed after Wilhelm, stomping his feet to bring his lower extremities back to life, tired and angry at having to delay his breakfast and much-needed sleep. He'd done his part. There were plenty of SS here that could do the Führer's bidding, whatever it was.

Karl clapped his gloved hands together a couple of times to awaken his numb fingers as he continued to trudge after Wilhelm through the icy snow up to the Berghof. When they rounded the corner to the back of the building, the winter sun's glaring light caught in the snow crystals all around them, and Karl had to squint, then close his eyes at the sudden brightness. When he opened them again, Wilhelm had already reached the house. Karl sighed and hurried after him. The Führer was a temperamental and impatient man prone to angry outbursts. Tired and hungry as Karl was, he was in no mood to add any more unpleasantness to this morning, which refused to come to an end.

Just as Karl joined Wilhelm, waiting to find out why their shift hadn't ended, the back door flew open and their commander appeared at the threshold. From the inside, Karl could hear screaming. Too early for any human to be in such a rage, he thought. The screaming grew nearer, and Karl could make out the words "traitor" and "coward." He swallowed hard. He knew why he was here after all.

The commander stepped aside as two SS guards pulled a man outside.

"Shoot him," the Führer screamed and slammed the door shut.

Wilhelm and Karl looked at each other, hoping it hadn't been a serious order and had only been uttered in a fit of rage. But Karl knew men had been shot at *Obersalzberg* in the absence of rage and for much less than treason.

He eyed the man carefully. He was no older than forty and wore, not a uniform, but the clothing of an intellectual, perhaps a professor? His thinning dusty blond hair was disheveled, and his glasses hung askew from his nose. He didn't fight back. His eyes were cast to the ground, shoulders hanging in defeat. Karl had never seen the man on the grounds before, nor did he know where to place him. Nothing looked familiar about him. But then again, he barely met any of the civilian or high-dignitary visitors who came to the Berghof at the order or invitation of the Führer.

"Shoot the traitor," their commander said, motioning to the two guards who had the man pinned between them. He waved his hand dismissively at them. "Take him to the wall at the back of the barracks. You know the spot."

With a brisk nod, he dismissed Karl and Wilhelm. They saluted and followed the guards who dragged the man down the slight slope to the barracks, where Karl had anticipated a hearty breakfast and his warm bed.

When they had reached the little yard, one of the guards shoved the man against the wall. His eyes were vacant, as if the spark of life had been drained from him already. As he had been taught, Karl formed a line with Wilhelm and the two other guards. On the command of one of the guards, he shouldered his rifle and prepared to fire. The man came alive. Panic contorted his face. He pressed his back to the wall, holding up his hands in defense. The guard gave the command. Karl swiftly tilted his rifle upward and aimed at the wall above the man's head. They fired their shots, and the man crumbled to the icy ground, which refused to absorb the blood offering that was seeping out of his body.

The thick, dark red liquid ran toward them with fervor. Karl took a step aside to avoid it meeting his boot. Soon it began to be swallowed up into the path its warmth had carved into the ice. Karl swallowed down the bile that rose in his throat. He was no longer hungry. All he wanted now was sleep.

Back at the barracks, Karl cursed under his breath as he undressed. Why hadn't he asked for leave to spend Christmas with his family? He wasn't stationed at the front lines and would have had a good chance of receiving permission. How he regretted now that he hadn't made the request. He surely could have used his charms or made up a plausible family reason to have it granted. He cursed his stupidity. Perhaps he could speak with his commander later today? Inventing a family emergency didn't seem too unreasonable to him now. Perhaps he could seek his commander out after he had gotten some much-needed sleep. *Perhaps*, he mumbled to himself as he drew the rough blanket over his body and drifted off to sleep.

Chapter 3

December 1942

Wallhausen, Germany

"He's here!" Gisela heard Irmtraud shout from their bedroom, which looked out the front of the house toward the street. Gisela and Irmtraud had been standing there for what seemed like hours, waiting for Erich to arrive. Only moments ago, Gisela had left the bedroom to help her mother in the kitchen, and now he was finally here. Erich would spend the Christmas holiday with them. Gisela felt almost giddy at the thought. She caught her broad grin in the hall mirror and promised herself to keep it in check.

Back in August, when Erich had been wounded, she had sat by his bedside until he was transferred to a hospital. He had promised to come visit as soon as he was better and was given leave. A terrible loneliness had settled over Gisela in the days after Erich's departure, alleviated only by his first letter, which arrived a week later. After that, the letters came regularly. In early October, Erich wrote that he had been released from the hospital and that he was back to flying. Gisela had not welcomed the news. From that moment on, she had been in a constant state of anxiety over Erich's safety. If the war would only end. It had to end.

Erich's car rolled up to the front of the house and Gisela threw all caution about her big grin in the wind and ran out the front door. Ripping open the driver's door, she dragged a laughing Erich out and pulled him into a fierce embrace.

"Alright, that's enough of that, young lady." Her father had appeared out of nowhere behind her, with a giggling Irmtraud next to him. Gisela pulled away and felt her cheeks grow hot. "Let Erich get out of the car and into the house, would you?" Her father said sternly. But the slight upturn of the right corner of his mouth told her that he had reprimanded her in jest.

Gisela stepped back, straightened her shoulders, and extended her hand toward Erich with exaggerated propriety and a playfully lofty expression on her face. He took her hand and shook it with a laugh. Her father extended his hand as well, and the two men shook heartily. Irmtraud went around the car to the trunk and busied herself trying to pull Erich's suitcase out of it. Erich came to her aid. Then, Gisela led the way into the house and to her and Irmtraud's bedroom, which they would give up once again as they had done when Erich lay wounded in August. Back then, he had brushed aside her father's argument that he must have been struck by friendly fire from a diving *Messerschmidt* since the bombers' gunfire could not possibly have reached the ground. Erich had simply dismissed it, and Gisela's father had never brought it up again. She hoped he wouldn't on this second visit, either. In fact, Gisela hoped there would be no talk of war at all.

But this was going to be impossible when her brothers came home for their Christmas leave in only a couple of days. At least two of them. They needed to count themselves lucky. Families with sons on the Eastern Front weren't so fortunate. Gisela was glad it was Waldemar who had received leave, and relieved it wasn't Karl. Not that she didn't think Karl deserved to spend the Christmas holidays with his family, but she could all too easily imagine how he would tease her relentlessly when he saw that she had taken a liking to Erich.

Gisela had managed to feign disappointment when her father had told her Karl wouldn't come home for the holidays, but she was looking forward to having Waldemar home from France. Her favorite brother would be kind, supportive, and happy for her. Heinrich, her oldest brother, would, as usual, not give a care in the world about her. Her only worry was that Waldemar would draw Erich into his endless discussions about the war. She wanted to have Erich to herself, at least most of the time, and was hoping her father, who had always abhorred all talk of war, would intervene and stop them if it became necessary.

⸺

Irmtraud had her ear pressed against the living room door as Gisela paced up and down the hallway, biting her fingernails. Occasionally, she stopped to look expectantly at Irmtraud, who merely shook her head and continued to listen intently.

When Irmtraud suddenly straightened, her face a mixture of shock and confusion, Gisela was by her side in an instant. "What is it?" She whispered. "What did they talk about?" Without realizing it, she had taken Irmtraud by the arms and shaken her. "What did they say? Irmtraud?" Gisela demanded, growing concerned and rather impatient.

Irmtraud pulled free and looked at her with narrow eyes that had suddenly grown dark. "He wants to marry you."

Gisela's hand flew to her mouth, and she stumbled backwards. If it hadn't been for the staircase banister behind her, she would have fallen. Then Gisela realized something and flew to Irmtraud's side, grabbing her arms once more. "What did father say?" She urged her sister, trying to keep her voice down to a mere hiss.

Irmtraud shrugged as if she didn't care. "I don't know."

Gisela pushed her sister away from the door and pressed her own ear against the wood. All she could hear was the low rumble of male voices. She couldn't make out a single word. Did Irmtraud really hear what she claimed she heard? Gisela stepped away from the door and scrutinized her sister's face. "You sure that's really what you heard?"

"Why would I lie about something like that?" Irmtraud shot back like a wounded animal. "Especially since I think this is an entirely bad idea."

"What do you mean?" Now it was Gisela whose eyes narrowed.

"You're much too young to get married."

"Hardly. I'll be nineteen in a couple of months."

"You barely know him. And who wants to get married in the middle of a war? Heinrich, Waldemar, and Karl might not even be able to be here. "

"People get married all the time." Gisela pointed out, annoyed. "No matter the circumstances. And the war will end soon," she added. "I'm sure of it. Hitler is winning this stupid war on all fronts."

At this, Irmtraud broke into hysterical laughter. Gisela stepped toward her. "Hush!" She hissed. "They'll hear us!"

When Irmtraud didn't stop, Gisela panicked and clamped her hand over her sister's mouth. Irmtraud shook her off and pushed her back angrily. "Have you not heard about Stalingrad?" She asked. "The 6th Army? Gudrun's brother is there. Trapped in the city. Surrounded by the Bolsheviks. Did she not tell you?"

Gisela shook her head slowly. She hadn't talked to Gudrun in a while.

"Father said they have no way of getting out. They're doomed to die." Gisela took a step back, shaking her head vehemently. "You would know," Irmtraud said, "if you had been doing anything other than fawning over Erich all the time. Gudrun and her mother are devastated, Gisela."

The door opened, and they both shrank back. Their father's face was unreadable. Had he heard them? "Gisela," he said, "please come in."

Gisela looked from him to Irmtraud. But her sister was still glowering at her, deep, angry breaths heaving her chest. Gisela entered the living room as her father gave Irmtraud a reassuring nod before closing the door behind them.

Inside, Erich stood by the window, his hands clasped behind his back. He looked almost serene. When he turned to her, a smile played on his face, but then he grew serious and cleared his throat. Gisela noticed that her father had remained by the door.

"Gisela," Erich said, "please sit. I have a question to ask you."

Gisela swallowed and sat down on the sofa, kneading her hands nervously. Erich joined her. He took one of her hands in his and cleared his throat again. "Gisela?"

She perked up and studied his face. She was surprised to find him looking nervous. His eyes were flitting back and forth, and he looked rather flushed. She resisted the urge to place her palm on his cheek to comfort and calm him. "Gisela," Erich said, "you're the most beautiful girl I know. Your presence makes me happy ..." He hesitated for a brief moment and looked at her father. Gisela followed his eyes. Her father seemed deep in thought.

Gisela felt Erich's fingers on her chin as he gently turned her face back toward him. "Gisela, you were a kind, caring, and steadfast companion to me when I lay wounded. I want to make you my wife. Will you agree to marry me?"

So Irmtraud had heard correctly. She had not made it up after all. Gisela felt ashamed of accusing her sister of lying. She deserved an apology.

"So," Erich said, "what do you say, Gisela Fahnrich?"

Gisela looked at her father, who simply shrugged his shoulders, but did she detect an amused twinkle in his eye? She straightened her shoulders and looked Erich straight in the face. "Yes," she said, "I will marry you, Erich Schmidt."

Erich whooped, and she had to laugh at his boyish jubilance. Then, in an instant, he grew somber. "You actually agree?" He asked, searching her face with such a lack of confidence that it reminded her of the boys in grammar school who were anxiously waiting for their voice to break. She nodded reassuringly, and he hugged her tightly for it.

"Should we wait until the war is over?" Gisela asked.

He let go of her. "Until after the war?" He looked startled. "That could be years."

"I'm sure it will be over soon enough," Gisela said as she watched her father come over and sit down in the armchair across from them, where in the evening, he liked to finish reading the pages of the newspaper he had missed at the breakfast table in the morning.

"It is up to you two, of course," her father said. "But Erich is right. This war might drag on."

Gisela remembered what Irmtraud had said in the hallway. "How can we celebrate when so many of our soldiers are suffering at the front?" She asked.

Her father and Erich looked at each other. "It doesn't have to be a big wedding," Erich said.

"If you want to wait, then you can wait, of course," her father assured her, not looking at Erich this time.

"I don't," she blurted, and the men looked at her in surprise. She felt her face burn and got up. "Let's get married. But without all the festivities. Let's get married while Waldemar and Heinrich are home." Gisela said, surprising herself.

A big grin stole across Erich's face. He got up as well and enveloped her in his arms. When he let go of her, he said, "And I won't take you away from your family. Not yet at least. Not now. Times are too uncertain. But as soon as this war is over, we will–"

Gisela took a step back. "What do you mean?"

"We will move to my village in Bavaria, of course. You will like it there. It is beautiful."

Gisela had not considered this. She had thought about Erich and about getting married, but certainly not about their life together after the wedding. She felt foolish that she hadn't considered where they would live.

"You'll be happy there, I promise," Erich said. "I will make you happy. And we will visit your family, of course. Whenever we can."

Gisela's ears were ringing. Erich's voice grew distant. She'd have to leave home. Wallhausen. Her family, her friends. A steep price to pay for the love she had for Erich. She felt her eyes burn and turned away quickly. "So much to prepare," she mumbled and rushed out of the room.

In the hallway, she ran into Waldemar, who had just arrived. He looked on in confusion as Gisela rushed past him. She had been so excited for him to come home, but now she felt smothered by the presence of so many people in the house. Usually, she would let him draw her into a big bear hug, but she needed to get away. To think. To come to grips with the fact that her life was about to change irrevocably. Irmtraud was nowhere to be seen, so Gisela rushed out the back door, grabbed her mother's bike, and pedaled like the devil was after her out the courtyard, past Erich's car, and down the road. She hoped Gudrun would be home.

"Perhaps you shouldn't have agreed so quickly to marry him," Gudrun suggested carefully as Gisela threw small sticks into the little pond behind her friend's house, where they had played many times during their childhood. Now, they no longer played, but it was still a place of refuge for them. A place where they could talk and laugh together, just the two of them. Without interruption. There, they dreamed and discussed their futures. Talked about boys and vented about their families.

"I love Erich, but why does my life have to change so drastically while his remains the same? It isn't fair!" Gisela protested, fully aware that she was pouting like a child. She watched the sticks floating peacefully on the surface of the water, and she could feel how it calmed her nerves, if only for a brief moment. She jumped when Gudrun threw a rock into the pond with a loud splash and drowned her sticks.

"Life is never fair," Gudrun said. "Perhaps it's time you realized that, too."

"What's that supposed to mean?" Gisela asked, taken aback by her friend's rebuke that had come out of nowhere.

"You have it all, Gisela. Your family is complete, you're beautiful, and now you have Erich, too..." Gudrun trailed off and threw another rock in the pond.

"Where is this coming from?" Gisela asked. "What are you saying? You have a family! You're beautiful!"

"Hardly as beautiful as you. And my mother is my only family now. My brother–" Gudrun choked.

"I heard about Stalingrad." Gisela placed a hand on her friend's arm.

"He's dead, Gisela!" Gudrun yelled like a wounded animal. She wiped angrily at the tears that rolled down her cheeks.

"I... I am so sorry," Gisela stuttered. "I didn't know." Did Irmtraud? She wondered. Did anyone in her family, in the village? She stared into the dark, murky waters of the pond at the spot where Gudrun's rock had sunk and thought she saw Fritz's face staring back at her. He was two years older than Gudrun and her, and he had often played with them when they were younger, before he joined the Hitler Youth. From then on, he had deliberately ignored them. Now he was gone. Dead. She shook her head in disbelief, drew her legs in, and rested her chin on her knees. For the second time in a day, she felt her eyes burning. Next to her, Gudrun sniffled.

"I will join the Lebensborn program," Gudrun said suddenly, her voice surprisingly firm and resolute.

Gisela lifted her head. "What is that?"

"They are looking for young, unmarried women to bear racially pure children."

"They are what?" Gisela jerked around to face Gudrun. Had she heard correctly? What was her friend on about? She had never heard of such a program, and she didn't like the sound of it.

"I've been offered admission to this program where I can help bear and rear children for the good of the fatherland, and I will get financial support."

"Whose children, Gudrun?" Gisela shook her head vehemently in utter confusion, ignoring the sick feeling that rose up in her. "I don't understand."

"There's nothing left for me here," Gudrun said. "And I'm certainly not going to be a burden to my poor mother. She has suffered enough."

"She needs you, Gudrun. Now more than ever."

"How would you know about that? Your mother is dead."

Gisela felt as if she had been slapped. Her cheeks were burning. She jumped up and stomped off without another look at Gudrun. She wasn't sure what had gotten into her friend, but she was too mad and disgusted to find out. Gudrun seemed changed, and Gisela didn't like this new Gudrun.

***

"Gudrun's brother has fallen," Gisela said breathlessly as soon as she swung open the door to the kitchen. Her father and mama, Erich, Irmtraud, and Waldemar were gathered around the kitchen table. Their conversation stopped, and their faces fell as soon as Gisela's news sank in.

"This is grave news," Mama said. "I must go see his mother. His poor mother!" The last words from her mama's mouth had seemed more like a yelp. She got up and left the kitchen. A few moments later, they heard the front door shut.

"Stalingrad will fall soon, too. It's only a matter of time," Waldemar said, his face dark. "The 6th Army is surrounded and cut off."

Gisela had completely forgotten about Waldemar's arrival and quickly went over to hug him from behind. "I'm sorry," she whispered in his ear. "For storming off earlier and not properly greeting you."

He patted her arm that was slung around his neck. "It's alright. I'm glad you're happy to see me after all."

"Of course, I am. I've missed you terribly!" Gisela sank down on the chair next to him, which her mother had left empty.

"I hear Erich here has been keeping you good company," he said, winking at her. She slapped his arm playfully and threw Erich a sideways glance. He was sitting next to her father. His face was unreadable, but his eyes were friendly. She knew they needed to talk about their future. But right now, Waldemar deserved her attention. And she wanted to hear all about France.

"Thank you for all those lovely postcards you sent me. They looked so... so French." Gisela had pinned them to the wallpaper on her side of the bedroom. They were colorful, happy, and flowery. Her favorite was of the Eiffel Tower, surrounded by blush pink peonies and the most beautiful golden cursive lettered greeting. She often ran her fingers over it while imagining herself being photographed below Paris' most famous landmark.

"I'm glad you liked them, little sister." Waldemar looked pleased.

Irmtraud leaned over and whispered, "How's Gudrun?" Gisela eyed her with a mixture of suspicion and relief. Was Irmtraud no longer upset with her?

"She's ... you know ... She's ... upset about it all, of course."

Irmtraud nodded knowingly. Gisela wasn't sure if she should share what Gudrun had told her about the program she wanted to join. It had made no sense to her.

"I'm sorry to hear about your friend's brother," Erich cut in. Gisela shot him a smile of gratitude.

"I wish there was more we could do," Irmtraud said suddenly. "The men go off to war, and we women just sit at home."

"You're a schoolgirl, Irmtraud." Her father's voice boomed from the other side of the kitchen table. "Many boys have left school to train to fight in the war. Why can't I do something?" Irmtraud demanded. "Contribute in some way?" She crossed her arms defiantly.

Gisela wanted to rebuke her by sharing Gudrun's other terrible news about joining that program she had mentioned but decided against it. She didn't want to give her little sister any ideas, especially not outrageous ones like that.

"We certainly need more nurses," Erich said. Irmtraud perked up immediately. "We don't have enough nurses in the lazarettes."

Gisela saw her father's face darken, but he didn't respond to Erich's suggestion.

"I wanted to go to nursing school after the school year is finished," Irmtraud said confidently, as if she didn't need anyone's permission.

"Why not go now?" Erich asked. Gisela shot him a look. Why would he suggest such a thing? "Your country needs you now," he said. "We are at war. What else can they teach you in a village school?"

"Irmtraud is too young, Erich," Gisela protested. "She's barely sixteen. And besides, by the time she finished nursing school, the war would surely long be over."

"As Irmtraud said earlier, there are boys as young as her in the navy and air force, training to join the war effort, Gisela," Erich said, leaning back in his chair to cross his arms.

"That's true," Waldemar added. "Boys in the Hitler Youth are encouraged to join the naval and air corps to train so they can join the fight when they turn eighteen," Waldemar looked at Gisela, lifting his hands as if to appease her. "But yes," he said, "perhaps it's best to finish school first."

"I'm done with school. Erich is right," Irmtraud said even more defiantly. She clearly understood that she had found an ally in Erich and didn't hesitate to use it to her advantage.

"A cousin of mine attended the nursing school in Kassel. It's not far, and you would be able to go home on the weekends," Erich said.

"In Kassel?" Gisela demanded. "Cities like Kassel are not safe. You know that, Erich. You helped defend it against the British. They have bombed it repeatedly."

Gisela couldn't believe what he was suggesting and wondered why he was encouraging Irmtraud. She looked to her father for help. He had narrowed his eyes, which were scrutinizing not Erich, but Irmtraud. Gisela hoped he wasn't considering giving in to her. Why didn't he say anything? How she wished Mama hadn't left.

"And we will continue defending Kassel. She's safe there. The Tommies' bombers are no match for our *Luftwaffe*," Erich replied rather arrogantly.

"She will finish school as planned. And that's my last word," her father said sternly as he rose from his chair. He turned to Irmtraud. "As long as you put your feet under my kitchen table, you will do as I say."

Irmtraud wasn't the only one who stared after him as he left the room. Their father was not strict, abrupt, or forceful. He'd always been a gentle and kind man of few words. As Irmtraud pushed her chair back and hurried after him, Gisela glowered at Erich.

"She'll get over it. You'll see," Waldemar spoke into the silence of the room before turning to Erich. "Tell me," he said, "now that you're becoming my brother-in-law, what in the world do you see in Gisela?" He laughed and slapped Erich's shoulder, ignoring Gisela, who glared at both of them. With a huff, she got up and left as well. While she usually appreciated Waldemar's jovial nature, which could defuse any tense situation, she certainly did not appreciate it today. Any more than she appreciated Erich's meddling in their family's affairs by encouraging Irmtraud to go to Kassel.

* * *

Gisela felt a hand on her shoulder and looked up from the book she had been trying to read. The words had blurred long ago. Erich stood over her, his broad smile revealing white teeth against a face still a little pale from his weeks in the hospital. It was hard not to return that smile, but she was still angry.

"I was looking for you," he said, dropping down onto the sofa beside her so the worn cushions dipped and bounced beneath them. "You're not upset with me, are you?" His tone was careful, his hand already finding hers. As he lifted it and brushed his lips lightly over her skin, something shivered through her. She pulled back quickly, turning to face him.

"I don't understand why you would encourage my sister like that," she said, folding her arms and crossing her legs.

"Gisela, I was in the hospital. I know what a shortage of nurses means for the wounded." Erich's eyes had shifted to his thigh, to the place where the bullet had torn through his leg. The joking tone was gone now. "Irmtraud wants to be a nurse," Erich said. "Your father should let her go to nursing school."

"She's too young, Erich."

He leaned back, watching her. "I find her very mature for sixteen."

"Erich, my father knows best, and I think you shouldn't have—"

"Shouldn't have what?" His voice was sharper now, and for an instant she saw him as he had been the day they met, the young pilot in the mud-smeared, torn uniform, demanding the nearest telephone as if no one would dare refuse him. That sternness had not frightened her then. It still didn't.

"You shouldn't have encouraged her. You don't know her. She doesn't need much encouragement. My sister needs the opposite, for her own good. Trust me."

"I'm sure she hasn't enjoyed being discouraged her whole life."

"She's discouraged me from marrying you," Gisela shot back.

His brows rose. "Why?"

"Same reason. I'm too young."

He laughed, a warm, quick sound that filled the sitting room. "She isn't wrong," he said. And when her eyebrows lifted, he added, "but that won't stop you, will it?"

She recognized the trap too late. Her mouth opened, then closed. She looked away, but he was already reading her. "I know your family is everything to you," he said quietly, leaning forward. His knee brushed hers. "That's why I want to be part of it."

Gisela had meant to stay angry. Instead, she found herself watching the faint crease between his brows, the line his jaw made when he grew serious. The room settled into stillness. Her book lay forgotten between them. She let her hand rest against his on the worn cushion.

Heinrich arrived from Italy a day later. He brought prosciutto, a welcome treat for their holidays. As expected, Gisela's oldest brother didn't pay much attention to his sisters. All they received was a meager greeting. However, Heinrich reveled in the news that he was gaining another brother and went out of his way to please Erich. In fact, brothers were occupying so much of Erich's time that she had no opportunity to be alone with him or discuss plans for their future together. With each passing day, Gisela grew more irritated with him and with all the menfolk in the house.

She spent the morning of Christmas Eve with her mother and Irmtraud in the kitchen, preparing their humble meal that would consist only of a potato salad and sausages. They baked Christmas cookies together as they had always done, but because they had so little flour and lacked other ingredients completely, the result was simple sugar cookies, which was still better than no Christmas cookies at all.

After they had finished, Gisela went to get ready for church. Her family never went to church, except for baptisms, weddings, funerals, and Christmas Eve, when it was their tradition to attend the late afternoon service in the village.

Today, Gisela hoped to spot Gudrun. It would surely sting for her friend to see Gisela with her brothers after she had lost hers, but Gisela hoped for a chance to speak with her, to somehow persuade her to abandon her plans to join the Lebensborn program. Despite the hurtful things Gudrun had said to her, Gisela had already forgiven her because of her loss. Gudrun was her oldest and dearest friend. Gisela hoped to be able to talk some sense into her before she ended up making a grave mistake. For that, Gisela decided she would need Waldemar's help. Her brother owed her. More importantly, he owed Gudrun.

Gisela had watched Gudrun fancy Waldemar since they were girls. Her friend had joined her and Waldemar for swims in the mill pond or cycling to the river for many summers. Gisela had always let Gudrun trail along, even nudging her friend closer while Waldemar pretended not to notice. He didn't seem to mind, until the day Gudrun invited just him for a swim. Waldemar had declined, saying she was too young for that sort of thing. Gudrun had nursed the slight for weeks, refusing to speak to Waldemar or Gisela.

Now, Gisela hoped to enlist Waldemar to help steer Gudrun away from the program. If he talked to her, showed her some kindness, perhaps she would reconsider. But would Waldemar be willing to do this? Perhaps, if she asked just right, he would agree. He was a kind man after all and liked to indulge his favorite sister.

Gisela caught her brother in his and Heinrich's room just before the family left for church. As usual, her father was the first one ready and was already waiting impatiently downstairs by the front door, holding a tall wooden-handled umbrella and wearing his hat and long wool coat.

Waldemar raised his eyebrows in surprise when Gisela entered after a brief knock. He was struggling to straighten his tie. Gisela went to help. "There," she said with a nod. "This looks good now."

"What is it, sister?"

Gisela decided to come straight out with it. Her father wouldn't tolerate them being late for church on Christmas Eve. "I need your help," she said.

Waldemar's eyes narrowed. "Is this about Erich?"

Gisela shook her head in confusion. Why would he think this was about Erich? "No, no," she said. "It's about my friend, Gudrun."

"Poor girl." Waldemar was slipping into his long grey army coat, which irritated Gisela. Why couldn't he go as a civilian? At least to church?

"Have you heard about the Lebensborn program?" She asked.

Waldemar stopped buttoning his coat and stepped toward her, his eyes suddenly fierce. Gisela shrank back in surprise. "You're not thinking about doing that, I hope?"

"So you know about it?"

"Gisela! You're not joining that program, you hear me?" Waldemar's voice was hard. She couldn't remember him ever speaking to her this forcefully.

"We are leaving!" Her father's voice bellowed from below.

"No!" She exclaimed. "No, not me. Not me, ever. Gudrun. She wants to. You need to help me to dissuade her."

Waldemar sighed in relief. "How can I help?" He asked more softly.

"You need to convince her to abandon this idea. You have to. Before it's too late."

"How? She won't listen to me. I don't think she likes me anymore, Gisela. She hasn't spoken a word to me since the day... you know..."

"Please, Waldemar," Gisela pleaded. "Try. Please talk to her. You owe me." She added quickly as she saw Waldemar's eyes darken. "What I mean is ... please just try talking to her. If you're kind to her, she'll listen. I'm sure." At Waldemar's sigh, she added, "She never stopped liking you, you know."

Downstairs, they heard the front door shut.

"Maybe she once liked me," Waldemar said. "Now she merely tolerates my existence because I'm your brother."

Gisela considered this for a split second, then shook her head. She had shared Waldemar's postcards with Gudrun, and her friend had studied them over and over again, running her fingers across his handwriting with the occasional sigh. Gisela knew her friend. Gudrun still had feelings for Waldemar. "Please, Waldemar," she said. "I don't want her to throw her life away like that."

"We need to leave. Father will be furious," Waldemar reached for the door handle without giving her an answer.

"Please," Gisela repeated, following him.

When they reached the top of the stairs, he turned to her. "I will try my best to... dissuade her, alright? I'll talk to her," he promised. "But you owe me now, sis. Big time!"

Gisela threw her arms around his neck and squeezed him tightly. "Thank you. Thank you! And this is why you're my favorite brother."

He unclamped her arms with a laugh and pulled her with him down the stairs and out the front door, where the family was waiting for them in their Sunday best. Her father shook his head in disapproval, then proceeded to walk down the street toward the village church. They all fell in behind him. Erich appeared by Gisela's side, snuck a peck to her cheek, then took her arm. She smiled at him broadly. There was much to be joyful about. Gisela felt blessed that she would be able to attend church this Christmas with her family intact and two out of three of her brothers home. Those who fought on the Eastern Front did not have the luck to be allowed leave. Why Karl hadn't joined them from Bavaria for Christmas, she didn't know. But Karl was Karl. He had never cared much for family time.

***

To Gisela's dismay, Gudrun was not at church. Her friend's mother attended with a neighbor who had accompanied the grieving woman. The mention of her son's passing by the village pastor during his sermon brought her and half of the congregation to tears. They all knew him. But where was Gudrun? Had she left already? She saw Waldemar thinking the same thing and noticed he looked as worried as she felt. She would need to pay Gudrun's mother a visit right after Christmas.

Her mind was taken off Gudrun for a while when the children performed the nativity play and the congregation sang the ancient Christmas songs she knew by heart. The time-worn organ accompanied their voices, echoing through the old village church as puffs of breath bloomed in the cold above their heads, and the light of flickering candles filled the little building with a warm glow.

After the service, the tolling of the church bell accompanied them on their silent walk home. When it finally stopped, Wallhausen lay quiet, the streets lit only by the light that fell from the windows of the houses. There was no snow this year, but the night was cold enough.

As they reached the house, a dark figure rose slowly from the front steps. Mama screeched. Gisela's father quickly strode ahead. Gisela grabbed Erich's hand. Then she saw her father fall into a big embrace with the man in the shadows. "Karl," she whispered as she recognized him, his black uniform barely distinguishable from the darkness that surrounded him.

Chapter 4

January 1943

Wallhausen, Germany

Sitting in the back seat, Karl cringed at the squeal from the car's transmission and rolled his eyes. His sister was at the wheel, torturing her fiancé's car, the beautiful Adler Trumpf. He wondered what had possessed him, why he had agreed to come along for the driving lesson. Although he had to admit, Gisela couldn't have done any better. Erich was good-looking, charming, a pilot, and owned his own car. Karl almost envied him. Almost. After all, he would have to deal with Gisela for the rest of his life. That was nothing to envy the man for.

"I give up. I can't do it," Gisela exclaimed and jumped out of the driver's seat.

"It just takes practice. That's all," Erich said, following her out of the car and putting his arm around her shoulders.

Karl rolled his eyes again at her crossed arms and pouting face, which he knew so well. He climbed out, too. "You're just a girl, sis. It will take you a while to get it," Karl said. "Erich is right, all it takes is practice. And you don't really need to know how to drive."

Gisela glowered at him, then turned to Erich. "How will I be able to practice?" She whined. "You're leaving me in two days."

"Maybe Father will let you practice in his car," Karl snickered.

"No, he won't. And you know that." She scowled at him, and Karl thought that Erich had just shot him a disapproving look. He shrugged it off. Gisela had annoyed him since the day she was born. He had been the youngest and his mother's favorite until the day Gisela came into the world. Her birth had changed everything for him. And he never let Gisela forget it.

"Would you like to drive back?" Erich asked, dangling the keys in front of his face. Karl snatched them and slid behind the wheel. He loved driving, and the SS had trained him to do all sorts of things. In Bavaria, he had learned to ski down a mountain, and he could drive anything, from a car to a motorcycle to a lorry. He had become an exceptionally skilled driver and was grateful that his commander had recognized his skill. Occasionally, Karl had even been asked to chauffeur Hitler's personal assistant and valet, Heinz Linge, on errands. He preferred that much more than standing guard and being assigned to shooting squads. The vehicle didn't matter. When Karl was driving, he felt independent and free.

Erich and Gisela climbed into the back seat, and Karl put the car into gear. For a while, they cruised along in silence, only interrupted by Gisela's occasional giggling. Karl didn't mind. He felt elated behind the wheel and enjoyed the low hum of the engine, his mind taking in the frosted fields and meadows they passed.

When they got home, Gisela was surprised to find her father waiting for them in front of the house. "Something has happened," she whispered more to herself than Erich and Karl, who both looked as concerned as she was at the unusual sight of her father waiting for them. He wasn't wearing a coat or a hat, even though it was freezing cold. He came toward them as soon as Karl had killed the engine, his face lined with worry. Behind him, Waldemar and Mama appeared on the steps of the house. Mama's face was red and tear-stained.

"What in the hell is going on?" Karl asked as he jumped out of the car.

"Irmtraud is gone," her father said, his voice breaking as the three of them walked toward him.

"Gone? What do you mean? Gone where?" Gisela asked, shaking her head in confusion.

"She left. To go to Kassel." Her father had fastened his gaze on Erich, who seemed to shrink.

"I don't understand," Gisela continued. But her father was neither looking at her nor hearing her. Gisela went to her mother and put her arms around her. A sob escaped Mama as Gisela stroked her back. "She left a letter," Mama finally said.

Gisela let go of her. "What did it say?"

"She went to Kassel to enroll in nursing school."

"She can't just do that," Gisela sputtered in her shock. Irmtraud was spunky and could be quite determined, but she was not thoughtless, careless, or irresponsible.

Her eyes fell on Erich, who had encouraged her a few days ago. Was he to blame?

"She can and she did," Waldemar said.

"We need to go after her." Gisela walked over to her father.

"I didn't mean to–" Erich was studying the tips of his shoes.

"Father," Gisela insisted, "we need to go to Kassel and get her."

"I will go." Erich straightened his back and looked at Gisela's father, who suddenly looked like an old man. "I put these ideas into her head, and I will make this right, Herr Fahnrich."

"I will go with him," Karl volunteered. Erich nodded in gratitude.

"You will bring her back home," Gisela's father said. It wasn't a question. He turned and started back to the house.

"You have my word," Erich called after him, then he turned and hurried to the car. Karl jumped into the passenger seat, and they drove off with gravel spraying.

Irmtraud must have left on the morning train, Gisela thought, as she followed her father into the house. If she had indeed caught the first train to Kassel, she had arrived in the city hours ago. It would take Erich and Karl a couple of hours to drive there. Gisela doubted they would be able to return tonight, even if they located her right away, and that was doubtful. The Fahnrichs had no relatives in the city, and as far as she knew, her parents did not have any friends or acquaintances there either. Perhaps Erich knew somebody in Kassel whom he could ask for assistance in locating her sister. Gisela ignored the knot in her stomach. For the first time in her life, she was afraid for Irmtraud. At barely seventeen in a city where she knew no one during wartime. Gisela shuddered at the thought. Erich and Karl had to find her, no matter what.

Gisela stood for a few moments, watching the now deserted road Erich and Karl had taken. Then she turned and walked back into the house and up to their bedroom. Hands shaking at the thought of what she might discover, she opened the wardrobe. She had expected to find Irmtraud's clothes gone, but it was shocking nevertheless to have the bare emptiness of her sister's side of the wardrobe stare back at her. Gisela had never expected to be the one left behind. She had always assumed she would leave first. But Irmtraud was never one who liked to be left behind, and now she had taken matters into her own hands. For the first time, Gisela would sleep alone tonight in the bed they shared.

It was barely dawn when Gisela woke from a night of tossing and turning. She got dressed quickly, then went to search for her father. She looked all over the house but was unable to find him. Mama was in the kitchen folding laundry on the kitchen table. Gisela noticed her hands were shaking. She went to her and rested her head on her shoulder. For a brief moment, her mother stilled.

"They'll bring her back to us," Gisela said, hoping her words brought comfort. She felt a sting of guilt that Erich had encouraged Irmtraud. Her mother sniffed back tears, then nodded resolutely and said, "If you're looking for your father, he went to the workshop."

To her surprise, Gisela found him in his office. She started to go in, then stopped when she realized her father was on the telephone. His voice was hushed. Gisela strained to hear, but she could only make out the occasional word. *Find... search... Irmtraud... network... SS... Karl.*

Chapter 5

February 1943

Kassel, Germany

Irmtraud put up the collar of her winter coat and hugged herself against the cold. A deflated grocery net dangled from her arm. The small store down the road from the nursing school was only a hundred meters ahead. She wouldn't be out in this miserable weather for too long. Food in the city was much scarcer than in a village like Wallhausen, where her family's vegetable garden and a cellar filled with potatoes, apples, and jars of canned fruit fed her family through winters and years of war.

Irmtraud put her hands in the pockets of her coat, clamping her frozen fingers around the ration card. While the nursing school provided meager meals from government bulk rations, the chief nurse and head of the school allowed her students to keep their individual ration cards and encouraged the girls to get whatever they could with them.

A small line of people snaked out of the building as Irmtraud approached. She had expected nothing less. Standing in line for food had been a constant exercise since the beginning of the war.

Irmtraud shuddered at the thought of having to stand in the cold. For a moment, she thought about abandoning her mission, but the forecast wasn't promising milder temperatures any time soon, and she needed to replenish the diminishing food supplies she stored under her bed.

When she finally made it inside the store with only five people left ahead of her in line, she tried to ignore the empty shelves that seemed to mock her as she inched toward the counter. When she finally got there, the clerk, who seemed about her age, pulled out a can of sausages and half a loaf of bread and placed them in front of her. Irmtraud held out her ration card so he could punch it. As he handed it back and she turned to go, she realized neither of them had spoken a word.

Back outside, it seemed the cold had lessened. Fat snowflakes began to fall. They stuck to her lashes, making it hard to see. Even so, Irmtraud enjoyed the cold wet on her face and the now muffled hustle and bustle of the street. Wiping her eyes, Irmtraud saw a mother and young son farther ahead. The woman pulled the boy into the shadows of an entrance to an apartment building, as she scanned the sidewalk that led to the small grocery store. Then, she pulled the boy back onto the sidewalk and towards the store. As they passed, their eyes cast to the ground in the drifting snow, Irmtraud noticed their gaunt faces and frail bodies that could not be disguised by their tattered coats.

For a moment, Irmtraud wondered if they were Jews in hiding. But from what she had learned, the last Jews of Kassel had all been deported to the East last year. Irmtraud stopped walking and decided to vanish into the same covered entrance that had been occupied by the mother and her son so she could watch them. She wasn't quite sure why. Out of curiosity? Empathy for the starving child?

Through the snow, Irmtraud saw the mother nudge the young boy to go inside the store, but he refused. The woman looked around to see if anyone was watching her, but no one on the street paid her any attention. The snowfall made the sad little pair look like phantoms in the graying daylight. Irmtraud watched the woman crouch and speak intently to the boy, her face only centimeters away from his. Then she let go of him, and he went inside. After what seemed like an eternity, he reappeared. Whatever he handed his mother, she hid it immediately under her coat. Then, she took his hand and hurried down the sidewalk toward Irmtraud.

As they passed her, Irmtraud stepped out onto the sidewalk. The mother and son looked at her with big eyes, startled at her sudden appearance. Without a word or thought, Irmtraud pushed her filled grocery net into the woman's arms and hurried away.

The red brick building that housed the nursing students was only a short walk from the hospital. As it appeared in front of her, Irmtraud felt a wave of relief. Inside, she shook off the snow and stomped her feet to loosen clumps that had collected on the bottom of her shoes. She greeted the watchman, who kindly tipped his hat toward her. The head nurse had told her that after she had arrived asking for enrollment at the end of December, her brother and another young gentleman had arrived, barely hours later, to pick her up. The head nurse had asked Irmtraud if she wanted to stay or leave. Irmtraud had asked to remain, and the head nurse had told the watchman to turn the two young men away. Weeks later, after she had become friendly with the watchman, he told her that the men hadn't been easy to get rid of. One of them had made threats he did not wish to repeat. There was only one of her brothers who would act that way. Irmtraud had been embarrassed and had apologized profusely.

She had also apologized to her parents. Irmtraud had felt immensely guilty for running away, but it had been the only way. She knew her father would have never agreed to let her go. She wanted to be a nurse, and right now, the program was fast-tracked. With any luck, she would be fully qualified by the end of the year. She had written to her parents shortly after her arrival in Kassel and admission to the school and informed them about her plans and the program. She missed her family dearly, especially her mother and Gisela, but she finally felt she mattered, and that what she did mattered. She would visit them in the summer. Hopefully, by then, they would have forgiven her.

The large dormitory Irmtraud slept in was occupied by twelve beds lined up against both long walls. She was surprised to find it empty. A glance at the clock on the opposite wall told her it was almost dinner time, and she suspected the others had already gone to the mess hall.

As Irmtraud passed the washroom, she heard hushed voices. She hesitated for a moment, then decided to go in. As soon as she entered, the voices fell silent. In the middle of the washroom, three of her fellow nursing students stood in a circle. A girl called Beate, who had grown up in Kassel, quickly put one of her hands behind her back, hiding something. Irmtraud pretended not to have seen it and greeted them with a friendly smile, which they returned. At the sinks, she washed her hands without another glance at them. But as she turned to leave, Beate stepped in front of her, blocking her way. Tall and wiry, Beate hovered over her. Irmtraud's eyes narrowed, but the girl seemed as friendly as always.

"Irmtraud, right?" Beate asked with a smile as warm as a summer's evening. Her hand was still tucked behind her back. Irmtraud simply nodded. Beate glanced at the other two, then she asked, "Why are you here, Irmtraud?"

Irmtraud was surprised by the question. "I assume for the same reasons as you," she said.

Beate nodded knowingly.

"What is this about?" Irmtraud asked.

"Can you forget you saw us in the washroom today?" Beate's smile had vanished.

"What is it to me?" Irmtraud shrugged. "I don't see anything out of the ordinary here. And if I had, it wouldn't have been any of my business." Irmtraud thought she saw a hint of relief flicker in Beate's eyes. "You don't need to worry about me. I really do mind my own business," Irmtraud reassured her.

Beate stepped aside and let her pass without another word. Outside the washroom, Irmtraud paused for a moment to listen intently, but no more voices came from inside. What had they talked about, and most importantly, what had Beate hidden behind her back? Irmtraud hadn't felt threatened, and it only now occurred to her that Beate seemed to have felt threatened by her. Irmtraud shook her head in confusion.

On her way to the mess hall, Irmtraud decided that she would make an effort to befriend Beate. Whatever she and the other girls had been up to was worrisome, but more than anything, she was curious.

Chapter 6

April 1943

Wallhausen, Germany

Gisela hastily unfolded the letter that had just been delivered and devoured Erich's words line by line. There was no extraordinary news, just Erich pacifying her that they would be together again soon. With the war continuing as it did, who knew when that would be.

After she was done reading, she pressed the paper against her chest, then carefully folded it to put it back in the fragile light blue envelope. She opened the drawer of her nightstand and placed it on top of the other ones already stored there. After Erich had failed to retrieve Irmtraud, he had left Wallhausen in a hurry. They had never had the chance to talk about their future together, and Gisela had been worried that Erich was reconsidering his proposal. But this letter, like all the other ones he had sent since his departure, had been tender and loving. He promised to see her as soon as he was granted leave. Now she could go back to worrying about his safety.

The same way she worried about Waldemar's. Her brother had been reassigned and had left Paris for the Eastern Front. Since the day his letter had arrived bearing the grim news, Mama had been constantly cleaning. Her father was quieter than usual. With little to do around the house and Irmtraud and Gudrun gone, Gisela was left to her own devices.

Karl, too, had left shortly after returning from Kassel, more in a fury than a hurry. Gisela had been glad he was gone again. He treated her like a child and never stopped demeaning her. But with the house this quiet and feeling this lonely without any of her siblings, she wondered if it would have been more bearable even with Karl there. Her days were occupied with helping her mother, when she let her, and with standing in line at the butcher or baker and helping her father with small tasks in his office. Most of his apprentices and employees had been drafted into the *Wehrmacht*. Only Georg, an old carpenter who had worked for her grandfather, was still here to help her father keep the business going. Not that there was much demand for furniture now. People were occupied with other things. Securing provisions had become far more important than acquiring a new dining room set. If only this war would end, and everything could go back to how it used to be. Gisela prayed for this daily, but deep down she knew things would never go back to how they were before. Her childhood was over, and she was left with only fond memories of her family being together. The four winds had scattered her siblings in all directions, and soon she would get married and leave home for good.

Gisela wiped her forehead with the back of her hand as she knelt in the fresh brown soil of her mother's garden in front of the house. It was enclosed by a green wooden fence and yielded flowers, gooseberries, and currants, and different kinds of lettuces throughout the summer. It was unseasonably hot for April, which usually brought a mixture of spring weather. The last snow had fallen in February, which seemed like an eternity ago. With little rain, March had warmed up quickly, too quickly for the freshly seeded radishes, which had grown too fast and would be shriveled and dry by harvest.

This morning at breakfast, her mama had interrupted the silent meal, asking her to prune the berry bushes and to sow the butter lettuce. Pruning the bushes was Gisela's least favorite chore in the garden. The thorns scratched her hands, and the height of the bushes made it a backbreaking task. Planting and sowing, Gisela enjoyed, however. Feeling the moist coolness of the soil between her fingers brought her joy, and she could spend hours doing it.

When the sun stood high in the sky, she took a break and sat down under the lilac tree. Its scent hung so heavily in the air that it was almost intoxicating. This spring, the lilac too had blossomed rather early. Usually, it would not bloom until the middle of May. Gisela leaned against the rough bark and pulled a somewhat shriveled apple from last year's harvest from her apron and bit into it. She leaned her head back and closed her eyes while she chewed. The sun warmed her face, and the insects around her filled the air with a comforting low hum. Somewhere close by, two doves cooed.

Gisela opened her eyes when she heard the faint call of her name. But it wasn't her mother who was calling her. As her father's voice drew nearer, she got up. Did he need her help? He rounded the corner of the house, striding toward her, his eyes fixed on hers. "You have a phone call," he said without breaking his gaze.

Gisela raised her eyebrows. Did she detect a hint of urgency in his voice?

"Come quick," he added and motioned for her to follow him. She wiped her hands on her apron and followed her father. *Who could it be? Erich? Irmtraud?* When they arrived in the workshop, her father stood back to let her enter his office while he remained at the door. The handset lay next to the phone. Glancing at her father, Gisela picked it up and put it to her ear. When she looked up, her father was gone.

"Hello?" She asked. Realizing it sounded more like a croak, she cleared her throat and tried again. "Hello?" She repeated more clearly.

"Gisela?"

The voice was unmistakable. "Erich," she breathed into the receiver.

"Gisela, I don't have much time." His words ran into each other. "I won't be able to come visit anytime soon. Not with the way this war is going." She wanted to interject, ask him what would become of their intended wedding, what would become of them, but he went on quickly. "Listen," he said. "I want to marry you. I don't want to wait any longer. I need you to be my wife." He sounded out of breath, as if he had hiked up a long flight of stairs.

Gisela shook her head in confusion. "I don't understand. How can we get married–"

"Marriage in absentia," he said.

There was a moment of silence, the three words hanging heavily in the air. "Gisela?" Erich asked, "Do you understand what that means?" She knew he wanted her to reply, but she couldn't find the words.

Gisela cleared her throat. "I ... I think I know what it means."

"No leaves are granted anymore. Not for something like a wedding," Erich said, his voice heavy with defeat.

There was silence again, as Gisela let this sink in. She fell onto her father's office chair.

"It's the only way we can get married, Gisela," Erich was saying. "This war will continue. Hitler won't give up. It could be years and years."

Again, silence. Gisela heard the doves' coo through the open window. She envied them. They were nestled together in the tree.

"We can have a proper party after the war," Erich added, as if to console her.

"It's not about the party, Erich." She couldn't believe he thought her this vain. If he really knew her, then he would know why she wasn't happy about this. "My family," she said. "I want my family to be there. With me. With us. And your family, Erich."

"That's impossible, Gisela, you know that. Your brothers won't get any leave either. And with Waldemar at the Eastern front now, who knows when and if–" If Erich hadn't cut himself off, Gisela would have. "Gisela, your parents can be there with you," he said. "When you get married to me in absentia."

Gisela shook her head at the image he had just painted for her. How sad and pathetic she would feel finding herself alone in front of the marriage registrar, and what about a church wedding?

"Only if we marry in the church after the war." She was surprised at her own words, surprised she even considered his proposal.

"We will," he said quickly, sounding relieved. "I promise you ... we will."

She could hear excitement and determination, as well as relief in his voice. Gisela knew he was waiting for her to match his excitement. But how could she feel thrilled at the prospect of getting married alone without Erich being there to hold her hand and kiss her?

"I got permission from my commander to go through with it and have already sent a letter with his permission to the registrar at the Wallhausen town hall," he said.

"You did? They know?"

"It's the done way these days." He sounded less animated now. "You will be taken care of, Gisela. You will have access to military allowances and pension benefits," Erich added in a matter-of-fact sort of way that made Gisela feel like marriage had nothing to do with love at all. "And you will be Frau Schmidt, wife of Erich Schmidt," he said in a lighter tone.

"I want to be your wife, Erich, but this is not how I pictured it." Gisela was twisting the cloth-covered cord of the handset around her index finger. Her arm was starting to get heavy from holding it, so she put her elbow on her father's desk. Her ear was starting to hurt with the receiver pressed against it. "And I haven't even met your family yet."

"You will ... This war—"

"Always the war. I'm sick of it, Erich. I'm sick of the war."

"Think of all the benefits of you being my wife," Erich said, trying to bring her back to the topic at hand. "You'll be protected in case I—"

"In case you what, Erich?"

"In case I die."

There was silence between them again.

"Please, Gisela," Erich said finally, "Marry me." His soft voice brushed her sore ear. "You pick the date. I can't wait for you to be my wife."

"I want to be your wife, Erich. There's nothing I want more."

"Then we are agreed." It wasn't a question. "I need to go," he announced. "I will write to you, of course, and you to me, yes? I hope when your next letter reaches me, it is from my wife."

Then there was a click in the line, and he was gone. Gisela took the receiver off her ear and gaped at it. Only when the voices of the men in the workshop reached her did she place the handset back on the phone. She leaned back in her father's chair with a sigh and continued to stare at the telephone, but it wasn't what she saw. The image in front of her was a bride in a graying white dress, wilted flowers in hand, standing alone in front of a registrar with only her parents behind her.

Gisela tore her gaze away from the black lump of bakelite that had brought her the unfortunate news. A ledger lay open on her father's desk. Under it, she noticed the corner of a strange card. Gisela leaned forward and pulled it out. It was the military conscription card of a Wehrmacht soldier. His name was Kurt. Kurt Vogel. She didn't recognize the name, nor the man in the photo. Why would her father have the conscription card of a stranger?

She took the card, slid it into the pocket of her apron, and left her father's office.

Gisela had searched the whole house, workshop, and garden for her father, but he was nowhere to be found. So she went to ask her mother where he was. She knew where to find Mama, in the washhouse at the back of the house. When Gisela entered, the thick humid air caught in her lungs. She could make out the shape of her mother in the foggy steam by the wood-burning stove, stirring a huge pot of suds and white linens.

Gisela placed a hand on her mother's shoulder. "Have you seen Father?"

Her mother turned to her. "Is he not in his workshop?"

Gisela shook her head, then realized that her mother might not see her in the steam that blurred everything around them. "He is not," she said. "Not anywhere. Has he left?"

"Not that I know of, child."

For a moment, Gisela considered showing her mother the conscription card. Perhaps she knew who this man was. Then she realized she had completely forgotten about Erich's proposal. Or perhaps she had pushed away the thought of it. She needed to tell her parents. Suddenly, it felt unbearably hot in the washhouse. Gisela opened the top button of her blouse and fanned herself with her hand, but it did no good at all. Tonight, she would tell her parents about Erich's call. Over supper. By then, she hoped she would feel more enthusiastic about the whole idea.

"Could you go up to the attic for me? Not the attic in the house, but in the workshop?" Her mother asked, interrupting her ruminations.

"Yes, of course, Mama."

"There's a bag of salt up there that I need. We are running low on laundry soap. There's none to be had. If I add some salt, it will stretch the little I have left. I need to get these linens whitened," she said with a hint of frustration as she stirred the pot with renewed fervor.

"I'll be right back with it."

Gisela felt her way to the door and stumbled out into the light and fresh air, breathing deeply. She realized that pearls of sweat had gathered on her forehead and wiped them away. She brushed back some flyaway hairs from her sticky temples and made her way back to the workshop. Gisela had no idea how her mother could tolerate the steam and heat of the washhouse.

As in busier times, the long workshop hall was filled with piles of wood and machinery, half-finished pieces of furniture, and swirls of sawdust in the air. Gisela headed for the staircase in the far back that was just off to the side of the large, gated loading doors. The doors were shuttered, as they so often were these days. Gisela remembered when they had stood open all day and every day, when the whole place had been alive with the hustle and bustle of workers and deliveries. Now, with everyone gone to fight in the war and barely any orders, the large workshop hall lay deserted. The only sound came from her feet crunching the shavings. As she walked toward the stairs to the attic, it occurred to her that she had never seen the floor of the building. For as long as she could remember, it had been covered in shavings.

Her father was still nowhere to be seen. Neither was Old Georg, the only employee he had left. Gisela climbed the steps that felt more like a ladder than proper stairs. When she reached the top, the small door to the building's attic was just across from her. It was closed, and there was no key in the keyhole. She knew that the door was locked, and she had to get the key from her father, who was who knew where. She sighed in frustration and gave the door a small kick. To Gisela's surprise, it popped open. So, it hadn't been locked after all. An oddity indeed, considering her father always locked every door, be it in the house or the workshop.

Gisela lowered her head so as not to bump it on the low clearance and stepped inside. The long attic was mostly empty. A few sacks of supplies were staggered along the wall opposite the windows, which appeared to be extraordinarily filthy, layered as they were with centuries of sawdust. Her great-grandfather had not only built their house, but also this building and their family's business. Gisela doubted these windows had been washed since they had been installed. The blurred sunlight shrouded the attic in a clouded haze.

She looked toward the sacks of goods stacked neatly against the attic wall but couldn't make out any that might be the sack of salt her mother had requested. It seemed as if her father did not use the attic at all for his business. There were no shavings on the floor. No wood was stored up here, either. Some old broken tables and chairs were piled in the far corner. A couple of almost medieval-looking trunks stood nearby. For a moment, Gisela wondered what old family treasures they could hold. Then she heard a sound like shuffling coming from behind the pile of broken furniture and held her breath. A mouse, perhaps? But a mouse wouldn't make such a big sound. Gisela held her breath and listened intently, but everything was quiet now.

She began to walk along the row of sacks stacked along the wall. Then she heard the same sound again. As swiftly and quietly as she could, Gisela glided across the floor toward the trunk and furnishings. She felt a tingle in the back of her neck. The hairs on her arms stood up. But, as usual, her curiosity had gotten the better of her.

Gisela reached the broken chair or table and stepped around them to see what lay behind. In the corner, on top of a pile of blankets, a pair of anxious eyes stared back at her. She had seen these eyes before. They belonged to the man whose photograph was fastened to the conscription card.

Gisela had stumbled backward. She had rushed out of the attic, flown down the stairs, and crashed into Georg, who had been attempting, in vain, to sweep up the shavings.

"Careful there," he had muttered and shaken his head while Gisela hurried toward her father's office for a second time that day. This time, she found him inside, sitting at his desk with the ledger open in front of him.

"There you are," he said, looking up. "Tell me about your phone call."

"Phone call?" Gisela stared at him.

"Your phone call with Erich," her father said, frowning, his eyes fixed on her. Gisela had forgotten all about it. Again. Her father's gaze made her uncomfortable. She reached inside her apron and pulled out the card. He watched her place it right in front of him. "Who is he?" She asked.

"Where did you get this?" He took the card and threw it in one of his desk drawers.

"It was on your desk. In plain sight." Gisela didn't want her father to think she had snooped around and gone through his papers and books.

"This is none of your business, Gisela. You had no right to–"

"Who is he, Father ... the man in our attic?" She heard her father inhale sharply and regretted her forwardness. "It seems," she said more gently, "that this conscription card belongs to him."

"Gisela," her father said haltingly. "You cannot know about this man." His voice was hushed as he got up, walked over to the door, and closed it. "I'm helping him. This has nothing to do with you. You must forget that you ever saw him."

"Who is he, Papa?"

Her father sighed. "He's the son of an old friend I fought with in the Great War. I wouldn't be here if it weren't for this young man's father. I owe him my life."

"Your friend's son is a soldier." Gisela pointed at the drawer that now held the conscription card. "Why doesn't he fight like everyone else? Like Erich? And Waldemar, and Karl, and Heinrich?" She studied her father's face and then leaned forward. In a hushed voice, she added, "He's a deserter. Papa, this is dangerous. They hang people for hiding deserters."

"And that is the reason why you must forget about this man."

"Does Mama know?" Her father shook his head with some vehemence. Gisela sighed in relief. "She wanted a bag of salt from the attic."

"I'll get you the bag," he said and got up. Before he opened the door, he turned to her. For a moment, he studied her face as if it held clues as to whether he could trust her. Then he narrowed his eyes. "Gisela," her father said. "Not a word to anyone, do you understand?"

"I do," Gisela said and watched as he left his office.

She swallowed hard. The thought of the stranger in the attic and the possibility of the Gestapo finding out about it left her stomach in knots. She went over to her father's desk and opened the drawer. She hesitated for a moment, but then she took the conscription card. It was best to have it disappear. If her father were questioned by the

Gestapo, there would be no evidence. Her only hope now was that her father's deed of repaying an old debt didn't end with him at the gallows.

Chapter 7

May 1943

Wallhausen, Germany

Gisela opened her eyes. The month of May was the most beautiful and sunny time of the year, but not today. Today, outside her bedroom window, a milky gray sky dipped everything in gloomy light. Today, she would get married.

Gisela was certain no bride had ever felt this miserable on the morning of her wedding. For a moment, she stared at the simple white dress that hung on the wardrobe across from her bed. It felt silly and pointless to dress in it. Erich wouldn't be there to see her.

Mama had sewn the wedding dress for her after she had refused to just wear the one Mama had worn when she had married her father. It felt sacrilegious to wear Mama's dress for this ceremony. Could it even be called a ceremony? Her parents had been shocked when she had told them about getting married to Erich in absentia. Her father had insisted she wait until after the war, but he eventually relented when her mother reiterated the benefits. Seeing both her parents' disappointment and disapproval had, in turn, made Gisela feel even worse about it.

The only highlight was that Irmtraud had come home for the ceremony. Gisela had called the nursing school and told her everything. When she told Irmtraud she needed her to be there, her sister hadn't hesitated. How she had missed Irmtraud. The night she arrived, Irmtraud had gotten into a shouting match with her father. But by the next morning, everything seemed as it had been before, and they were happily chatting over breakfast in the kitchen.

Last night, Irmtraud and Gisela had talked for hours. About Kassel, the nursing school, and Erich. Gisela was dying to tell her about the man in the attic but knew she couldn't. She had tried to forget about him, but she couldn't do that, either. There were days when she didn't think of him at all, but then she noticed her father taking food from the kitchen, and she was reminded of who it was for. She hadn't dared go into the workshop again, let alone the attic. It was for the best. The less she knew and saw, the better.

Irmtraud seemed changed. She appeared much older and wiser, and it made Gisela feel years her junior. To her dismay, Gisela found that her sister had also lost some of her youthful zest. Nothing that Irmtraud had told her explained the change in her. Gisela wondered if Irmtraud had a secret of her own she had not shared. When this wedding, if you could even call it that, was over, she would try to find out.

Gisela got up with a groan. It was time to get ready.

———

Gisela was glad that her father had agreed to get the car out and drive them to the town hall. Her mother had cut some lilac and pressed the small bouquet in Gisela's hand. The pungent aroma made Gisela feel nauseated. Sitting beside her in the back seat of the car, Irmtraud held Gisela's hand and smiled at her encouragingly. It did nothing to calm her nerves.

It was a short drive. Gisela hoped no one spotted them when they filed out of the car in front of the town hall, which was located right at the center of the village. To her dismay, a line of people was queuing up in front of the butcher. To Gisela's great relief, her father came around to help her out of the car and block her from the curious eyes of onlookers while Irmtraud and Mama waited by the steps of the tall narrow building that had dominated Wallhausen's village square for hundreds of years Then the four of them climbed swiftly up the stairs, and slid inside the half-timbered building that was in desperate need of a fresh coat of paint.

The registrar's office was on the second floor, so they had to climb again. Gisela held her dress so as not to step on its hem as the narrow staircase creaked under their weight. She felt winded and unable to catch her breath when she finally stood in front of the registrar's desk.

"Normally, we would now go into our ceremony room at the end of the hallway, but that won't be necessary in this case," the registrar said, pushing a document in front of Gisela.

"This won't do." The stern lines of her father's face were more pronounced than usual. "We will use the ceremony room," he said. "Like everyone else."

"But I haven't set it up," the clerk sputtered.

"Why didn't you? Isn't it your job?" Her father demanded.

Gisela placed a hand on her father's arm. "It is alright," she said. "I can just sign, so we can leave."

"My daughter is getting married today, and you will get the room ready," her father told the now harassed looking clerk. "Is this understood?"

Had he even heard her? Gisela just wanted to sign and get out of here. And out of this dress. But the registrar had already scampered away. Gisela felt someone squeeze her hand. Without looking, she knew it was Irmtraud. Again, she thanked the heavens that her sister had come to be by her side through this.

After a few minutes, the clerk reappeared. Her father linked arms with her on her left, and her mother hooked her arms with her on the right. Together, they led her into the ceremony room, followed by Irmtraud. The registrar closed the doors behind them, and Gisela took a deep breath. In a few minutes, she would be a married woman. She closed her eyes and tried to picture Erich. But every time she thought she had gotten hold of an image of his face, it vanished into the dark.

***

"Now that you're happily married–" Irmtraud ducked to dodge the pillow Gisela had thrown at her head. "What I'm trying to say is–" She chuckled at Gisela's eyeroll. "I will miss you." Against her will, Irmtraud realized that she suddenly felt rather somber.

"And I will miss you. Do you really have to go back to Kassel so soon?"

"I have no choice. I'm grateful the head nurse let me leave at all." Irmtraud had received leave for three days and two nights. She needed to catch the early train tomorrow morning for her hospital shift with the other student nurses. Her thoughts turned to Beate and the other girls in her group, and she felt the urgent need to tell Gisela about what had been going on. She had always shared every secret with her sister, as Gisela had with her. But would her sister understand? Gisela had always been averse to any form of risk. She would most certainly chide Irmtraud for putting herself in danger and beg her not to continue. But what kind of nurse would she be if she didn't participate in helping those unfortunate souls the Nazis had deemed unworthy of life? Suddenly, Irmtraud felt a hand on hers.

"Why are you so pensive?" Gisela asked with a mixture of concern and curiosity.

Irmtraud studied her sister's face for a moment. "Have you heard about the T4 program?"

"I have heard Father mention it, but that was a long while ago. Must have been at least two years since I overheard him and Mama talking about it."

Irmtraud nodded and realized that back then, she would have been too young to want to know or understand. "It's been *officially* discontinued." She made sure to emphasize "officially," so Gisela would catch on.

"So they no longer euthanize people who are terminally ill?"

Irmtraud's eyes narrowed. "Not only the terminally ill, Gisela," she said quietly. "But also, the old, the mentally challenged, children with handicaps. Children, Gisela!"

Her sister stared at her. Gisela opened her mouth to speak, but Irmtraud cut her off quickly. "The program was officially discontinued, but the chief physician at the hospital still kills people by injection."

Gisela's hand flew to her mouth. Irmtraud nodded. "We are helping the head nurse to either smuggle those patients out of the hospital, or we hide them in a backroom of the basement and care for them there until we can get them out." The words were just tumbling out of Irmtraud now. "We falsify documents and declare a patient dead, forging the doctor's signature. Two men come to the hospital once a week to pick up corpses. We pay them to also bring our "dead." Irmtraud raised her eyebrows. "They take them back to their families, or they hide them. I don't know where."

Gisela was staring at her, a mixture of shock and fear in her eyes. She wrung her hands and sat straight up, as if she was about to jump off the bed. "That's too dangerous." Gisela almost shouted the words.

Irmtraud had expected her sister would react this way, but she had also hoped she would understand. Now, Gisela snatched at her hands. "You can't go back," she said. "You need to stay here."

Slowly, Irmtraud pulled her hands out of Gisela's. "You know I won't do that."

Gisela got up and started pacing up and down past the foot of the bed.

"Gisela," Irmtraud said, as gently as she could. "I wanted to become a nurse so I could help people. Now, I'm not only helping the sick. I'm also helping those who are condemned to die. And not of incurable illnesses, but at the hands of a Nazi doctor."

"But what if he finds out what you and the others are doing? Don't you see how dangerous that is?"

"I do," Irmtraud said, "I know." There was nothing else she could say.

Gisela sat down on Irmtraud's side of the bed. "Is there nothing that could convince you to stay?"

Irmtraud shook her head, her eyes wandering to the window and the darkness outside.

"Can you please be careful then?" Gisela pleaded. "And if you're in danger, promise me you will flee, and come home straight away?"

"Of course, I will." Irmtraud leaned over and hugged Gisela. "I promise," she said. "I promise you."

The next morning, Irmtraud got up before dawn to get ready to leave. After she had finished packing, she gently shook Gisela's shoulder to wake her. Her sister groaned and turned away from her. "Gisela," Irmtraud whispered. "I'm leaving." There was another groan. "Won't you tell me goodbye?"

Gisela snapped back around, her eyes wide open. "I'm coming with you to the station. I'm seeing you off." Gisela threw back the duvet.

"No need," Irmtraud shook her head. "Father is taking me. And, besides, there is no time. I have to leave this instant."

Irmtraud picked up her bag with a sigh as Gisela jumped out of bed, pulled open the doors to the wardrobe, and began rummaging through it.

"I'm taking you to the train station," Gisela said, grabbing a trench coat she had found and throwing it on over her nightgown. "Are you coming?"

Sighing, Irmtraud followed her sister out of the bedroom. Father and Mama were already waiting by the front door. Their father greeted Gisela's get-up with a shake of his head, but he agreed to let Gisela take Irmtraud to the train station instead of him. Mama placed a hand on Irmtraud's cheek and managed a smile despite the tears that stood in her eyes. Then, everyone hugged and promised to write to each other, and Irmtraud and Gisela slipped out of the house and into the dewy morning.

Wallhausen lay still. The streets were empty. They encountered no one on their way to the train station, so it was even more surprising to find the platform crowded when they arrived. Irmtraud found a far corner that was a little less crowded, and for a moment they huddled together in the damp, breezy morning air.

Gisela was biting her lip and pushing a small rock around with the tip of her shoe.

"I'll be back as soon as I can," Irmtraud promised. For a moment, Gisela narrowed her eyes and stared back at her, but she didn't speak. "What is it? What's on your mind?" Irmtraud asked, searching her sister's face. Something was bothering Gisela, and she had no idea what it could be. Gisela's stare was starting to make her uneasy, but her sister still didn't say a word. Instead, she started pacing up and down. "What is it?" Irmtraud asked, yet again.

Gisela came to a stop in front of her, took a step closer, then scanned the platform around them. "I ... I have a secret of my own."

"What do you mean?"

Gisela drew even nearer, her voice hushed. "I wanted to tell you, but I didn't know if I should betray his trust."

"Whose?" Irmtraud felt the unease creep into every bone of her body.

"Father's." Gisela gazed at the ground, found the rock, and started to nervously shuffle it around again. Irmtraud went very still, holding her breath. This was not what she had expected, or rather, whose name she had expected. "He's hiding a deserter in the workshop attic." Gisela had said it so quietly that Irmtraud wondered if she had heard correctly.

"What?" She whispered.

Gisela clutched her arm. "Mama doesn't know. I discovered him by accident."

Irmtraud heard the whistle of a train in the distance, then the chugging that drew nearer and nearer. She grabbed Gisela's hand. "You must help Father keep this secret," she hissed. "At all costs."

The train came to a screeching halt in front of them. Irmtraud grabbed Gisela by the shoulders and pulled her sister into a tight hug. Then she whispered a quick goodbye into her ear, let go of her, and climbed onto the train. She threw a last look at Gisela over her shoulder as her sister slowly raised her hand in goodbye.

Irmtraud quickly found a seat by the window. Not far off, Gisela stood holding her trench coat closed with folded arms, the hem of her nightgown peeking out the bottom. Their eyes found each other as the whistle blew, and the train jerked into motion. Irmtraud pressed her hand against the dirty windowpane and thought she saw Gisela giving her a determined nod before she disappeared.

An hour later, the train came to a screeching halt. Irmtraud rubbed her eyes. She must have dozed off. A look out the window told her they had not yet arrived in Kassel but seemed instead to be in the middle of nowhere. Outside her window, fields that had just come into bloom stretched toward dark woods. The passengers looked around nervously, trying to make sense of the sudden stop. Then the conductor appeared. "The Eder Dam has been bombed," he announced. There were several gasps from the passengers as he continued. "The Fulda River has swollen enormously, and Kassel has been flooded." There was silence. No one dared to speak. "And so has the train station," he added. "We cannot get to Kassel."

Irmtraud swallowed hard, wondering how she would make it back to the city, or if she would even be able to get into Kassel if it was flooded.

Clearly wondering the same thing, a man got up and raised his hand. "How are we supposed to get there?"

The conductor sighed and slowly breathed out the next few words. "You cannot get there. Kassel looks like Venice." The man frowned but sat back down. "We will reverse and go back," the conductor said, "We have no choice." There was a swell of disgruntled murmuring from the passengers as the conductor moved on to spread the bad news to the next car.

Irmtraud looked out the window. They couldn't be far from Kassel. Maybe ten kilometers. She could walk. And when she got back to Kassel, she would find a way around the flooded districts of the city. The nursing school and hospital were situated on a slight hill and had hopefully been saved from the floodwaters.

Looking around, she could tell that some passengers were not resigned to going back and seemed to consider that same option of walking. They had gotten up and were looking out their windows, trying to get a lay of the land. When, minutes later, the conductor came rushing back, Irmtraud stood up, stepped in front of him, and said, "I'd like to get out."

The conductor looked at her as if she were mad.

"Kassel can't be more than ten kilometers from here," Irmtraud said, and noticed other passengers listening.

"You want to walk there?"

Irmtraud straightened her shoulders and nodded.

"But it's flooded, girl. It's not safe."

"I want to leave this train. Please open the door for me." Some passengers got up and moved closer as Irmtraud spoke.

"You're mad, but suit yourself," the conductor said and went to the nearest door. Irmtraud quickly grabbed her bag and followed him. Out of the corner of her eye, she saw others do the same.

As she hopped off the train and into the tall grass next to the tracks, the conductor shook his head. His whistle hung loosely between his lips, ready to send the train back.

Two more passengers exited after her. One was a young man with tousled black hair with a backpack on his back. He wore a bright red knitted sweater that had several holes where the yarn had unraveled. His trousers were dirty and stained. The other passenger who had jumped down into the grass was an older man with a briefcase, who was wearing a suit.

The conductor waited a brief moment, but no one else appeared to want to get off the train. Finally, he blew his whistle so loudly that Irmtraud covered her ears, then yelled at them to step back farther into the grass that was clustered with stinging nettles. He swung himself onto the train as it started to reverse back in the direction they had come from. A few moments later, the train picked up speed. They stood and watched it vanish into the distance.

"Kassel is in this direction. We should follow the tracks," the man in the suit said, and started walking. "At least until we come to the flooding. Then we need to find a way around it."

The young man started after him. "You coming?" He asked Irmtraud over his shoulder.

Irmtraud tightened her grip around the handle of her bag and started after them, wondering if it had really been a good idea to get off the train and follow two complete strangers into the unknown. She pictured Gisela's horrified face, which made her even less confident.

By noon, when the sun stood high, they came upon the first flooded fields. A few hundred meters farther, the railway tracks, too, were covered in water. They went into the woods on the other side of the tracks, which lay a little higher and were not so wet.

Like ducks walking in a row, they had followed the tracks with Irmtraud in the rear, staring at the back of the young man. They had not spoken since they started walking. Now in the woods, they walked side by side. "I'm Herr Müller," the older man said into the silence that was only interrupted by the occasional sound of a woodpecker.

"Jan," the young man said, looking at her expectantly.

"Irmtraud." She didn't feel like telling them but didn't want to appear rude since the men had shared their names.

"What business does a girl like you have in Kassel?" Jan asked.

She glanced at him, studying his face for a moment. He was tanned, and there were smudges of dirt on his cheeks and chin. For a moment, she wondered about his occupation and why a young man his age was not serving at the front. "I'm in nursing school," she said. "In Kassel. I need to get back."

"Don't we all," Herr Müller grunted, then pulled a kerchief out of his suit pocket to wipe his shiny forehead.

"And what do you do, Jan?" Irmtraud asked, not finding it necessary to hide her curiosity.

Jan glanced at her. "I'm on a pilgrimage of sorts."

"Shouldn't you be in the Wehrmacht?" Herr Müller had stopped walking and turned around to face Jan. "Young men your age are all serving their country. Why aren't you?" he asked, his eyes narrow.

Irmtraud stepped forward and held up her hands. She didn't want a fight to break out between these strangers. All she wanted was to get back to Kassel as quickly as possible. For a moment, she considered abandoning the men and going on alone without them, but they were heading where she was. "I'm sure Jan has a reason why–"

"Quiet," Jan said and held up his hand.

Irmtraud wanted to protest, but Jan placed a finger on his lips, then pointed at the treetops. Blue sky peeked through the lightly swaying trees. Then, Irmtraud heard it, too. The all too familiar sound of bombers. She covered her ears as the rumble grew into a ferocious roar. She crouched down and squeezed her eyes shut, trying to shut out the world around her, but she couldn't. She felt the tremor in her stomach. Her bones vibrated, and then she felt an arm around her, holding her tight. She opened her eyes. It was Jan who had put his arm around her. She breathed in his musky, earthy scent and leaned in against his shoulder.

When the roar overhead had subsided, Jan let go of her, and she stood back up. She saw the concern in his face. His scrutinizing gaze made her feel uncomfortable, so she started walking. Soon, she heard the two men behind her. No one talked for a while, and Irmtraud was grateful for it.

After about two kilometers, the forest thinned, and then they reached its edge. They stepped out into the open and stopped, shocked at the sight. Surrounded by hills on one side and a swollen river that looked more like a lake on the other, the city lay in front of them. Some of the districts were completely covered by floodwaters.

No one spoke. They stared in silence at the devastation ahead for what seemed like a long time before Herr Muller said, "I guess we should have listened to the conductor."

He sat down on a tree stump with a huff. He had finally loosened his tie and taken off his suit jacket, which he now laid neatly over his right knee.

"We have to stay away from the river," Jan said. "Get to the hills and then make it down." He was pointing to the hills on the left that bore a monument and a statue of Hercules that the Hessian landgrave had built in the early eighteenth century to signify his wealth and power. Irmtraud had visited the monument a couple of times on her walks in the beautiful park that lay below. The hospital and dormitory were located at the foot of the hill, a short walk from the park, just off the wide, tree-lined avenue that led all the way to the center of the city. Irmtraud found the park, then followed the avenue, which she could see clearly. It looked like the hospital and nursing school had been spared from the waters.

She turned to Jan. "I like your plan. It should work."

"It's the city center I need to get to," the old man grumbled.

"You won't be able to get to it. Can't you see?" Jan was clearly getting irritated by Herr Müller. "But I'm sure the waters will have subsided in a couple of days," he added more kindly.

"I should go home then. I don't know what I was thinking, getting off the train.

"You will walk back?" Irmtraud couldn't imagine going back.

"I'll go back to the tracks and follow them until I get to a village with a train station. There are several along the line." The old man got up, swung his suit jacket across his shoulder, and headed back in the direction they had come from. "Good luck to you, " he said without looking back.

Jan turned to face her. "So, it's just us now," he said with a wink, then marched past her toward the hills.

Irmtraud stared after him, then in the direction Herr Müller had taken. With a sigh, she followed Jan. She had to get back to Kassel. Her work at the hospital was dangerous, but for the first time in her life, she felt needed. She was making a difference. She was saving lives.

———

Irmtraud followed Jan on a well-used trail into the hills. She was glad for the green canopy that kept them hidden from the outside world and from any enemy bombers on their way to their next target. She didn't speak, nor did he. They walked on silently, but Irmtraud still wondered why he needed to get to Kassel and what his occupation was. His unkept appearance gave her no clues. "I'm thirsty," she said finally, trying to get his attention. Jan stopped walking and turned around to face her. "Very thirsty," she added and wiped her forehead with the back of her hand.

Jan looked around in all directions for a moment, then nodded. "Alright," he said. "It's not directly on the way, but I know of a spring a little over a kilometer from here."

"You know these woods really well, don't you?"

Jan grinned at her, then left the trail to cut through the underbrush. Irmtraud followed him reluctantly, knowing her stockings were done for and she'd suffer from the stinging nettles.

When he noticed that she couldn't keep up with him, Jan slowed his pace. On a couple of occasions, he held back branches for her so she could get through. On the last occasion, he caught her by the arm with his free hand. She looked up at him in surprise, but he was not looking at her. His gaze had caught something else, and by the look on his face, which had grown dark and distorted with anger and fear, it was something terrible

Jan was biting his lip. Worry swam in his eyes. Irmtraud started to ask him what was wrong, but he shook his head and, taking her hand, crouched, pulling her down with him. She noticed that he barely breathed. Then she heard the far-off shouts of men. Jan motioned for her to lie down between the ferns. Like a stealthy cat, he did so first, and she followed suit, trying to avoid making any sound. Flat on her stomach, Irmtraud realized the fern covered them completely. The smell of the forest floor was oddly comforting, and she relaxed a little.

The shouts came closer. They were more like barks. Soldiers? Gestapo? Irmtraud felt herself starting to tremble. Then she heard urgent, anxious pleading uttered in French. Then shots. The shooting silenced whoever had begged in French.

In the next second, the wood was filled with the hollow, tortured screams of men. Irmtraud had never heard men scream before. She had never heard any human make a noise like this. It was like the scream of a badly wounded animal, or of a pig about to be slaughtered. She had witnessed that a few times in her childhood, from the window of her classroom. Next door to her school was a small meat processing shop. Before being slaughtered, the pigs would be hung by their hind legs, head down. Their screams had curdled her blood.

More shots followed. Irmtraud felt Jan squeeze her trembling hand. And then there was silence, a leaden kind of silence that quieted the birds in the woods. The stillness was interrupted by the far-off sounds of trucks rumbling away. Then the only sound that remained was Jan's and her breathing.

Jan rolled onto his back. She followed suit, inching closer to his body. He took her hand again, and together they looked up at the canopy overhead. It calmed her. "What...what happened there? The words came out louder than Irmtraud intended.

"SS shooting French prisoners of war, I assume," Jan said finally. "There's a camp not far from here. At least there was." He looked at her. There were new dirt smudges next to the old ones on his cheeks and forehead. "You still thirsty?" He asked.

Irmtraud stared at him for a moment before she shook her head. Then the burning thirst in her throat and her dry mouth forced her to nod instead. Jan squeezed her hand in acknowledgement. He slowly sat up and scanned the area around them. The woods were still. No one was here. He stood up, still scanning the trees, and pulled her up. "The spring is not far now," he said and started moving stealthily through the sea of ferns.

Irmtraud didn't follow him. He noticed and turned around.

"What is it?" He asked in a hushed voice.

"Who are you, Jan? What do you do?"

He shook his head. "I cannot tell you that. It's too dangerous." He started walking again and motioned for her to follow him, but

Irmtraud remained rooted in place, her bag by her feet. She crossed her arms. She was determined to find out who and what he was and would not take another step until he told her.

"I told you. It's too dangerous," he said over his shoulder. "And none of your business."

Irmtraud could tell he was annoyed, both by her questions and her insistence. But she didn't feel like following him any farther without knowing who she was following.

"I thought you were thirsty," he asked, turning around again.

"I am. But I find it rather disconcerting to follow a man I don't know through the forest." Irmtraud still didn't move.

"You know my name. You've seen that you can trust me. I've kept you safe so far, have I not?" Now it was he who crossed his arms.

Irmtraud couldn't deny that, or the fact that she trusted him. She felt safe and oddly reassured in his presence. "Alright then, Jan. I'll trust you," she said, "for now. And I will trust that you're not the type to lead a girl astray." She uncrossed her arms, picked up her bag, and went to the spot where he stood. A little smirk played around his mouth as she passed him. She heard him follow her.

As Irmtraud trudged through the fern, her thoughts returned to the Frenchmen. She swallowed hard and hoped fervently that they would avoid coming upon the men's bodies or any other surprises. She couldn't handle much more. A simple train ride back to Kassel had turned into an odyssey.

They reached the spring a couple of hundred meters later. The water seeped from a pile of rocks, and Irmtraud had to wait patiently for her hands to fill with water to drink. "Not much of a spring, is it," she said, putting her wet hands on her neck for some relief. The water was pleasantly cool. "How do you know it was here?"

Jan scrutinized her, then spoke, although haltingly. "I know these woods," he said. " I might have spent a night or two here."

"You have?" Irmtraud's eyes fell on his dirtied trousers.

"We should get going," Jan said. "We still have quite a few kilometers ahead of us." He bent to fill a small flask he had pulled from his satchel. "Do you want me to carry this for you?" He asked, pointing at her bag. Irmtraud shook her head, but he took it from her anyway. She wanted to protest, then thought it would be best to let Jan carry it, that way she could at least keep up with him.

To Irmtraud's great relief, the rest of their journey to the city was uneventful. As dusk dipped their surroundings into an evening glow, their surroundings became familiar to Irmtraud, and she cried out in relief when they finally stepped out of the woods onto a street lined with a few houses. The Hercules Monument loomed on the hill above. They had made it.

Jan held out her bag to her. "This is where I leave you," he said. "You're familiar with the area?"

"Yes, yes, I am." She thought she had sounded a bit too happy.

"Well," he said, "I'll be off then. Stay out of sight as much as you can. The curfew, remember. And if anyone stops or questions you..."

"I'm sure the city's police have other worries with this flood."

They both looked down the street and into the city below, where dark water glistened in the evening light. As predicted, the flooding had not reached this area of town, and Irmtraud was grateful for that. At least the last part of her journey would be without hazards.

"The floodwaters seem to be receding," Jan said, interrupting her thoughts. He was pointing to the far-off city center. "That's good," he mumbled to himself.

"Thank you for getting me here, Jan. I'm truly grateful."

"It was my pleasure, Irmtraud." He grinned at her, then abruptly turned on his heel and disappeared back into the woods.

Irmtraud stared after him, taken aback by his abrupt departure. Her thoughts ran wild. Where was he off to? What was he up to? For a moment, she wondered if she'd ever see him again. Finally, she shook her head and started down the street that would feed into the avenue she needed to follow for about a kilometer before she got home. She looked down on her skirt, scratched-up legs, and torn stockings, and thought it best to heed Jan's advice and stay out of sight.

Taking back streets that ran parallel to the avenue, walking in the shadows of the dying daylight, Irmtraud realized how hungry she was, and how sore her legs were. If she hurried, she could still get back to the nursing school in time for supper. Thoughts of hot soup, even if meatless, and a slice of dark bread made Irmtraud pick up her pace. As she rounded the last corner and the nursing school came into view, Jan seemed nothing but a distant memory.

Chapter 8

June 1943

Wallhausen, Germany

Gisela sat at the kitchen table with her parents. They had eaten a while ago, so the table was clear of dishes. Her mother's hands rested on the tablecloth while Gisela, with her index finger, traced a few faint stains that had never come out in the wash. Waldemar's unfolded letter with the torn-open light blue envelope next to it lay in front of her father. They hadn't spoken a word since he had finished reading it to them. Now he sat tapping his fingers and staring at it with a mixture of apprehension and fear.

Kursk. Gisela had never heard of the place. Waldemar was there, and so was Erich now. She hadn't heard from her husband in two weeks. No letter. No phone call. And now Waldemar said he had joined Erich at the Eastern Front. They were fighting in the same battle. While Waldemar was fighting on the ground, Erich was attacking the Soviets from the air. The realization that the man who was now her husband was at the dreaded Eastern Front made Gisela's head spin. Two of her favorite people stared death in the face.

A numb, heavy silence filled the room. Gisela's father watched her as she clasped and unclasped her hands. Then he got up abruptly, grabbed the letter, and headed out the back. Gisela chased after him. She knew where he was going.

When he had almost reached the entrance to the workshop hall, he noticed her and stopped walking. "Go back to the house, Gisela," her father said without turning around.

"I have as much a right to know as you do. Erich is there. Waldemar said so."

"I don't know if the man can tell us anything. If he does, I will let you know."

But Gisela didn't go back. She put her hand on her father's arm. "Please."

Her father studied her face for a moment, then sighed and opened the big, tall doors in front of them. Sawdust danced in the air as they stepped into the long workshop hall. Gisela resisted the urge to cough as she climbed the stairs behind her father. Ducking, they entered the vast attic space and headed for the far end where the man was hiding.

He had heard them coming and appeared before they reached the pile of wood and broken furnishings. The men shook hands. Gisela stayed behind her father. The stranger no longer wore a Wehrmacht uniform, but clothes she recognized as her brothers'. If her presence surprised him, he didn't let it show. Instead, he simply ignored her.

"Tell me what you know about Kursk," her father said. "My son and son-in-law are there, facing the Soviets."

"Operation Citadel." He sounded defeated. He looked at them and frowned. "So," he said after a moment, "it has been set in motion." It wasn't a question. His voice was resigned.

"Please, tell me everything you know about it," Gisela's father urged. Suddenly, Gisela wished she hadn't followed him. She didn't want to hear what this operation meant for Waldemar and Erich. She noticed the man looking at her. A glint of recognition swam in his eyes. "My daughter's husband is there, too," her father said. "He's a *Jagdflieger* in the *Luftwaffe*. She deserves to know."

The man nodded, as though he understood perfectly. Gisela hadn't gotten a good look at him the first time she had seen him. She studied his face and thought he couldn't be more than ten years older than her. Yet, the stubble on his chin bore gray patches, and so did his hair. He appeared in need of a haircut and a shave.

"The planning of Operation Citadel began after Stalingrad." He lowered his eyes, his voice hushed. Gisela wondered if he had been in Stalingrad, and that's why he had deserted. "Hitler wants to regain the initiative on the Eastern Front by eliminating the Soviet bulge at Kursk. A decisive victory in the Kursk region would weaken Soviet forces and allow the *Wehrmacht* to regain lost territory. The goal of this new offensive is to encircle and destroy a large portion of the Soviet forces in the region by striking the Soviet defense positions around the city. A very large number of our troops, among them my unit, or whatever was left of it, have been moved to the region since spring. That's when I... left. I didn't want to see another Stalingrad." His last words were barely audible.

"Will they win?" Gisela blurted out.

The men looked at her. Neither spoke. Their eyes fell to the ground, avoiding her imploring gaze. Suddenly, the vast empty attic seemed to close in on her from all sides. Gisela took a few steps backward, trying to control her breathing, then she turned and ran. Down the stairs, through the workshop hall. Outside, she found her mother's bike leaning against the side of the house where she had left it yesterday. She grabbed it and started pedaling. There was only one place she wanted to be right now. Where she felt close to Erich.

———

The meadows lay still in the late afternoon sun. A few storks were feeding close to the bank of the river. Not a soul was around, and Gisela was grateful for it. She pushed her bike toward the old oak whose branches now only bore a few leaves here and there. It appeared to be dying, but Gisela knew the battered old oak was as alive as ever. She sat down in the damp long grass and leaned her back against its trunk. The cold, damp, and rough bark was uncomfortable, but she didn't mind. It gave her an odd sense of comfort, stilled her agonizing thoughts, and quickened the beating of her heart. After a while, she felt herself relax, but when her thoughts turned to Waldemar and Erich, and to tanks and planes and bombs, she choked on a sob, gave in, and let the tears run. Gisela had no idea how long she had cried. Occasionally, she wiped her cheeks and nose on the sleeve of her dress. Finally, she had no more tears, and sobs became stuttered sighs. How she wished Irmtraud were home. She had never missed her more in her life. Gisela realized how utterly alone she was. It was just her and her parents now, and she did not want them to worry any more than they already did. Finally, she pulled her legs in, rested her chin on her knees, and sat watching the storks.

Gisela realized she must have fallen asleep. The lavender haze of dusk that hung over the surrounding meadows told her that it was getting late, and dinner had long passed. She got up, put her hand against the rough bark of the ancient oak, and closed her eyes as if to say a prayer. She stepped closer and leaned her forehead against the gnarled sentinel. This tree had seen so much conflict and war. Medieval lords feuding and oppressing the local population. The devastating Thirtieth War, when marauding armies of Croatians and Wallenstein's mercenaries had plundered and raped the villagers of Wallhausen and laid waste to their fields, taking or slaughtering their cattle, hogs, and sheep. The French who had come through in later centuries, their armies taking whatever they needed without a thought as to how the people would survive the approaching winter.

Gisela left the old oak and walked over to her bike. She had no desire to go back home, but she didn't want to worry her parents either, especially now, with Waldemar at the Eastern Front and Irmtraud back in Kassel. She wanted to be the one child who would not cause them any worry. They needed her now, and she understood that she needed to be a constant in their lives, not add to their many worries and sleepless nights.

Gisela reached the house right as night fell. A black car she didn't recognize was parked out front. Her heart dropped. She knew the very few cars that were owned by villagers. She had never seen this one before. And it was late. Who was paying them a visit at this hour? Her grip on the handlebars tightened. She swallowed and pushed her bike through the gate and around the back, leaning it against her father's car. When she opened the back door, she heard the muffled voices of men in the living room. But as she passed the kitchen, her mother called her name in a hushed voice.

Gisela found her mother leaning over the sink, busying herself with washing dishes, something she had never done at this hour. Her eyes were red from crying. That in itself wasn't unusual these days, but when Gisela noticed her mother's hands trembling, her stomach knotted, and she felt panic rise in her.

Her mother turned to face her. The terror in her eyes made Gisela take a step back. Her breath caught, and she had to cough. Her mother's eyes widened as they flew to the open door. Mama stepped closer and grabbed Gisela with her wet hands. She shushed her vehemently, then pulled her to her chest, stroking her hair. It was the kind of rough stroke that bore the marks of panic and fear. Gisela pulled free and stared at her mother, but her terror-stricken face provided no clues.

When her mother finally let go of her, leaving wet handprints on her upper arms, she went to the door and closed it as quietly as she could. Then her mother turned around to face her and mouthed the single word, "Gestapo," with trembling lips.

Gisela caught hold of the back of one of the kitchen chairs to steady herself. *Gestapo.* Her thoughts went immediately to the man in the attic. Were they here for him?

She and her mother froze when they heard the living room door open. Heavy steps came down the hallway. Through the frosted, textured glass of the kitchen door, Gisela saw the shapes of her father, followed by two men, pass by the kitchen to the back of the house. Her nails dug into the back of the chair, and she stared at her mother as they heard the back door open. Mama was shaking her head vehemently, but Gisela knew what she had to do. She tore open the kitchen door and ran after her father, ignoring her mother's hushed and desperate pleas.

Gisela caught up with the men as they stepped into the workshop. They didn't notice her. Peering past them, Gisela was surprised to see Georg taking long planks of wood over to the circular saw. He usually went home in the late afternoon.

"Do your employees always work this late?" One of the Gestapo growled. "Surely it's against town ordinances to use a circular saw this late in the day?"

With a swift movement, Georg pulled his cap off, revealing his shiny, bald head. "Good evening," he said, with a slight bow. "I'm just setting up for tomorrow morning. I have no intentions of sawing tonight, sir."

The Gestapo officer walked toward the old man, coming to a stop just inches away from his face. Clasping his hands behind his back, he scrutinized her father's oldest and only remaining employee. Then he turned toward the stacked planks of wood, pretending to inspect them.

"You shouldn't make your men work so late, Meister Fahnrich," he said over his shoulder. Then, as he returned to his companion and Gisela's father, he finally noticed her. "Who do we have here?" He asked and turned to face Gisela.

"That's my daughter," her father's eyes narrowing as he said, "Go back to the house, Gisela."

"Not so fast, Herr Fahnrich." The Gestapo officer stepped forward, smiling. "Perhaps your daughter knows something about the deserter." Gisela's heart dropped. She saw the panic in her father's eyes.

"What deserter?" Gisela asked. She didn't know why, but she thought it best to delay with questions rather than flat out deny any knowledge. She saw her father's eyes widen in shock, before he quickly recovered.

"We are looking for a soldier, a deserter, who abandoned his unit and his fatherland in a time of great need. The coward needs to be brought to justice. He was last seen in Wallhausen."

"And why would you think he's here, in my father's workshop?" Gisela crossed her arms, wondering and not wanting to know why they would suspect her father. She glanced at Georg, who was getting ready to leave, wondering if the old man knew anything about the soldier.

"We are searching all the houses and businesses in Wallhausen," the Gestapo officer smiled at her again, but there was nothing friendly in it. "Your father was just letting us search his."

"That's enough with your questions, Gisela," her father said suddenly. "Let the men do their job. Go back to the house."

But Gisela didn't want to go back. If they discovered the deserter, her father would be shot alongside the man he had been hiding. She didn't know what else she could do. She had tried to stall for time and distract the Gestapo with her questions, but her father didn't seem to understand that she had only been trying to help him.

"Go, I said. Now!" He repeated.

As if the words were directed at him, Georg picked up his satchel and left the workshop through the side door that led to a back alley. They heard him turn the key in the lock. Then the workshop was completely quiet.

"It was nice to make your acquaintance, Fräulein Gisela," the other Gestapo officer said. Only now did she realize how young he was compared to his colleague. She nodded at him as the two men turned and proceeded down the workshop hall.

"Go back to the house. Listen to me, for once," her father hissed before following them. The Gestapo were already inspecting every nook they passed and headed toward the stairs that led up to the attic.

Gisela stood rooted in place. She couldn't bring herself to go back to the house. She realized her hands had become fists, her fingernails were digging into her palms as she stared after them. She jerked around when she heard the metallic "krring, krring" of her father's desk phone. The shrill, bright trills echoed through the workshop.

"You have an office in here?" One of the men asked her father.

"Gisela," her father called, his voice laced with urgency and confusion, "would you get that?"

The older Gestapo man put his arm out and stepped in front of him. "Let me," he said and walked toward her father's small office.

Who was calling this late at night? Gisela glanced at her father and saw that he was wondering the same thing. The concern on his face made her swallow.

They followed the Gestapo into her father's small office in time to see the older officer pick up the telephone handset and listen for a moment. Then he held it out to Gisela's father. "For you," he said, "Meister Fahnrich."

Her father took the receiver and, with some hesitation, put it to his ear. Gisela's heart sank when she saw a flicker of shock cross his face. As he pressed the receiver harder, Gisela could see his knuckles turn white. So did his face. Finally, her father stumbled backwards, falling into his desk chair. His jaw had tightened, a deep crease forming between his brows as the weight of the message sank in. For a heartbeat, his eyes flitted to her. Gisela swallowed hard, staring at him, trying to make out anything, trying to find any clue, to understand whatever terrible message it was that they had received.

Finally, her father dropped the handset onto the desk. "You will have to excuse me now," her father said, getting up with some difficulty. He was shaking. "We are finished... here. Search... if you must." His breath was ragged, his face white as death.

"Father! What's the matter? Who was that?"

"Meister Fahnrich–" The older Gestapo officer began, but her father cut him off.

"I have to …" he said. "I have to go." His eyes searched his desk. Gisela wondered what he was looking for. Then he headed for the door. The pain written on his face made Gisela's heart stop.

"Herr Fahnrich! You can't just leave. We have not allowed you to–"

Gisela's father turned around, his face hard. "You will have to excuse me," he said. "I have to go tell my wife that her son, a soldier, has died for his fatherland."

A terrible sound ripped the air. Everyone stared at Gisela. She realized the scream she had heard was her own. While she gasped for air, her father continued relentlessly.

"Search for the deserter," he said. "You're looking for yourself. All my sons–" His chest was heaving uncontrollably now. He got hold of the door frame to steady himself. "All my sons are serving the Führer. All of them. Now let me be." He almost shouted the last words.

Gisela stared after him, her head spinning. Waldemar. Erich. Heinrich. Karl. She gasped. Her eyes stung as she ran after her father. She had lost all fear of the Gestapo. She didn't care about them or the man in the attic.

She found him in the kitchen, consoling her mother, who grasped for Gisela. The three of them stood there, holding each other. Gisela only let go when her mother wailed Waldemar's name. She stumbled backwards, shaking her head. Her father tried to grab hold of her, but she escaped and ran out of the kitchen, up the stairs to the second floor, where Waldemar and Heinrich's room lay undisturbed, as if they had never grown into men who now died for the Führer.

Gisela threw herself onto Waldemar's bed and buried her face in his pillow. Of all her brothers… She hated herself for the thought. But Waldemar?! "Not Waldemar," she screamed into the pillow, her tears soaking the red and white checked pillowcase. Gisela sniffed and caught a wisp of her brother's smell. She curled up like a baby, heavy sobs rocking her body.

Gisela didn't know how long she lay like that. An hour? Maybe two? She was no longer crying. She felt numb. Cold. On this June night. She got up slowly and wiped the wet strands of hair out of her face. The room felt eerie to her now, and she wanted to escape it. Closing the door behind her, she promised herself never to set foot in it again.

Downstairs in the kitchen, Gisela found her parents in an embrace. She joined them, resting her head against her mother's shoulder.

"What about the man in your attic, Father? I'm sure they'll be back." Gisela was surprised at her own words. Why did she care about that man? Waldemar was gone forever. He had died for Germany, while this man had refused to fight.

"What man?" Her mother asked, letting go of both of them. Gisela realized her mistake. She wanted to say something to distract her mother but found no words.

Her father held up his hand wearily. "Not now, Gisela." His voice caught. She watched as he shuffled out of the kitchen, suddenly looking ten years older than he had only hours ago.

"What man?" Her mother asked again. Gisela put an arm around her mother's shoulders as she began to cry again, sobs rocking her body. Gisela joined in, her tears freely falling once more. *Waldemar!* She silently screamed as if he could hear her. Then she let go of her mother.

"Please, be with Father."

Dabbing her face with an already tear-stained kerchief, Mama nodded slowly and left the kitchen. Gisela stared after her for a moment. Then, she wiped her eyes with the back of her hand and left the kitchen, too.

In the hallway, Gisela grabbed the bundle of keys that sat on top of the console table underneath the beautiful picture of the woman who had given birth to her and left the house through the front door. She walked a short distance down the road before turning into the narrow, dark alley that led to the side door of the workshop. Despite feeling utterly drained and numb, Gisela knew she had to take care of the man in the attic. Her father wouldn't. He couldn't. Not now.

She stared at the bundle of keys in her hands. She had no idea which of them would unlock the door. She had no choice but to try them all. She glanced around. The alley was deserted. The village was sleeping peacefully. She was sure she was the only one out and about at this hour.

Gisela swallowed down the tears that threatened to well up again. Grateful for the dim moonlight that fell into the narrow alley, she chose an old, long, round-bladed key with simple teeth that she had never used before. It looked like the kind of key that would fit this door that had been here for a century, ever since her great-grandfather built the workshop. Putting it in the rusty keyhole, she felt it turn with ease. Gisela pushed the handle down, and the door swung open.

The workshop was dark, still, and deserted. Gisela wondered who had switched off the lights. The Gestapo? She decided to leave them and feel her way through the shadows toward the stairs. In the corner near her father's office, she heard a faint rustling. Mice. It had to be mice. She found the stairs and climbed slowly, careful not to miss a step in the dark.

The rusty hinges screeched as she pulled open the attic door. Stepping inside, Gisela held her breath and listened. Nothing moved. She walked quietly to the end of the attic, stepping over patches of moonlight as if they were hot coals. Ahead of her, the pile of broken furnishings lay quietly in the dark. Drawing close to it, Gisela paused and waited for the man to say something or appear. When nothing happened, she took a breath and stepped around to peer into the hiding place. There was nothing there. No blankets. No personal items. Just the dark attic floor. The man was gone.

Chapter 9

July 1943

Kassel, Germany

Sitting down next to Beate on her bed, Irmtraud studied the tiny note on top of the rough gray blanket in front of them. A short list of names was written in pencil. The writing was smudged along the edges and creases of the paper. Occasionally, Irmtraud or Beate would glance in the direction of the door, hoping they would remain undisturbed for a few more minutes.

When the door did open and a pair of nursing students came in chatting happily, Beate grabbed the note and stuffed it in her cardigan sleeve. Only a few people were aware of their attempts to try to save the most vulnerable, those who had been chosen for death by the hospital's chief physician, Dr. Engelhardt, a fanatical devotee of the Führer's cause, who saw it as his duty to carry on the government's dismantled T4 program.

Irmtraud got up and brushed down the skirt of her uniform. She took off her cardigan and flung it onto her bed, which was next to Beate's. It was a hot summer's day, and the air in the patient ward would be stifling. "We better get going," she said. "Shift starts now,"

Hiding the note in her pillowcase as she stripped off her own cardigan, Beate groaned and got up. They had a long shift ahead of them. In addition to their regular duties, the head nurse had planned at least one trip to the basement of the hospital for them. While the cool basement would be a welcome respite, it was also dangerous.

* * *

By noon, the heat had become unbearable. Nurses and students had opened all the windows in all the rooms and wards, but it did no good. The air hung thick and heavy without the slightest breeze. Given the humidity and darkening skies, Irmtraud suspected a thunderstorm wasn't far off. Nevertheless, she chose to eat her lunch on one of the benches in the park adjacent to the hospital. Anticipating the storm, people had hunkered down. Irmtraud studied the skies that lay to the East and thought of home. Of how the thunderstorm had most likely already passed through Wallhausen. She thought of Waldemar and found that she had difficulty swallowing suddenly.

Gisela had called with the terrible news. Irmtraud had spoken with her mother after, but her father had refused to come to the phone. She missed her family more than ever now, especially Gisela. Waldemar's death had driven her into a deep depression for a couple of weeks, and only Beate had managed to pull her out. At the same time, it made her more determined than ever. How could she leave now? Waldemar wouldn't want her to. While being home and being with her parents and Gisela would be a balm to her soul, she was glad to be in Kassel, in the nursing school and at the hospital, where she had a purpose, and felt she could make even a small difference in this cruel, war-torn world.

Since the ordeal of getting back to Kassel in May, Irmtraud found that she sometimes thought of Jan. But when his face appeared in her mind's eye, she quickly chided herself for the distraction. She wanted to do everything in her power to help those whose lives the regime had deemed worthless. Witnessing her sister's sadness on the day that should have been the happiest of her life, and now Waldemar's death made Irmtraud more determined than ever to fight the cruelties of the government and help ease the burdens of this war. She was appalled by the stories some of the wounded soldiers recovering at the hospital had shared with her. Irmtraud would abhor war for the rest of her existence. But Hitler was pressing on, even after the fall of Stalingrad, and now Kursk. After Gisela's confession on the morning of her return to Kassel, Irmtraud understood that her father and sister had been doing their part to support those who resisted the regime. Even so, she still couldn't fathom it. A German soldier, a deserter unwilling to fight in Hitler's war, hiding in their workshop attic. It had made Irmtraud see her father and Gisela in a completely different light.

Startled by the quick sound of footsteps, Irmtraud looked up to see Beate coming to stand in front of her, obviously in a hurry, panting and holding her side. With her face red from exertion and her head haloed by the black clouds of the coming storm, Beate looked unearthly, like some menacing goddess.

"You need to … come … quick," she gasped. "The head nurse … she … needs us … now."

Forgetting her uneaten lunch, Irmtraud jumped up.

"Dr. Engelhardt just left. We need to act quickly," Beate said over her shoulder as she led the way to the patient ward, where the head nurse was already waiting for them. She nodded when they stood in front of her, then pointed with her chin in the direction of a bed where a young girl around the age of ten lay with closed eyes. Irmtraud remembered tending to her yesterday. The girl's small frame was visible under the thin blanket that covered her despite the heat.

Irmtraud followed Beate to the girl's bed. Seeing the small paper name card affixed to the metal headboard marked with a red X, Irmtraud shuddered. She wondered why the girl had been condemned to death but knew that this wasn't the time to ask questions. Beate was already unlocking the wheels of the bed. Together, they rolled it out of the sick ward and down the hallway toward the old elevator. Irmtraud prayed that it would work today. She studied the girl's face while they waited, Beate scanning the hallway left and right. The girl's eyes were still closed. She looked as if she were sleeping peacefully. Too peacefully. The child looked dead, Irmtraud thought, and chided herself for thinking it. It didn't appear that she was breathing. Irmtraud put her ear to the little girl's face. The small, shallow breaths reminded her of the ones her grandmother had taken right before she had died in the bed Irmtraud had once shared with Gisela. For a horrible moment, Irmtraud wondered if they were too late and Dr. Englehardt had already administered his lethal injection.

Finally, the elevator pinged, the doors opened, and they pushed the bed in. It took up most of the space. Beate hit the button that would take them to the basement of the hospital. As the doors closed, Irmtraud turned to Beate. "Do you know what she's suffering from?"

"Tuberculosis," she whispered matter-of-factly.

"Why wasn't she isolated? Or sent to a sanatorium?"

Irmtraud felt a flash of anger. Why was this child in a regular hospital? With the right treatment, in a sanatorium, she would have a chance to be cured. And why had Dr. Engelhardt condemned her to die? Why her?

"They killed them there, too, you know," Beate whispered. "In the sanatoria." At Irmtraud's puzzled look, she added, "They killed most patients in the sanatoria when they started the T4 programs. It's no safer than an ordinary hospital. And she has bone TB. It's not contagious. Her parents lived in the city and wanted her close. Understandably."

Irmtraud nodded. What mother would want to send their child far away in times like these? She had heard about TB and how it could affect organs other than the lungs. Judging by the girl's fragile frame, she was at an advanced stage. Was that why Dr. Engelhardt wanted to get rid of her?

The elevator jerked to a sudden stop. The doors opened, and they pulled the bed into the dimly lit basement. It was dark except for a flickering utility light over a door to their right. Beate and Irmtraud pulled the bed in the other direction, into the dark and damp to their left.

Irmtraud stopped suddenly, startled by the faint, feeble voice of a child. Beate turned around. "What's wrong?"

Irmtraud thrust her chin toward the girl whose eyes had fluttered open, and who now looked around anxiously. "Nurse, where are you taking me?"

Irmtraud grabbed her hand, but it was Beate who spoke softly and soothingly. "We are taking you somewhere safe. Then back to your parents."

The girl looked around wildly. "But this doesn't look very safe. I'm scared." She grabbed at Irmtraud and pleaded, "Please, nurse. I want to go back."

"We are saving your life, child," Beate said. Irmtraud could hear the rising impatience in her friend's voice. "Nothing will happen to you," Beate tried to reassure her. "I promise. You need to trust us. All we want is for you to be back home with your parents."

The girl's lips parted as if to protest, then she nodded weakly.

"What's your name?" Irmtraud asked, even though she had learned her name from the little note from the head nurse that was now stashed in Beate's pillowcase.

"It's Sofie," the child whispered. "With an *f*."

Irmtraud smiled. "It's nice to meet you, Sofie with an *f*. I'm *Schwesternschülerin* Irmtraud. With a *d*. At the end, that is."

Sofie smiled at her. Irmtraud winked, and they started moving again, pushing Sofie's bed past cellar doors, down the dark basement hallway, Irmtraud still holding onto her hand.

When they finally reached the end of the hallway and came to a halt, Beate pulled a key from the pocket of her uniform and opened the door to the right. Inside, two hospital beds stood against opposite walls. The room was lit with a warm light. A couple of rugs covered the floor. There were even pictures on the walls. Of saints, Irmtraud realized. Their haloes shimmered in the room's warm glow. One of the beds was empty. The other one was occupied by an old woman who smiled kindly at the sight of them. A tray of food stood on a side table to her left. "Let me," Irmtraud said, and proceeded to lift the girl out of her bed. She was as light as a feather. Through her nightgown, Irmtraud could feel every bone. She carried the child over to the empty bed and put her down gently.

"We will take care of you down here until we can take you to your parents," Irmtraud promised, and covered her with the thick blanket that had been folded at the foot of the bed. The girl nodded a thank you and sank deep into the pillow, pulling the blanket all the way up to her nose, so that only her eyes peeked out.

Irmtraud placed a hand on her forehead and smiled at her. "We will bring you some nice soup later today," she promised. "It's only for a few days. Frau Frieda here will keep you company until we can return you to your parents."

The girl's eyes wandered across the room to the old woman in the other bed. Her toothless grin spooked her, and she withdrew even more under the blanket.

"I will keep you good company, little one," Frau Frieda said with a smile that did not reveal her gums this time.

"She has the best stories, believe me," Irmtraud said. "Funny ones, too," she added with a look in Frau Frieda's direction that she hoped would tell her to keep it light. To her relief, the old woman nodded knowingly.

"We have to go now, but I will be back with your soup later. I promise," Irmtraud said as they left the room, carefully closing the door behind them. Beate locked it, and together, they pushed the bed back toward the elevator. In her mind, Irmtraud counted the days until the two men who helped them transfer patients would come and pick up the girl.

⸻

It turned out to be exactly five days before they finally came, well after dark, to take the little girl home to her parents. The men had appeared in the head nurse's office dressed as janitors right after Dr. Engelhardt left. The doctor had learned of the girl's "death" days earlier from the head nurse and had not questioned it. Considering her weak condition, Irmtraud was not surprised he had accepted her 'passing' so easily. Now, she only hoped the child would survive the transport.

Irmtraud had finished her shift, but insisted on seeing the little girl off, so she had been waiting in the head nurse's office. She nearly choked on the water she was drinking when she saw that one of the men was Jan, wearing oversized blue coveralls and a cap.

"Who is he?" The head nurse asked, scrutinizing Jan.

"Filling in," the other man said, putting his meaty paw on Jan's shoulder. "You can trust him. He's my nephew. Jan is his name."

Irmtraud rolled her eyes at Jan's grinning at her from ear to ear.

"Do you know each other?" The head nurse asked, hands on her hips. She had clearly noticed their little exchange and didn't seem happy about it.

"Jan helped me get back to Kassel in May when the city was flooded."

"I see." The head nurse studied him for a moment, then turned to the older man. "He will do. Let's get the patient out of here."

The four of them went to the basement, and the head nurse unlocked the room. Inside, Frau Frieda and Sofie were playing cards. Frau Frieda had left her bed and was sitting on Sofie's bed in her robe, dealing.

"Isn't Skat a little too difficult for the child, Frau Frieda?" The head nurse asked.

"It's not Skat we are playing, sister. Neither have I tricked Sofie here out of her pocket money."

Irmtraud walked over to them and took a look at the cards. "Black Peter," she said. "And it looks like Sofie is winning."

"Again," Frau Frieda gave an exaggerated huff, throwing her hands up. She hobbled slowly over to her bed and, with some effort, climbed back in. "I see you haven't come to get *me* out of here."

Irmtraud wanted to respond, but the head nurse shook her head. Frau Frieda had no place to go. About a month ago, after Dr. Englehardt had condemned her to death with the stroke of his red pen because of her old age and inability to take care of herself, the head nurse herself had moved Frau Frieda down to the basement herself. The old woman's broken hip was healed, but she had no family to take care of her. Frau Frieda was a widow, and her only son had fallen in Stalingrad.

"Are these men here to take me home to my mama and papa?" Sofie asked.

Irmtraud went over and sat down beside her, stroking her head. "Yes, they are," she said. "You can finally go home." Sofie rewarded her with the biggest smile, then gazed at the men apprehensively. "These men are nice," Irmtraud reassured her. "I even know one of them. He once rescued me, too, just as he will rescue you now. So, you can trust him. I trust him." Irmtraud chose not to look at Jan as she said all that. She was certain he understood that Sofie just needed some words of encouragement.

"Will you come with me?" Sofie asked.

Irmtraud started to reply, but the head nurse cut her off. "You'll be in the best hands," she told Sofie.

"I wouldn't mind," Irmtraud said as the little girl clutched her hand. "My shift is over–"

"You can't go about the city dressed in your uniform. You will raise suspicion."

"I can quickly change, then accompany them." Irmtraud got up. "It's no bother," she said. "Really."

"Oh, please, please let her come," Sofie begged, sitting up now.

All eyes were on the head nurse. Irmtraud could tell that she wanted to refuse. But who could deny a dying child a wish, any wish. The head nurse softened. "Alright then," she said. "Sister Irmtraud shall accompany you. We will get you ready for your departure while she goes to change out of her uniform."

Irmtraud was back in the room in less than ten minutes, this time wearing a polka-dotted dress that she had hastily grabbed from her suitcase. In the elevator, she had cursed at herself for forgetting her cardigan. The temperature had dropped in the last couple of days, and the evenings could get a little chilly.

By the time she got back to the basement, they had already wrapped Sofie in a big blanket. She looked like a larva in a cocoon, ready to become a butterfly. The head nurse frowned at Irmtraud, clearly disapproving of her choice of dress. Sofie, on the other hand, was beaming at the sight of her. To her surprise, Jan was, too. She had only been gone for ten minutes, and those two greeted her as if she had been gone a year. She chuckled to herself.

"Let's get going, everyone," the head nurse said, and Jan walked over to Sofie.

"Not everyone," Frau Frieda called from her bed

"We just can't let go of you, Frau Frieda. You belong with us," Irmtraud said as she poured more water into the old woman's glass. "I will see you tomorrow."

Frau Frieda responded with a disgruntled mutter and turned on her side, away from them.

"Goodbye, Frau Frieda," Sofie called as Jan swept her up into his arms.

"Frau Frieda is sleeping now. She needs her rest," Irmtraud said, following Jan and Sofie out of the room. The head nurse locked the door. Then she and Jan's uncle followed them to the elevator.

The car Irmtraud assumed Jan's uncle used to get patients out of the hospital and away from Dr. Engelhardt's deadly injections stood outside. She was surprised to find out that it belonged to Jan. He held the door for her as she slid into the back seat. Then he carefully placed Sofie next to her. Irmtraud put an arm around the girl as Jan took the driver's seat while his uncle got in on the passenger side, and they drove off into the night without any headlights.

They made their way slowly through side streets and back alleys to avoid police patrols or worse, the Gestapo.

"How come you are allowed to drive in the city after curfew?" Irmtraud asked.

"My uncle is an air raid warden," Jan said. "Too old to be of service otherwise," he added with a chuckle, for which he received a clip to the back of his head from his uncle. "I'm just his humble driver. He doesn't see well at night, or so he claims."

"And they made him an air raid warden?" Irmtraud asked.

"Not too many men left at the home front. And with all the bombardments Kassel already endured, they want to be vigilant and more prepared."

Sofie snuggled close to Irmtraud in her cocoon, and Irmtraud held her tight as they chugged through the streets and alleys until they came to a halt in front of an apartment building. Jan turned off the engine and got out and held the door open for Irmtraud while his uncle waited in the car. He scooped Sofie up once more and carried her to the front door of the building, where a man stepped out of the shadows, giving Irmtraud a start. Without a word, he opened the front door for them, placing a finger on his lips.

Inside, they followed him up the stairs to the third floor, where he carefully and quietly unlocked a door. As soon as they were in the apartment, Sofie's father took his daughter from Jan. Sofie wrapped her arms around his neck, nestling her head against his shoulder. In the living room, he placed her on the sofa and kissed her forehead. Sofie's mother came in from the kitchen, bursting into tears when she saw Sofie. Her father extended his hand to Jan. "I will never forget what you have done for us, for Sofie."

"We just do the transports. It's the nurses who saved her life," Jan said with a look at Irmtraud.

"Thank you," the man said, extending his hand to Irmtraud.

She took it and smiled at him shyly. "I'm just a nursing student."

Sofie's mother came over and threw her arms around Irmtraud's neck. "You're my angel. Thank you for saving her."

Irmtraud felt awkward being hugged by the stranger. She noticed the rounded belly. The woman was pregnant.

"We need to get going," Jan said, taking a step toward the hallway.

Irmtraud went over to Sofie and took her hand. "You'll be a good girl for your parents, will you?" Sofie nodded vigorously, then leaned back into the sofa pillow and half-closed her eyes that had dark, deep shadows under them. The transport home had taken a toll on her. But she looked so content. It reminded Irmtraud of when she and Beate had taken her down to the basement, how she had been sleeping so peacefully, the contentment on her face a mirror of pleasant dreams. Dreams of home.

They left the apartment and crept downstairs to the front door. Sofie's father accompanied them. Before he locked the door behind them, he shook Jan and Irmtraud's hands again. Then they joined Jan's uncle in the car and drove slowly away.

"We will take you back to your dormitory," Jan said. "Unless, you–" Jan paused, watching her in the rearview mirror.

"Unless I what?" Irmtraud's eyes narrowed.

"Unless you'd like to join me for some dancing."

"Dancing?" Irmtraud stared at him, and Jan's uncle chuckled.

"Yes, swing dancing, to be precise." Jan brought the car to a stop.

His uncle scanned the street nervously. "We need to keep going," he said.

"Not until Irmtraud has agreed to dance with me tonight."

"I've never swing-danced before. Besides, I doubt that's allowed. I heard swing dancing has been banned. Along with its music. Besides, I don't imagine there's any dancing anyway these days."

"Oh, there is," Jan said. "Believe me. In this very city. In the cellars under the old vineyard."

"Kassel has a vineyard? In the city?" Irmtraud had never seen a vineyard, let alone in a city. This part of the country was not where grapes grew. The only time she had eaten grapes was on her family vacation in the south of Germany when she was a child. She remembered the small green grapes and their sour taste and pulled a face.

Jan saw it in the mirror and laughed. "Wine not to your liking?"

"I was thinking about the grapes I once had. That's all." She had never tasted wine. Her father drank beer occasionally or pulled out his home-distilled black currant liquor for guests. Her mother even had some occasionally, claiming it was good for digestion. But Irmtraud herself had never had alcohol of any sort.

"Don't worry," Jan said. "We won't be drinking wine tonight. That's a rare commodity these days. And Kassel's vineyard grew its last grapes in the Middle Ages. They built the city around it. There is nothing but gardens up on the hill now."

"We need to get going," Jan's uncle's voice was urgent.

"So, you're in?" Jan looked at her expectantly, his eyes practically nudging her.

Irmtraud looked away. "I don't think I can," she muttered. "Dance while others suffer."

"We need to keep up our spirits. Especially in this war. Besides," Jan added, "it's a form of resistance. You'll see." Apparently unbothered by her concerns. Jan got the car rolling and drove toward the center of the city.

After a few moments, a hill topped by a familiar structure appeared in front of them. "That's the vineyard?" Irmtraud asked.

She had passed this part of the city a few times since coming to Kassel. The vineyard with its terraces loomed like a forgotten fortress in the dark. The grand stone arches, once symbols of civic pride and architectural ambition, now bore the scars of war, crumbling mortar, soot-streaked façades, and missing balustrades where Allied bombs had shaken the hillside in previous bombardments of the city. Jan explained how it, and the gardens and park that made up the terraced hill, had once been a promenade for the city's elite. Known centuries ago for its vineyards, it was a little oasis in the hustle and bustle. Tonight, in the dark, the arches cast deep, long shadows.

Jan stopped the car, and both he and his uncle got out. Then, while Jan's uncle got into the driver's seat, Jan opened her door.

"I thought your uncle didn't drive at night?" Irmtraud asked with a concerned look as Jan helped her out of the backseat.

"He'll manage. He always does," Jan said. And, with that, he banged twice on the top of the car, and his uncle slowly drove off.

Once he had rounded the corner, Irmtraud turned to Jan. "Where are we going?" She asked. "It's way past curfew." She looked up the hill, concerned.

"Not up," he said, motioning to the dark shadows under the arches. "We are going down." There's a door that leads to the medieval cellars. Bomb shelters at times of raids, swing dance clubs when not in use." He winked at her.

"But it all looks deserted. No one is out. No one is supposed to be out."

"We are just late to the party," Jan said with a husky laugh as he pulled her along with him.

Irmtraud wished she had not let him talk her into this. A shiver was crawling up her spine. She knew she shouldn't be here. It felt wrong and dangerous. "What... what if we get caught...," she said between breaths, struggling to keep up with him.

"We won't. I promise," he said, coming to a halt in front of an old metal door so suddenly that she crashed into him. She blushed and mumbled a quick apology. He put an arm around her and kept her close while he rhythmically knocked on the door. Irmtraud felt safe, and to her surprise, not awkward in Jan's arm. She knew she ought to wiggle free, but her body leaned into his. He gazed down at her and smiled.

The door opened and they stepped into the dark. The faint sound of jazzy music reached them. They walked along a long, dimly lit hallway deep into the hill. It smelled of damp stone and, as they walked farther, also of cigarettes. Every few meters, a flickering utility lamp provided some light. The music grew louder and was mixed with voices and laughter now. Irmtraud threw Jan a sideways glance. His face shone with excitement. It was contagious. She started to feel his thrill.

At the end of the hallway, Jan pushed open a pair of tall doors, and they stepped inside. Irmtraud froze, and her mouth dropped open. She'd never seen anything like it. There was a jazz band playing in the far-left corner of the huge underground room. The trumpet's brazen cry cut through the air, followed by the pulsing of a stand-up bass. The musicians half danced along with the crowd. It was infectious.

Bare bulbs in wire cages swung overhead, casting golden pools of light across arched brick cellar walls and the blur of fast-moving feet. Men swung girls around, up in the air and through their legs. Girls in calf-length skirts twirled, their bobby socks flashing white as they jitterbugged with boys in loosened ties and suspenders. Laughter and whoops bounced off the walls.

The couples spun and kicked in time with the music, their energy explosive and their face and expressions determined and defiant. Irmtraud couldn't take her eyes off the dancing. Jan had been right. This was rebellion. This was resistance. Life pulsing against all the death this war had brought. Her thoughts turned to Waldemar, and she had to swallow.

Someone brushed against her arm. A girl her age, flushed and breathless, leaned in and shouted over the music. "First time?" Irmtraud nodded dumbly. The girl grinned. "Then don't just stand there. This isn't for watching, it's for living."

It was Jan who followed the girl's command and pulled Irmtraud with him onto the dance floor. Before she could protest, she was drawn into the fray, and into Jan's arms, and into a whirl of brass and bass, and something she hadn't felt in months. Pure joy.

CHAPTER 10

AUGUST 1943

OBERSALZBERG, BAVARIA, GERMANY

Karl glanced at the man sitting in the back of the car he was driving. He was heavy-set, too heavy for a physician. Not a paragon of youth and health in Karl's book. But Dr. Morell was the Führer's personal physician who had come on the night train from Berlin to Munich, and Karl had been tasked with picking him up from the train station and bringing him down to Berchtesgaden and up the mountain to the Berghof.

The doctor pulled out a kerchief and wiped his large forehead. Sweat stains marked the collar of his shirt. It was a hot August afternoon, and Karl had folded back the soft top of the black Mercedes-Benz cabriolet to allow for some relief from the stifling heat. The small swastika flags on the fenders flapped in the wind. With every kilometer they climbed, the air became cooler. Especially in the hot summer months, Karl was grateful to be stationed on the Obersalzberg, in the mountains, where it was cooler.

Karl returned his focus to the winding, narrow road he had driven up and down numerous times in the last few weeks. The

Führer himself had discovered how good Karl was behind the wheel last month when his personal driver had fallen ill and Karl had taken his place. Hitler had been so impressed that he had told Karl's commander to transfer him from watch duty to chauffeuring dignitaries and visitors up and down the mountain. Karl had been excited and considered it a stroke of luck. He would much rather drive around all day than stand for hours keeping watch. Or worse, fight like Waldemar somewhere in the East and end up rotting in the ground of some faraway, godforsaken place.

The news of Waldemar's death had hit him harder than he ever could have imagined. He'd had nightmares for weeks after receiving the news. But, of course, he didn't let on to anyone how he felt. And no one asked about his well-being when he woke up screaming. Everyone had someone to mourn these days.

His mother had written to him. A single-page letter that told him that Waldemar had fallen at the Battle of Kursk. Her message had been matter of fact, but the tear stains on the paper told him of her pain at losing Waldemar, a son she hadn't borne but had raised like her own. After he had finished reading the letter, Karl had run off, deep into the nearby forest. Straying from the path, he had cut across several kilometers, fighting underbrush and branches, until he finally came to a breathless stop in front of a tall pine and crumbled against the tree. The shock of the news had kept him there for the rest of the day. Only in the evening, after his anguish had settled enough for him to feel in control again, did he hike back. The return journey had turned out to be more difficult than he expected.

He had lost his way. But he hadn't minded. One always found one's way back. One way or another.

The gate appeared ahead, and Karl slowed down the car.

"Almost there, sir."

Behind him, Dr. Morell merely grunted in response. When they reached the Berghof, Karl got out to open the door for his passenger. As soon as the doctor disappeared into the house, Karl took the car, parked it in one of the carports, and unfolded the top to secure it. The air was heavy, and thunderstorms could roll in quickly in the mountains.

He took his SS uniform jacket off and pushed up the sleeves of his shirt, exposing his muscular, tanned arms. Then he went over to the shed where the cleaning supplies were stored, found a bucket and sponge, and washed down the car. Afterwards, he took a cloth and wiped it until it gleamed in the evening light. Leaning back against the car, Karl took out a cigarette and lit it. Life wasn't bad at all these days. The war was far away, and he was in the most beautiful region of the Reich.

Karl looked up at the sound of boots on gravel and saw Wilhelm coming his way, his face unreadable in the fading light. He stopped a few paces from Karl and glanced at the freshly cleaned Mercedes. "You are good with cars, aren't you," he said, admiring Karl's handiwork.

Karl took another drag from his cigarette. "Better than with people."

Usually, Wilhelm laughed at his jokes, but tonight he only nodded slightly, then looked toward the Berghof.

Karl arched an eyebrow. "What is it, Wilhelm?"

Wilhelm hesitated, then pulled a folded piece of paper from the right pocket of his pants. Karl took it, flicked the ash from his cigarette, and unfolded the sheet. The lines were precise and impersonal. Orders, stamped and signed. Karl read them twice to make sure he wasn't misinterpreting the words. *Report to Standartenführer Müller at 0600 tomorrow. Special assignment. Confidential. Eastern operations.* A chill crawled up Karl's spine despite the warm evening air. *Eastern operations.*

"They're pulling me out of here," Wilhelm said quietly. Karl didn't want to meet his eyes. "Not just me, a few others, too. But it seems not you. Someone up there must still need you, and decided it wasn't your turn yet," Wilhelm added without making any attempt to hide his bitterness.

Karl folded the order slowly and carefully. Handing it back, he looked a Wilhelm, the man who had become his friend. It would be a matter of sheer luck to ever see him again. Karl knew that, and he knew too that the day would come when he, too, would be called to the front, away from clean mountain air and quiet routines. "Do you know what the assignment is?" Karl asked.

Wilhelm hesitated, gazing toward the mountain peaks looming in the distance. "Rumors only," he said, finally. "Something about a *cleansing operation*. In the occupied territories in the East. Civilian zones." His voice dropped, and he continued in a hushed tone. "I will need to bury my conscience." Karl felt a sudden surge of something. Revulsion? Dread? Maybe guilt. "I'm not sure I can do this," Wilhelm added, his voice almost inaudible.

Karl watched as Wilhelm turned on his heel and disappeared into the waning light. For a moment, he stood alone, the last of his cigarette burning to the filter. Behind him, the roof of the Berghof glowed in the dying sun. As sure as the setting of that sun, Karl understood that his day of departure from the Obersalzberg would arrive sooner or later. Then he, too, would find himself on the front lines, fighting the Führer's total war. Hitler needed soldiers and officers who were fiercely and unwaveringly loyal to him. They were becoming a rare commodity these days, and no amount of skilled driving would prevent Karl from eventually being called up.

Walking toward the barracks, he tried to ignore the pressure building in his chest.

Chapter 11

October 1943

Wallhausen, Germany

Gisela made her way to the root cellar in search of vegetables. She had promised her mother this morning that she would cook a hearty soup for lunch. Most days, her mother made lunch, which was the hot meal of the day, but Gisela had insisted on taking over some of the cooking.

In the cellar, it felt like it was winter already. The cold, damp air made Gisela shiver, and she pulled her cardigan more tightly around her. Hugging herself, she passed a couple of doors. The bin where her family stored their potatoes sat just under the only window. Today, the freshly harvested potatoes shimmered golden in the faint light that fell through the dusty panes. By spring, whatever was left would be covered in sprouts.

Gisela put a handful of potatoes in the small sack she had brought. Then she turned towards a door in the darkest corner of the cellar, where her mother kept her canned treasures. She hated going into the storage room because she had to feel her way through the dark and fumble for the light switch.

Gisela sighed in relief when the single bulb that dangled from the ceiling came on, lighting up the room. Besides her mother's canning jars, there were crates of other root vegetables and apples. She added some apples to her sack, along with an onion that was already sprouting, and found a couple of beets and turnips to add to her collection. Gisela didn't like beets, especially not in soup, but these were difficult times, and they were lucky to have vegetables and fruit from their own garden. She could not fathom how people in the cities managed. She thought of Irmtraud. When Gisela had asked her about food supplies in Kassel in her last letter, her sister had not answered, which made her worry even more about Irmtraud. Of course, Gisela did not share her worries with her parents. They already had enough to be concerned and fearful about.

Gisela ran her fingers along the rows of preserving jars lined up on the rickety shelf that she estimated was at least as old as her family's house. She was hopeful that perhaps one of these jars would contain something she could add to make her soup more flavorful. But her mother's canning jars contained mostly currants, blackberries, and gooseberries. Finally, Gisela found a jar of pickles. She had learned in school that the Russians used pickles in their soup. What did they call it? *Rassolnik* or something like that. She wasn't sure if her mother would approve of pickles in a soup, but she was willing to take her chances and try something new. She grabbed the jar and carried it upstairs with the rest of her harvest.

In the kitchen, Gisela caramelized the onions in a drop of oil in the big enamel pot her mother had designated a long time ago for soup making. Then she added the potatoes to brown them slightly before adding water and the rest of the root vegetables. While the soup simmered, she went out the back to the window planters her mother kept on the south side of the house. The herbs looked ready to give up for the approaching winter. But she found a few blades of chive that hadn't wilted fully yet, and some dry thyme. There was still plenty of cold-tolerant parsley, and she harvested a good handful.

Back in the kitchen, Gisela tasted the watery soup, added salt and pepper, and chopped up the herbs. She would add some flour later to thicken it. Her eyes fell on the jar of pickles, and she glanced over her shoulder at the door. Her mother was in the laundry kitchen and wouldn't witness the affront of adding pickles to a soup. So she popped open the jar, cut a few into small pieces, and added them to the broth. After a couple of minutes, she took a spoon and tasted her creation. She liked what she tasted and decided to chop up the rest of the pickles and add them as well. With another look at the door, she poured a little of the jar's liquid into the pot, then put on the lid to let her soup simmer for a few more minutes. She checked the breadbox to see how much of the loaf her mother had baked yesterday was left and was glad to find half a loaf. She sliced it all up, tasted her soup one more time, then nodded to herself in satisfaction.

Gisela carried the soup plate up the narrow stairs to the workshop attic as carefully as she could without spilling it. Two pieces of yesterday's bread were stuffed in her apron pocket. Two weeks after disappearing, the soldier had returned.

Georg had come to the house one day and asked to speak with her, which had surprised her at first. But since her father had withdrawn and now left the running of the business to Georg, she understood why the old man had come to her. In a hushed voice, he had confessed how he had hidden the deserter in his coal shed. But now that the Gestapo had given up their search and left Wallhausen, Georg thought it best for him to return to the workshop attic. The old man had mumbled something about feeding another mouth, so Gisela had agreed to take care of him, knowing her father would not be able to.

Since that day, she had taken full responsibility for the man, delivering his meals and other necessities to make his stay in the attic bearable. He had asked for some charcoal sticks, and she had found some in Heinrich's desk, along with a few sheets of sketch paper. Art supplies were hard to come by these days, and she had been reluctant to hand her brother's special paper over to a stranger. Heinrich had always liked to draw. His pictures hung on every wall of his room, at least until Hitler came to power. Then, he had given up his art for the Führer and the *Reichsdienst* that followed. When he had joined the *Wehrmacht* and became a soldier, Gisela had wondered if Heinrich would ever return to drawing.

After he heard about Waldemar's death in the Battle of Kursk and how it had changed her father, the deserter had repeatedly offered to leave and find another place to hide. But Gisela wouldn't hear of it. She feared the man would be seen and arrested, and questioned about his previous whereabouts, which would lead back to them.

Gisela didn't remember much about that terrible night, except for the fear of the Gestapo and the grief about Waldemar's death that had penetrated down to her bones. How she had felt physically ill, then and in the following days, reeling from shock and grief. And guilt. Guilt for immediately thinking of Erich and wondering if he was still alive. There had been no news of any kind from or about Erich. At this point, she figured no news was good news.

Gisela had no idea how to go on without Waldemar. She had always missed him terribly when he was gone, and now that he would never come back home, that pain had become a permanent ache that at times took her breath away. Gisela sometimes wondered if Erich's death was next, and if it would feel less painful because he wasn't her blood. She wondered if one could get used to death and loss. Grow numb to it with time, if it happened this often.

Seeing her father suffer added to Gisela's grief and pain. He had gone numb. Waldemar had fallen, and in response, her father had fallen silent. He no longer spoke to her or her mother. For most of the day now, he sat in his big armchair in the living room, staring out the window. Occasionally, he would shuffle out the front door into the garden and stand by the fence and stare in the direction of the train station as if he hoped one of his children would return. But as soon as he saw someone come down the sidewalk, he went back into the house. Her father no longer worked or even set foot in the workshop. He had become an old man overnight. With Georg's help, her mother was trying her best to keep the family business going, while Gisela helped keep the household running on the little income they had.

Ducking her head, Gisela entered the attic, careful not to spill any of the good soup she had brought. She carefully glided across the attic floor. The man appeared and came toward her, taking the still-warm plate. He set it on the floor, then sat down. Gisela pulled the two slices of bread from her apron pocket and handed them to him.

He shook his head vehemently. "Two slices are too much."

"Please, take them. What you cannot eat for lunch, you can save for tonight," Gisela said, still holding the bread out to him.

He didn't protest any further and mumbled, "Thank you."

For a moment, she watched him eat. Then she noticed the charcoal stains on his fingers and asked, "Have you done any new drawings?"

His face lit up, and he nodded, getting up quickly and disappearing around the pile of broken furnishings. He reappeared with a piece of paper and held it out to her. Gisela took it. He had sketched a landscape with a gnarly tree in the background. The longer she looked at it, the bleaker it appeared. Gisela wasn't sure if it was the dark gray of the charcoal or the leafless tree, but it suddenly struck her as a landscape of war. A kind of no man's land. A desolate, wintry landscape void of any beauty. She handed it back to him.

"It's for you," he said, between spoonfuls of soup. She noticed him studying her. The light had disappeared from his face. "You don't like it?"

Gisela looked at the drawing again. "It's masterfully done," she said. "Really. It's just... just a bit dreary."

He cocked his head. "It's the charcoal, isn't it?" He laughed. "I wish I could have painted you something in watercolor."

"In despair, the devil will eat flies," she said, joining in his laughter. After a moment, she added, "In any case, I thank you for the drawing."

"You're welcome." He was cleaning his plate with a small piece of bread.

Gisela watched him for a moment and realized how little she knew about him. She didn't want to think of him as a stranger any longer. "Your name is Kurt Vogel, correct? I saw your conscription card in my father's office." He looked up at her with raised eyebrows as if her question surprised him. "Do you have a family? Where are you from exactly?" She hoped she didn't sound like she was interrogating him.

The man smiled, then gave a slight laugh that reminded Gisela of Waldemar. For a moment, the sudden pang of sadness took her breath away. "Please call me Kurt." He smiled at her encouragingly.

"Then please call me Gisela," she said, matching his smile.

"I'm from Dresden. I was an art professor at the university there." He cleared his throat. "I have a wife and young daughter in Dresden." He looked down at the empty soup plate. "I hope they are well."

"You should send a letter to your wife, or to someone who knows her, who could tell her that you're alive and well."

"I think that'd be too dangerous right now."

He was probably right, Gisela thought, and took the empty soup plate.

"Have you heard from your husband?" His question took her by surprise, but she quickly shook her head. There hadn't been any word from Erich. None. She didn't know if he was alive, missing in action, or dead. That was the case for many of the men who had fought at Kursk. "You will. Soon, I'm sure," he said, and got up.

Gisela nodded and forced a quick smile. "I'll be back tomorrow," she said and turned to leave.

"Don't forget your drawing."

She took the picture from him without looking at it and left the attic. As she descended the stairs, Gisela glanced at the picture. "Erich," she whispered, and wiped at the tears that ran down her cheeks.

Every family meal was a quiet endeavor now. Gisela watched her parents spoon their soup in silence. Only the occasional slurp or chewing sound interrupted the oppressive hush. After a moment, her mother looked up in surprise, still chewing. "Pickles?" She asked.

Gisela laughed and nodded. "Works, doesn't it?"

"It does. Not bad at all." Her mother smiled, and Gisela realized that it had been a long time since she had seen her mother's face light up.

"The Russians like to cook with them, so I thought I would give it a try."

"Nice flavor, Father, isn't it?" Her mother looked at Gisela's father, but he spooned on silently without looking up or acknowledging that he had heard her.

After lunch, Gisela helped her mother clean the few dishes, then retired to her room for a nap and some reading. She was supposed to prepare the garden at the front of the house for winter but would wait until tomorrow.

She grabbed Hermann Hesse's *Peter Camenzind*, the book Irmtraud had been reading right before she had run off to Kassel, from the nightstand, and turned to where she had left off the previous night. While she somewhat blamed Erich for Irmtraud's departure, she also wondered if Hesse's book had anything to do with it as well. Like her sister, the protagonist in the story left his village to go study in the city. Gisela had partly started to read the book to find out if the story had indeed encouraged Irmtraud to leave home.

Her eyes wandered to her sister's empty side of the bed. Gisela had placed the drawing there, unsure what to do with it. She leaned over, picked it up, and looked at it again. It reminded her of Kursk and Waldemar and Erich, and this damned war. Kurt's masterful artistry had brought the war painfully to life on a piece of paper.

Gisela suddenly remembered his conscription card. It was hiding in the lowest drawer of her nightstand. She fished it out and stared at it for a moment but then stuck it between the pages of the book she had already read. It would be a better hiding place than her nightstand drawer. With another look at the drawing, Gisela promised herself that she would go to the workshop later in the afternoon and ask Georg to cut her some wood, so she could frame and hang it on the wall across from her bed. She would take it down when the war was over.

***

The next day, Gisela spent the afternoon preparing the garden in front of the house for winter. The air was chill, and the ground was still damp from yesterday's shower, but the sky was remarkably clear for a cold October afternoon. Usually at this time of year, a stiff wind chased rain clouds across the sky, but not today. Today was the perfect day to attend to her mother's many plants, all of which Gisela had to trim, in addition to weeding the flower beds one last time and covering the cold-sensitive bushes with brushwood.

The street in front of the house was deserted. No one was out. It was an eerily quiet afternoon. Gisela didn't mind. She worked on in silence, occasionally humming one of the songs her mother had taught her. As the light began to fade, she picked up the pace. She wanted to get done with the garden today, and there were only a few minutes of daylight left.

When Gisela was done putting down the last of the brushwood, she got up, beat the dirt off her hands, and stretched her aching back. She gathered up all her tools and, with a satisfied look at her day's work, she left the garden and went inside to wash up before supper.

***

Gisela didn't know how long she had been asleep. It couldn't have been long. She had gone to bed early due to her aching back and fallen asleep in an instant. What had woken her? She opened her eyes, expecting to be enveloped in total darkness, but her bedroom was engulfed in a deep orange glow as if she had descended into hellfire. Gisela rubbed her eyes in confusion and shook her head. She looked at the clock on the wall. It was just past midnight. She threw back her blanket and got up.

Going to the window, Gisela could not believe what she saw outside. She grabbed her cardigan and ran into the front yard. Gazing skyward, she took a step back in bewilderment. Her foot caught a garden spade she had forgotten in the grass. She stumbled and caught herself, unable to take her eyes off the sky. It was ablaze.

Gisela's mind started to race. She shook her head in a mixture of astonishment and fear. She couldn't understand what she was seeing. The entire sky glowed deep orange and crimson, as if the edge of the world had caught fire. It was a sky on fire. But not from dawn or sunset. From war, mute and vast.

Gisela sank her knees in the wet grass. Something huge was burning to the West. She clutched her side. "Kassel. Irmtraud," she breathed, barely audible. Then she threw her head back and let out a scream that sounded like an animal.

Behind her, Gisela thought she heard her mother call her name. A moment later, she felt Mama's arms around her. They held each other, tears streaking their faces, staring at the inferno of the sky. Even from seventy miles away, the air felt changed and heavy. Kassel was burning.

The next morning, snow fell, thin and brittle. From underneath her big down blanket, Gisela stared out the window, watching the snowflakes sail past as if they had been sent to extinguish the fiery sky, which now shone gray. The world was as cold and desolate as Kurt's drawing. Snow in October was a rarity. She wondered if the snowflakes were ashes.

Gisela had barely slept for what had remained of the night after they had tried for hours to reach the hospital in Kassel by telephone. They weren't surprised they couldn't, but they kept trying, nevertheless. They had to. Eventually, her mother had sent her to bed, but she didn't find much rest. Worries about Irmtraud plagued her. Whenever Gisela dozed off, she woke up, startled. Each time, the orange sky had grown a little dimmer.

She turned and yawned into her pillow and closed her eyes again. The night seemed like a bad dream, and she wondered for a moment if she had indeed witnessed it or if it had just been a nightmare. She listened intently, but everything in the house was quiet, filled with a hushed silence, the kind that echoed inside.

Her heart began to race again when she thought of Irmtraud. Since they were unable to reach her by telephone, she needed to write to her immediately. Perhaps, she should get on a train to Kassel. But none would be running, nor would her mother let her.

A sharp, official-sounding knock on the front door interrupted her thoughts. Gisela's eyes flew open. Her heart rose in her throat the way it always did now when someone unexpected came to the door. Perhaps it was someone who brought news about Irmtraud. She got up quickly, pulling her cardigan over her nightgown.

Gisela looked in confusion at the old postman, Herr Rossmann, standing on the step, hat in hand, face unreadable. "Fräulein Fahnr—Frau Schmidt," he said, correcting himself and clearing his throat. "This arrived today." Gisela stared at the envelope in his hand. Was there news from Irmtraud? "No return. No postmark either," he added.

He handed her a thin, gray envelope, creased at the edges. Her name was written in a hand she would know even blindfolded. Erich's. She gazed at it for several seconds before taking it. The old man gave her a short nod and walked away.

Gisela went back to her room and sat at the edge of her bed. She did not open the envelope immediately. Her fingers brushed the corners, then traced her name written in pencil in Erich's hand, smudged at the *m* and *t*. She imagined its contents had been folded by cold hands, maybe dirty, hungry ones.

When she finally opened the envelope and unfolded the sheets, she noticed a soft tear at the edge of the first page and the faint scent of burnt wood. The letter was also written in pencil. The thin paper was creased and smudged with dirt. For a moment, Gisela stared at Erich's handwriting without reading a single word. She ran her fingers across the first page. For months, she had been waiting for news from him. She began to read with trembling hands, the words swimming in front of her.

September 14, 1943. Somewhere in the East. My dearest Gisela. If this letter reaches you, then the world is kinder than I have believed these past few months. I'm alive, and that must count for something, even here, where the snow doesn't melt and men forget their names. We were shot down near Kursk. The Soviets found us in the wreckage. I was wounded, but lucky, if such a word can be used here. They took me and many others prisoner. We traveled for weeks on trains and on foot until we arrived in this godforsaken place. They house us, men who once wore uniforms, in this camp of frozen earth. Some of the men speak to themselves in the night. But I think of you, your smile, the smell of your hair, and your stories. May you not forget me, Gisela. I write in the hope that this letter will reach you, so you know I'm alive and that I think of you every day, every hour, every minute, and every second of the day. Hopefully, peace will find us before time forgets us. I do not know how long I will be kept prisoner here and when I will return, or if. And when this war finally ends, and if I do not return, I want you to find a new husband. I'm glad you have your family to give you comfort. Please send a letter to mine, so they too know that I'm alive. All my love, your husband Erich. "Let happy memories sustain you if your strength fails you; they are always there, and their current does not run backwards, even across foggy country, it floats toward the future." ~Rilke

Tears began to fall on the thin paper as Gisela read the last lines. She panicked and tried to dab at them with the sleeve of her cardigan. Finally, she set the letter carefully aside and looked at it from a safe distance, folding her hands and mumbling a short prayer of gratitude. Erich was alive. And one day, he would return to her. But then Gisela's thoughts turned to Irmtraud. She swallowed hard and slid off the bed and onto the floor and her knees, wringing her hands. *Oh God, please, please, I beg Thee, let them both return to me.*

CHAPTER 12

OCTOBER 1943

KASSEL, GERMANY

Irmtraud's heart jumped when the lights in her dormitory flickered and went out. It jumped again as the air raid sirens started to wail. Although she had experienced the shrill, penetrating sirens in Kassel before, they still gave her a start and made her pulse quicken with anxiety. Sometimes the siren's wailing had been answered with scattered bombings that rattled the hospital and dormitories. They had never received a direct hit. A big red cross had been painted on the roof of the hospital to spare them. Of course, every so often, the sirens shrieked in vain. Then everyone felt relieved that it was a false alarm.

Not knowing if bombs would fall this night, Irmtraud got up from her bed without any urgency. She had grown numb to the warnings. Straining her eyes in the thin darkness, she checked the wall clock. It appeared to be shortly after nine thirty, her usual bedtime. She had just finished her long shift half an hour ago and had settled down on her bed with some reading to distract her racing mind when suddenly the lights had flickered, and the sirens had started howling.

She knew the drill. It was all hands on deck when air raid warnings went off. The hospital personnel would move the less incapacitated patients to the basement. Unfortunately, those who couldn't be moved remained upstairs. Most of the time, the head nurse would be the one staying with these patients while everyone else kept those in the basement calm. Much to everyone's relief, the chief physician never joined them. Air raids happened mostly at night, and he usually left the hospital around suppertime and returned the next morning.

Irmtraud groped for the cardigan she had left at the foot of her bed and pulled it on. She felt for her white, starched nurse's cap she'd left next to it, and secured it high at the back of her head with the hairpins she always carried in her pockets. Then she slipped into her shoes, laced them up, and headed with the other student nurses out the door and over to the hospital. Outside her dormitory room, someone came running toward her. She realized it was Beate. "Christmas trees are falling," she called, trying to catch her breath.

Irmtraud knew what that meant. Target flares. The slow-falling canisters of brightly multi-colored, burning magnesium flares lit up the sky like a Christmas tree right before bombing raids. When Irmtraud had first seen them, she had stood, staring in awe at their beautiful, eerie glow in the night sky. Now, she knew they were deadly, signaling that bombs would follow soon, and telling where they meant to hit. Terror crept up in her.

Beate took Irmtraud's hand, and together they hastened to the hospital. Irmtraud felt her heart hammering against her ribs. She noticed that the city had also gone dark, except for the green, yellow, and red lights that fell from the sky. Slow and deliberate, they drifted down on silken threads, casting an unnatural glow over the rooftops.

"Like stars," Beate muttered next to her. But they were not stars. They were floating beacons to mark the city's heart. They drew death like moths, and Kassel was the flame tonight.

A flare caught on the steeple of the hospital. Hissing as it burned in place, it lit up like a ghost, visible before it vanished. For a moment, everything seemed to stand still. Then the sky cracked open.

"No!" Irmtraud wasn't sure if she or Beate had screamed. She turned and found Beate's face contorted by flashes of light and terror. Hospitals were not supposed to be targets.

Then came the sound. A low, far-off rumble, like thunder being dragged across iron. Irmtraud's stomach turned. The real bombs were coming now, guided by those glowing markers.

They ran into the hospital building and were greeted with the chaos and rush of the evacuation. Hospital personnel were flying up and down semi-dark hallways that occasionally lit up from flares and bombs, casting weird, distorted shadows. A long line of patients was already waiting by the elevator to be taken to the basement. Those able to walk were helped downstairs by nurses and their assistants. Like a beehive that had been prodded and smoked, the hospital boiled with restless motion. Nurses rushed between wards, and stretcher bearers yelled over each other. The air was thick with frenzied footsteps, shouted orders, and fear.

Irmtraud felt Beate letting go of her hand. With a look at the long line of patients, Beate said, "I will see if I can help some of them down the stairs to the basement." She didn't wait for Irmtraud's response and ran off in the direction of the elevator.

For a moment, Irmtraud looked around, not sure where to turn, what to do. Her head was spinning and her heart racing. She couldn't think straight. A young girl on crutches hobbled past her. The children's ward would need help moving the youngest of their patients, so she ran that way, past the elevator and its long line of patients, past Beate, who was desperately trying to convince an old man to let her help him.

Irmtraud found the children's ward almost empty. A couple of kerosene lamps on side tables provided some light. Only two of the smaller beds were still occupied. A pair of little boys who couldn't have been older than two and four looked at her with big, round eyes. She pulled the blanket off one of them and got ready to scoop him up into her arms.

"No, not him," the head nurse called from behind her.

Irmtraud whipped around. "Why not?"

The head nurse came over and carefully lifted the boy's pajama top. He lay completely still as if frozen, watching them with anxious, panic-stricken eyes. His tiny, mangled chest was covered with a big square of gauze. Dried blood had seeped through the bandaging.

"He has a bad case of TB. The doctor performed a thoracoplasty yesterday," the head nurse said, and gently pulled down his pajama shirt. She gazed at him for a moment, then patted his head. "He lost three ribs, and I don't want his sutures to become undone. I have strict instructions not to move him. He wouldn't survive."

"Then I will stay here with him," Irmtraud said.

"No, you won't. You will go to the basement. Now!" the head nurse snapped. "It's an order. I will stay with him tonight," she said more gently as she pulled a chair up to the boy's bed. "Go." She motioned to the other bed. "Take the other boy with you."

"Are you sure?" Irmtraud could feel a knot forming in her stomach. The head nurse glared at her. "Go! Now!"

Irmtraud swallowed, gave her a quick nod, and headed to the other bed. She was within arm's reach when a blast hit, close enough to rattle her teeth and send dust pouring from the ceiling. Too close. Closer than bombs had ever been dropped. It would only be a matter of time before the hospital would be hit directly. She had seen the flare, the prophet of destruction.

The little boy in the bed screamed. The head nurse took his hand and whispered something in his ear. Irmtraud rushed over to the other child, threw back his blanket, and scooped him up. The little boy wrapped his arms around her neck, holding on so tightly that Irmtraud struggled to breathe. She pushed through the door and ran out into the hallway. Patients were still waiting by the elevator, looking around anxiously and covering their heads in anticipation of the bombs.

"Everyone to the stairs, if you can," Irmtraud yelled. Some obeyed her command and began to shuffle in the direction of the stairs.

She had almost reached the stairway when a blast threw her to the ground. The boy slipped from her grasp. For a moment, Irmtraud forgot where she was. The blast had knocked the wind out of her. She gasped and tried to get up, but the ringing in her ears made her stumble and fall back down. Dust, debris, and smoke burned her eyes and throat. The hospital had been hit. In the darkness, on her knees, coughing, Irmtraud crawled, groping for the boy. She found him not far off and, with some effort, pulled him onto her lap, but his limp, lifeless body fell to the side. Irmtraud tried to make out his face in the dark. Blood came from his ears and nose. A large swelling bloomed on his forehead. Irmtraud felt his pulse and put her ear to his mouth. She drew a sharp breath and started rocking his body back and forth. He was gone.

Irmtraud tried to make out the stairs in the dark. She knew she needed to get to the basement. Now. The sirens were still wailing. Between their howls, she could hear the high-pitched whistle of falling bombs like the screams of banshees. The deep, bone-cracking booms that followed split the air all around her.

She inched along in the direction of the stairs and thought she saw the mangled silhouette of the iron banister appear like a broken spine jutting out of a pile of rubble in front of her. She managed to get up and reach for it, but it fell over onto the wreckage that occupied the space where the staircase used to be. An arm stuck out from underneath the concrete, and she wondered if it was one of the patients she had sent this way. Irmtraud shuddered and hugged her body. She looked around, trying to get her bearings, and wiped her face with the back of her hand. Her forehead felt wet. She realized she was bleeding. Oddly, she didn't feel any pain.

It dawned on her that she was cut off from the basement, and the patients down there were trapped. She groped her way through the darkened corridor, stumbling over shattered plaster and limp bodies as she moved toward the children's ward. But it was gone. In its place was a gaping hole in the floor, smoking and silent. Here and there, small fires lit up the devastation.

Irmtraud swallowed hard and sank to the floor. She pulled her legs in and wept. About the destruction. About the little boys and the head nurse and all of the others. All lost. Outside, bombs kept coming. The relentless roaring overhead made her teeth chatter and her bones vibrate.

She felt a hand on her shoulder and looked up.

"We need to get to the air raid shelter. Now," Jan said, pulling her up.

"You came," she breathed, shaking her head slowly, as if her mind couldn't quite catch up to the fact that Jan was standing before her.

"Of course," he said simply. He placed a hand on her cheek. "I'm glad you're alright. I was on my way to the hospital when I saw it get hit... I feared the worst." He looked around, then back at her. "We need to hurry."

Jan took her hand, and Irmtraud stumbled after him, out into the open. She almost fell when her leg hit the mangled form of the bench where she used to sit during her breaks. Jan caught her and put his arms around her, leading her away from the burning building. She turned and gasped. The hospital was gone. All that was left was a burning skeleton of brick.

As if by instinct, Jan ducked his head, pulling her down with him, as more enemy bombers approached overhead. They passed. But a moment later, the earth vibrated from the explosions, and their ears rang from the thunder of the blasts and the shattering of glass. They kept low for a moment longer, trying to catch their breath in the smoke-filled air that smelled of scorched wood, hot metal, and something else. Burnt cloth, blood, and the faint, sickly sweetness of burning flesh. "We need to keep going," Jan choked out. "Can... can you run?"

Irmtraud nodded, and they started running. Jan led them through small streets and alleys. She didn't recognize any of them. To their left and right, houses had been bombed to smithereens, and some of them were burning. Here and there, they heard the screams and wails of people. Irmtraud decided to look straight ahead at Jan's back and not at the destruction around them. In the distance ahead and to the east of them, the city seemed to have erupted into an orange glow. It almost looked like the painting of a fiery blood-orange sunrise. Kassel was burning.

Jan stopped a few times so she could catch her breath. He constantly scanned their surroundings. Irmtraud didn't like the concern she saw written across his face, or the fear that had darkened his eyes. It made her afraid, too. Filled her with a kind of fear she hadn't known before. One that settled heavy and deep in her bones and told her that no one, not even the strong ones, would survive this.

They pressed on through the smoke and rubble, only to halt when their destination came into view. Barely a few hundred meters ahead of them was the cellar beneath the old vineyard that served as a bomb shelter. Not so long ago, she had danced there with Jan, the air thick with a different kind of smoke, and smell, and laughter. Pure and unadulterated. The joy she'd felt there now seemed distant, almost unreal, like something borrowed from another life, another time.

A wall of fire had completely engulfed the ancient vineyard. For a moment, all they could do was stare at the scene before them.

"Jan ... the people in the shelter ..." Irmtraud breathed.

Jan didn't respond. Instead, he took her by the hand and pulled her toward the river. But there, too, the firestorm was already raging. Buildings burned all along the bank. There was no way to reach the water. They tried going west, but after they had rounded a couple of streets, their path was cut off by the same raging firestorm.

Jan looked toward the hospital. He stopped, let go of her hand, and took a few steps away from her, as if he wanted to be alone. Irmtraud let him. She looked at his silhouette, framed against the wall of fire that now approached them from that direction as well. They were encircled, trapped. Irmtraud felt faint and swayed. She bent over and heaved. "We will never make it out," she sobbed, staring at the approaching wall of fire.

Jan returned to her and took her face in his hands. "No ... we won't," he said with tears in his eyes.

Irmtraud took a step back and shook her head vehemently. *No! It couldn't be. Not now. Not like this.* She didn't want to die. Panic tightened her throat. She choked and coughed. Jan pulled her in, pressing her against his chest. She wrapped her arms around him as the fire grew closer and louder.

The heat became unbearable. Irmtraud struggled to breathe. Her lips tasted of ashes. She thought of her family. Her parents. Gisela. A wave of guilt washed over her. Sobs were rocking her body now, and Jan held her even tighter, pressing her hard against his body. She wriggled free, and what she saw made her heart stop.

"Don't look. Don't look," Jan shouted over the rumble of the fire. Irmtraud closed her eyes and let him hold her. He kissed her hair. The hot wind tore at her clothes. Her heartbeat pounded in her ears, a steady, slowing drum. Terror took hold of her, and she wanted to scream. But there was no breath left for it. Just a final thought... quick, small, and all-consuming like the firestorm raging around her.

Forgive me!

Chapter 13

December 1943

Wallhausen, Germany

Christmas had always been Gisela's favorite time of the year, but not anymore. Just last year, Erich, Waldemar, and Irmtraud had been here, celebrating the holidays at home. She couldn't imagine it would ever be her favorite time of the year again. Not without them. It was a painful season now, a time when she acutely felt all that she had lost, and all those who were gone.

Still, her mother had insisted on lighting a new candle every Advent, as they had always done in anticipation of the holiday. On one of the Advent Sundays, Mama had even been able to convince Gisela to bake some simple cookies with her, something Gisela had always looked forward to since she was a child but had no desire to do this year. Who would they be baking for? And wasn't it frivolous to use the flour they had left for such extravagance? She had finally fought back when her mother demanded they put up a tree on Christmas Eve. To no avail. Her mother won that battle, too.

Gisela stared at the skeletal, scraggly tree in disgust. Irmtraud would have been appalled if she had seen it. Her sister had always insisted on the tallest, fattest tree. Her father had laughed at Irmtraud's insistence, but always eventually gave in and got her the tallest one. Then Irmtraud and Gisela would decorate it, and the tree would stay up until Irmtraud's birthday on the tenth of January.

Today, just two days after Christmas, Gisela stood in front of the embarrassment of a Christmas tree taking down the few wooden ornaments she had used, intricately carved scenes of the nativity. Her mother had made them many years ago. Gisela remembered how she and Irmtraud had watched in awe while Mama worked, amazed at her craftsmanship. Sighing deeply, Gisela's eyes drifted to the window beside the tree. It was rimmed with frost, the pale winter light pressing in. Staring at it, Gisela had a sudden image of their mother showing Irmtraud and her the ornaments so many Christmases ago.

The last time Gisela had heard from Irmtraud was in a letter she had sent the week before the bombs fell on Kassel. Irmtraud had written in her usual hurried scrawl, complaining about the cold floors at the hospital, and asking for wool socks if Gisela could spare them. Gisela had read that letter a hundred times since, the ink now smudged from her thumbprints.

Irmtraud's body had never been found. The hospital had taken a direct hit. Its basement, used as a bomb shelter, had completely collapsed under fire and stone. The rest of the building had disintegrated in the firestorm that followed and had burned for hours. It had been over two months now since that fateful night, but Irmtraud's name still didn't appear on the Red Cross lists. There was no confirmation of her death, and she had no grave.

Gisela had written to the Red Cross office every week since the destruction of Kassel. The same notices came back. The same kind of letter each time, kind words, but missing the words she longed for most. The not knowing had been the hardest part, until one day it wasn't. Now the hardest part was knowing without proof. The certainty no one had spoken aloud, but everyone had quietly agreed on. Irmtraud wasn't missing. She was dead.

Silence had settled into Gisela's chest much as it had into her father's. Some nights, she dreamed Irmtraud was calling her from underneath the rubble. Most mornings, she woke without remembering what day it was.

Outside, snow was falling, slow and muting, as if the world had agreed to cover the destruction and the dead. Gisela placed the last of the ornaments in its small box. For a moment, her fingers rested on it and made her chest ache. *You should be here.*

⁂

The snow stayed until New Year's, then temperatures rose, and heavy rain set in. It did not let up for days. Gisela could feel herself falling into a depression. She felt utterly alone. At times, she even joined her father in the living room, staring out the window without purpose. In silence. All day long. Until he shuffled out of the room without a word and crept up to his bedroom.

The days ran into each other without relief, and with the same mind-numbing routine of tasks. The only highlight was when she visited Kurt in the attic, who would tell her about this or that piece of art. He painted each work as vividly with his words as the artist had with their brush. Kurt told her stories about his life in Dresden and about his family. Sometimes he would draw while he talked, always handing Gisela the drawings he had made before she left.

One day, Georg handed her a dusty old roll of wallpaper. At her surprised look, he explained that one could draw on the back of it if one was desperate for paper. She had accumulated quite a collection of Kurt's drawings, which now covered most of the walls in her bedroom. Only the first one he gave her was framed, and it held a special spot on the wall opposite her bed. It was the first thing she saw when she opened her eyes in the morning, and the last when she closed them at night.

Oddly, the drawing made her feel especially close to Erich. She had not heard from him since the arrival of his first, and only, letter after his capture. Now more than ever, she needed to feel close to him. She had begun to forget his face. He almost seemed like a distant memory. Kurt's drawing helped her to hold on. To wait for Erich's return. One day, he would be back. She would wait for him, no matter what. She had promised herself that much.

* * *

The knock on the door was so faint that at first Gisela thought she must have imagined it. But then it grew louder. More insistent. She had been sitting in the living room with her father since breakfast, staring out the window with him. But she hadn't seen anyone approach the house or come up the front steps.

Shaking her head in confusion, Gisela got up. But when she got into the hall, she found that her mother had been faster and was already at the front door, unlocking it. Mama had insisted on keeping it locked from the inside since last October. Gisela understood. It gave her mother comfort and the illusion of control, as if she still had a hand in protecting those she loved. Gisela knew this was an illusion, a fragile sense of safety and protection.

As the door swung open, Gisela cried, "Gudrun!" Rushing past her smiling mother, she threw her arms around her friend. "You're back!"

"I am," Gudrun said, her voice filled with hesitation, her body stiff. Gisela let go of her, feeling silly.

"Come in, child," Gisela's mother urged, pulling Gudrun into the house and locking the door again. Mama took Gudrun's coat, and Gisela led her friend into the living room.

"Good day, Herr Fahnrich," Gudrun said to Gisela's father. But the old man didn't react. He just continued staring out the window, unmoved.

"He hasn't been the same since... since Waldemar's death, I'm afraid," Gisela said, swallowing hard. She eyed her friend carefully. Gudrun looked crestfallen. Tears stood in her eyes.

"My mother told me that Waldemar had fallen," Gudrun murmured, her eyes downcast, as if she stood at Waldemar's grave. "I'm so sorry, Gisela," Gudrun said, sniffing back tears.

They stood in silence for a moment, trying to regain their composure. Gisela was kneading her hands, missing Waldemar terribly at that moment, and unsure what to say to her friend. Not only was the air thick with their grief, but they also hadn't parted well. It had been almost a year and a half since she had seen or spoken to Gudrun.

Gisela's mother came in, balancing a tray that bore four porcelain cups and a steaming, chipped teapot that smelled faintly of chamomile. "A bit of hot tea will warm you up," she said softly to Gudrun with the practiced calm of someone trying to keep the world steady.

Mama set the beautiful tray with its ornately carved handles down on the small coffee table with deliberate care. She had made it with her own hands in happier days, proving herself as gifted a craftsman as Gisela's father. "Come, sit," she added, gesturing toward the chairs before pouring the tea.

"Have some, dear," Mama said, placing the delicate white Meissen cup and saucer patterned with blue flowers on top of a book on the little side table by his armchair. She then handed Gudrun and Gisela their own cups and, folding her skirt beneath her, sat down on the sofa opposite them.

Gisela took a careful sip of the hot liquid that smelled of dry meadows. Although she had numerous questions she wanted to ask her friend, she was glad her mother was here to ease the conversation.

"How have you been, Gudrun?" Mama asked. "You were gone for so long."

Gudrun gazed into her tea as if it might offer her an answer she could share. Then she put down the cup. "I'm well, thank you," she said. "I'm home now. With my mother. She is glad I'm back. She needs me."

Gisela couldn't help but notice Gudrun's stiffness, and the flat, uncanny monotone of her voice. She took another sip, letting the warmth run down her throat and settle in her chest as she watched Gudrun over the rim of her cup. Her friend's posture was too straight, too careful, like someone who had needed to watch herself for a prolonged period of time.

"That's good," Gisela's mother said gently. "Family matters more than ever these days."

Gudrun offered a polite nod but didn't look up. Her hands, folded in her lap now, were still.

Gisela hesitated. Her mind circled the questions she wanted to ask. Where exactly had Gudrun been? The purpose of Himmler's *Lebensborn* program, which Gudrun had told her she wanted to join before she left Wallhausen, was to produce children. Aryan children, as the government always emphasized. Did Gudrun have a child?

As if she had heard Gisela's thoughts, Gudrun glanced at the door to the hallway. Her voice dropped as she said, "There's a little one. A boy. His name is Dieter."

Gisela's mother's cup clinked gently against the saucer. "Yours?" she asked softly.

Gudrun paused. "Yes," she said, and this time she looked at Gisela. "He's mine."

The room fell quiet. Outside, the wind moved through the bare branches, scratching faintly at the windowpanes. Gisela wanted to ask who the father was. If Gudrun had loved him. If it had been her choice. But the words caught in her throat. Instead, she reached for the teapot and said, "I hope to meet little Dieter sometime." She smiled at her friend encouragingly, hoping Gudrun would sense that she was still there for her.

"I hope so, too. He's with my mother right now," Gudrun said softly.

"Spoiling him, I'm sure," Gisela's mother said with a warm smile, which Gudrun returned, nodding.

"I heard about Irmtraud," Gudrun said carefully, and Gisela saw the smile leave her mother's face. "I'm so sorry about your loss. For both. Waldemar and Irmtraud." She placed a hand on Gisela's arm. "I know what it is like to lose a sibling. And I know how close you were with them both."

Gisela swallowed hard and looked back into what was left of the amber liquid in her cup. "Thank you, Gudrun," she murmured.

The room had fallen quiet once more, matching her father's silence.

"I need to get going. Dieter will be hungry soon," Gudrun said, getting to her feet.

"I'm glad you came by," Gisela said as she followed Gudrun into the hall and helped her into her coat. Gudrun turned to her with a smile but then stopped short, eyeing something behind Gisela. "I didn't know you could draw like that," she exclaimed. Gisela turned around. The door to her room was ajar and offered a glimpse of the drawings on her bedroom wall.

"Oh, no. I didn't draw them. A ... a friend drew them for me," she said, clearing her throat.

"I see," Gudrun said, still admiring them. Then she suddenly stepped around Gisela and went into the bedroom. "Your friend is very talented," she said, walking around the room with her arms crossed, scrutinizing them.

Gisela cleared her throat nervously. "Have you read Hermann Hesse's *Peter Camenzind*? You might find it—" Gisela cut herself off and swiped the book off her nightstand to thrust it into Gudrun's arms.

Gudrun looked at her in surprise and then at the book in her arms. "I have not," she said, opening the book with some curiosity. "Thank you for letting me borrow it."

"I am just glad to have my friend back. It's been very lonely around here," Gisela said quickly and pulled Gudrun with her out of the bedroom.

"And I'm glad to be back." Gudrun hugged her, then slipped out the door, which Gisela locked behind her. How glad she was that her friend was back and had called on her. They had not parted well, but everything seemed forgotten and forgiven now. One could not hold a grudge in times like these. And Gudrun had a child now and would need her support. But then she let out a slow sigh of relief, went over to her bedroom and gently closed the door, chiding herself for not having done so earlier.

Chapter 14

April 1944

Munich, Germany

The train platform in Munich was covered in a thin layer of frost. Not completely unexpected this time of spring, but surely this would be the last. Karl was wearing his full SS uniform with his topcoat and polished boots. A small travel bag sat by his feet. A stiff breeze was blowing, although the sun wouldn't be up for another hour. Behind him, other shadowy uniformed figures lurked in the dark, waiting for the first train of the day.

Karl hadn't slept the last few nights. Since the arrival of his orders. After Wilhelm had received his orders last August, Karl had spent the night walking the forest trail behind the Berghof, the same path he had once stumbled along in grief for Waldemar. But with Wilhelm's warning ringing in his head, there had been no release in nature. Only questions, and the words *cleansing operation* echoing endlessly in his mind.

A low mist curled over the tracks as the whistle of the arriving train, bound for Budapest, shrieked through the darkness. There, Karl had been told, he'd be participating in *Operation Margarethe* and working at a coordination center for SS special actions in the General Government. *Not the front line*, he had been reassured. Nevertheless, not knowing the specifics of his new assignment made him uneasy.

It was only weeks later, standing at the edge of a small Hungarian town in the outer foothills of the Carpathian Mountains near the northern border region, that Karl began to understand his assignment. Together with his unit, he was ordered to round up the Jewish and, if feasible and productive, also the Roma population of the towns and villages of the region.

Officially, Karl's assignment had been to assist with "security enforcement" during the operation. Drive a Wehrmacht lorry. Shuttle the men of his unit from town to town and village to village. He understood now what "security enforcement" really meant.

Day after day, they herded people into trucks like livestock. Men, women, children. To be taken to bigger towns, where in ghettos, they waited for days, sometimes weeks, to be loaded onto trains to be taken north. Through Slovakia. Into Poland. To a camp called Auschwitz. Karl had heard the place mentioned in conversations at Obersalzberg a few times. By the snippets of the descriptions he had caught, it sounded like a factory. Now he knew what kind of factory.

How he missed his previous assignment. Even fighting the Soviets at the Eastern Front, which meant almost certain death or capture, was more appealing.

He hadn't had to fire his weapon once here in Hungary. He hadn't needed to. He'd just stood there, part of the machinery of terror, his presence giving legitimacy to the horror. A lieutenant barked orders. And they forced people out of their homes and onto the trucks amid faces contorted by terror, screaming, and wailing. Even the roaring of the trucks' engines as they carried off their human load couldn't cover the sound of terrified people.

At the end of one such day, some of the men joked and lit cigarettes. One of them offered Karl a light. He didn't take it.

Instead, he stared down the road where the trucks had vanished, leaving nothing but muddy tracks behind. Here and there, a piece of luggage or a garment was strewn about. In his mind, he saw the frightened faces of women and children, and the accusatory stares of hopeless men, all of them blurring into a grotesque sea of humanity. One child's arm still reached upward, frozen in mid-motion.

Karl shuddered and vomited behind the *Wehrmacht* lorry.

That night, he drank half a bottle of schnapps and stared at the ceiling of his barracks. Outside, a dog barked and was silenced. Tomorrow, it would happen again. In another town. And then another. And each time, he would tell himself that he was only the driver of the lorry. Only logistics. He never pulled the trigger. He never gave orders. He just followed them.

But each time, something in him crumbled. He had tried to bury his conscience, as Wilhelm had suggested back in August. But time and again, it reared its head. He hadn't slept well in weeks and hardly ate, choking down food only to prevent himself from fainting.

Now, sitting on the edge of his cot, Karl realized he had made his decision. He rummaged through his bag, retrieved a journal and a pencil, and started writing. In the final lines, he wrote: "Waldemar died in the snow with a rifle in his hand. I die in pieces with blood on my hands. One of us had the better fate." Then, Karl closed the journal, hiding it once again in the inner lining of his bag.

"You're here for *Operation Margarethe*."

It wasn't a question, but Karl straightened his shoulders and said, "Yes, sir."

"What makes you think you'll fare better at the front? Especially the Eastern Front? Haven't you heard that the Soviets' Red Army has begun a major offensive in the East, and is gaining ground?"

Karl simply nodded in response, hoping the *Oberscharführer* would grant him permission to be transferred to the front. He looked at the documents Karl had handed him.

"You seemed to have served the Führer well, so I will grant you your request. You will leave in the morning. Help hold back those Bolsheviks." His superior scribbled something on his paper, then stamped it. Karl clicked his heels and saluted the man, a mixture of relief and anxiety washing over him. The Eastern Front had moved closer and closer over the last few months. The Wehrmacht was losing one battle after another, trying to hold the Soviets back. To no avail. The Russians advanced, and the Wehrmacht had begun to retreat. Karl was sure of one thing. His efforts, however minor, would probably be completely in vain. A lost cause. A damned cause. Was that what he was giving his life for?

Karl stepped out of the office into the wet evening air, his breath catching. Around him, the outpost lay quiet. Nothing but the distant sputter of a diesel generator broke the leaden silence. He lit a cigarette with unsteady hands, the first he'd had in weeks. He could still hear the stamping of his transfer echoing faintly behind him, like a final judgment. Or perhaps more like a signed death sentence. But it had been all his idea. He'd asked for it, *begged for it*, really. Like a condemned man asking for a different rope. But at least there, he told himself, his death would be honest. No more standing guard while the helpless were loaded into trucks like sacks of grain. The war on the Eastern Front was brutal. But the men they fought had rifles, not dolls and bundles clutched to their chests.

He walked slowly back to his barracks, gravel crunching under his boots. Inside, the room was dim. A single kerosene lamp provided some light. The low murmur of men preparing for sleep filled the air. Someone in his unit had dozed off with a newspaper over his face, another snored softly in the cot next to Karl's.

He sat down quietly on the edge of his own cot, careful not to wake anyone. He wanted to be alone with his thoughts. He carefully fished around in his bag for his journal again. This time, he found it right away. He opened it but could only stare at the blank page. The pencil hovered, then fell to his lap.

Outside, another dog barked, brief, sharp, and fearful. Then silence.

Karl lay back, staring at the wooden beams above, still feeling the cold metal of the lorry's steering wheel in his hands, still seeing the children's faces. One had smiled at him, too young to know what was coming, or understand the fear in her parents' eyes.

The half empty bottle of schnapps sat untouched beside Karl's cot. He no longer needed its dulling warmth. He whispered his brother's name into the dark. Not for guidance. Not for comfort. And not out of grief. But for reassurance that he would soon find a similar fate.

CHAPTER 15

NOVEMBER 1944

WALLHAUSEN, GERMANY

It was a cold Tuesday in November when, early in the morning, Gisela got ready to battle the weather and line up in front of their village grocer to see if she could secure some meat, flour, and milk. She wasn't too hopeful, but she needed to try. Their pile of potatoes in the cellar was already dwindling, and other food had become scarce.

For the first time in her life, Gisela learned what it meant to be hungry. Not the passing kind of hunger one felt when skipping breakfast or eating a late lunch, but the type that gnawed at your stomach, causing a kind of dull, persistent pain that settled low in the belly and did not go away, no matter how slowly one chewed the single boiled potato that now passed for a whole meal. She had grown up thinking hunger was a sensation, something sharp, temporary, and tolerable. But this seemed permanent and intolerable. Like a cold that seeped through the walls and down into her bones.

Before wrapping her scarf around her neck, Gisela looked in the front hall mirror. She no longer resembled the beautiful woman in the portrait. Dark shadows under her eyes and sharp cheekbones had changed her appearance. Her hair had lost its shine and felt brittle to the touch. Gisela huffed at her reflection and wound the scarf twice around her neck, not bothering to knot it. She grabbed her coat and threw it on. It now hung loosely on her, as if it belonged to her brothers or her father. Throwing another look of disgust at her reflection, she stormed down the hallway, past the picture of the woman who had borne her, and out the back of the house to get her bike.

It was her bike entirely now. She stared at it for a moment, swallowing down the tears that threatened to cloud her vision. Irmtraud would never ride it with her again. Gisela had never felt lonelier in her life. She dabbed her eyes with one end of the scarf and angrily kicked the bike's tire, sending it crashing to the ground.

She righted the bike, wrestling with it for a moment, and stared at the saddle, her eyes drifting to the seat post clamp. Swallowing, she bent down and released it. For a couple of minutes, she tried to wiggle the seat loose without much success. Then, glancing back at the house to make sure no one was watching her, she lifted her foot and kicked it into submission. That had done the trick. Gisela pushed the saddle lower, then clamped it into position. With a satisfied grunt, she swung up onto the bike. As she rode down the street, the cold wind taking her breath away and stinging her face, she thought of the woman who had left her the old bicycle. She might not be as tall and no longer as beautiful as her birth mother, but

Gisela knew that she now had a strength, an inner core, even the war had not managed to snuff out.

———

A long line of women had already formed in front of the only grocery shop in their village. Wallhausen had a butcher and a couple of bakers, but it was only at the grocer's where one could get their hands on milk, cheese, and flour. Gisela also hoped that she would be able to purchase some meat, since these days the butcher was only open every other week.

She parked her bike and got in line behind a short, older woman wearing a beautiful but well-worn winter coat that sported a fur collar. Her gloves were also fur-rimmed, and so was the fancy hat she was wearing. These, too, showed signs of wear. Every few minutes, the woman took a kerchief from her purse to blow her nose. After a few minutes, the line finally started moving. The shop had opened, but Gisela knew it would be sheer luck if she ended up with anything on her list today. She put her collar up and hugged herself against the cold, stamping in place to keep the blood to her lower limbs moving as she dug her hands into the pockets of her coat, fingering her ration card.

A few Wehrmacht lorries rumbled down Main Street, which had been renamed Adolf-Hitler-Street. The woman in front of her turned to face her. "They're taking the old men to the front now," she said. "My husband was picked up yesterday." The woman blew her nose again, and Gisela realized she had been quietly crying.

She thought of her father. They wouldn't! He had fought in the Great War and had served the Fatherland.

"My husband did his duty in the Great War," the woman added, echoing Gisela's thought. "He still limps from his injury," she said, wiping her nose again, fighting back more tears as she turned to face the front of the line.

Gisela stared at the shoppers ahead of her, then at the back of the old woman. The thought of her father having to fight knotted her stomach. He was a broken man, in no condition to take up a rifle. She shuddered, then turned, left the line, and pedaled home.

With each corner she rounded, the knot in Gisela's stomach tightened. As she approached the house, she saw her mother standing by the gate as if waiting for her. She was dabbing her face. Gisela's heart sank.

They called it the *Volkssturm*. A last effort to turn the war in their favor. Rumors had long spread that Hitler was losing, and that the Americans and Soviets were closing in from the West and East. Gisela felt dread, but also hope that this might finally end, even if it meant Germany losing yet another war.

Her mother described how her father had been dragged out of the house and into a Wehrmacht lorry. Perhaps he had even been in one that had passed her while she stood in line at the shop. It stung to picture her father, huddled in the back of a Wehrmacht lorry, silent, broken, and hopeless. If only she had known. But what could she have done?

And now, he was gone. He had grown so frail over the last months. How could he survive combat? She had heard that they now used old men and young boys as a last line of defense at the outskirts of cities, along roads that led to them, and at bridges. Perhaps her father wouldn't see any fighting at all. Maybe it wouldn't come to that. *Maybe.*

How many more people she loved had to die? Waldemar and Irmtraud were dead. Erich was imprisoned in some faraway Soviet labor camp. Heinrich, Karl, and now her father had to fight in this devastating war. Gisela felt utterly helpless. All she could do was watch as one after another member of her family was sent to their deaths.

———

Still wearing her winter coat from this morning, Gisela stared at the small onion that had already sprouted and the small, stale piece of bread that sat beside it on the kitchen counter. She was embarrassed that this was all they had to spare and share with Kurt. With a sigh, she scooped them up and stuffed them into her pockets.

They had had no luck in securing enough coal for the coming winter. Everything went to the war effort. All resources were sent to the frontlines. Her mother insisted that they conserve what little coal they did have. So, they wore their hats and coats in the house, and an extra pair of socks if needed. It was only November, and on a couple of mornings last week, Gisela had woken up to white wisps of breath escaping her mouth. It had been very difficult to crawl out from underneath her heavy goose-feathered duvet and leave her warm bed.

Gisela shivered, put up the collar of her coat, and stepped out the back to bring Kurt his ration for the day, however meager. But when she opened the door to the workshop, she fell backward. The place was in utter disarray, as if a storm had swept through it. Planks of wood were no longer neatly stacked against the wall but tossed aside. The table saw had toppled over. The blade now hung askew. Gisela walked slowly through the mayhem, stepping carefully around emptied boxes of nails and broken furniture. What had happened here? She looked toward her father's office, swallowing hard. The door was ajar, but it lay quiet and dark. When she got closer, she saw something on the floor. After a few steps, she realized it was a hat. *Georg*, she mouthed. The hat was torn on one side, and someone had stepped on it. She picked it up and took it inside the office.

The floor was covered in papers. Some of the drawers of her father's desk stood open, while others had been ripped out, emptied, and thrown on the floor. She stared at the chaos in disbelief. Then she looked at the ceiling.

Gisela ran across the destroyed workshop and up the stairs to the attic. The door was ajar. Her stomach dropped. She ducked and went inside, her eyes falling on the single small sack of flour leaning against the attic wall. That's all they had left.

The pile of broken furniture that had sheltered Karl had been taken apart. Gisela knew he was no longer there, but she looked anyway. All his things were gone, even the roll of old wallpaper and the pieces of charcoal. Had he been arrested? Taken to the front with Georg and her father? Shot?

She sank to the floor, drawing her legs up and hugging them, rocking back and forth. The men were gone. All of them. Now it was just her and Mama. How could they go on all by themselves? Just the two of them. They no longer had any income from the family's carpentry business. How would they survive the winter?

When Gisela finally returned to the house, she went to her mother's bedroom. Mama lay on her bed, on top of her duvet, fully clothed, staring at the ceiling. Gisela went to her and sat beside her. Her mother's face was red, but she was no longer crying. "What are we going to do, Mama?" Gisela whispered.

For a long time, her mother didn't answer. Then, finally, she turned to Gisela and patted her hand. "We will do everything necessary," she said, "to survive. For your father, for Waldemar, and for Irmtraud," she added, quietly. Clearing her throat, she added, "And for you, and your Erich." His name hung in the air like dust.

Gisela nodded, watching her mother's hand resting on hers. *Survive.* The word felt small. She was tired of holding her breath just to make it through the day. She wanted more than rations and silence and waiting for news that never came. She wanted her family back. She wanted things to be the way they were before this terrible war. She wanted something that felt like life. But wanting was dangerous these days.

Gisela leaned down and rested her head against her mother's chest. Her apron smelled faintly of flour, which gave her odd comfort. "I will try my best, Mama."

Her mother put her arms around her and patted her back. "That's all we can do now," she said. "Try. And not look down. We cannot lose hope, you hear me?" Gisela didn't answer. She didn't need to. Hope wasn't optional. It was survival. Once you let go of it, everything else went, too.

Gisela dug her bare hands into the pockets of her coat. She was walking beside Gudrun, who was pushing Dieter in a pram that was so old-fashioned it looked as if it came from the turn of the century. Its curved iron frame, painted black and chipped with age, creaked faintly as it rolled. The large, spoked wheels, made of solid rubber, were worn smooth from decades of use. Brass fittings, only slightly dulled with time, still glinted at the hinges and joints. Gisela wondered where Gudrun had found it. Perhaps she had borrowed it from a neighbor. Or maybe she had found it in their attic. Perhaps Gudrun's mother had spent her infant years in it. Then another thought came to Gisela. Maybe it had been given to her by the Lebensborn program.

Gisela gazed at Dieter, whose little nose peeked out from underneath the blanket that covered a bulging duvet. A small strand of his wispy, white-blond hair had escaped from underneath the knitted, woolen bonnet Gisela had made for him. His eyes were closed, and he seemed to have drifted off to sleep as they rattled down the cobblestoned street that led to the river. Gisela hoped that today, she would find the courage to ask Gudrun about the program.

Putting her arm through Gudrun's, she helped push the pram onto the bridge. She was glad her friend had returned, and her dreary days were interrupted with visits from Gudrun and Dieter. But she could not deny that her friend had changed since her return. She appeared rather quiet and withdrawn. Less outspoken and opinionated. Gisela glanced at Gudrun. Her eyes were sunken, and she looked pale. Gudrun had never been the frail type. She was tall and bony. Strong. Now, she seemed delicate and fragile.

Gisela knew everyone was going hungry these days, but as a new mother, Gudrun needed sustenance. For little Dieter. "How are you getting on?" She asked.

"What do you mean?" Gudrun had stopped walking and let go of the pram, rubbing her gloved hands together.

"Do you and your mother have enough to eat?"

"As much as everyone else, I suppose," Gudrun said and started pushing again.

"Do you have enough milk? For little Dieter, I mean?" Gudrun did not react, so Gisela took her by the arm, forcing her friend to look at her. She was taken aback by the tears swimming in Gudrun's eyes. "What is it, Gudrun?" Gisela whispered. "You can tell me."

Gudrun sniffed back tears. "I have less and less milk. I'm so worried. I don't know how else to feed him. I don't know what to do," she blurted out and started sobbing.

"Can the program not help?" Gisela asked carefully.

"I ... I didn't leave under the best circumstances," Gudrun said hesitantly, not looking at Gisela. "And I'm not going back there," she added more forcefully.

"What happened?"

The question hung between them until, finally, Gudrun looked at her; her face was hard, but looking into her friend's eyes, Gisela saw nothing but hurt and guilt swimming in them. "I don't want to talk about it," Gudrun muttered. Then added, "I'm too ashamed."

"You know you can tell me anything, Gudrun." Gisela fought the urge to put her arms around her. Instead, she took her friend's gloved hand and squeezed it. " I won't judge you for it, I promise."

Gudrun sighed deeply. "I ran away from the program," she said. "They were going to take Dieter from me." Her voice was so low that Gisela had to strain to hear.

"Why?" She asked, shaking her head in dismay. "Why would they take him from you? I thought you were there to raise the child you bore?"

"I had to sign something when I arrived in that castle in Bavaria." Gudrun was shaking her head. "I was so overwhelmed by the luxury of the place and the welcome they gave me. I just signed what they put in front of me. You should have seen the place, Gisela," she said. "There was a game room, a beautiful library, the most lavish sitting room, grounds like a park, and even a cinema. Can you believe that? And the food... I have never had such good food in all my life."

The words were tumbling out of Gudrun now. "I had a thorough medical examination when I arrived. I had never experienced anything like it. All the other girls did, too." She paused and swallowed hard. When she continued, shame had crept back into her voice. "They calculated our periods. One day, a group of young SS officers arrived. They spent the evenings with us. We played games, watched films, and wandered the park. They even organized a dance for us. These were the best days. They were good-looking young men. You would have–"

Gudrun stopped and lowered her eyes to the ground, shaking her head. Gisela placed a hand on her friend's shoulder. When Gudrun finally met her gaze again, she had a far-off look on her face, as if she was somewhere else and not really seeing Gisela at all.

"They told us we had to pick one of the SS officers that we liked," she said. "The one I chose, Dieter's father, came and spent three nights with me. I got pregnant right away." Gudrun's voice dropped. "They took good care of me those nine months, but I had a very difficult birth. I was allowed to nurse Dieter at first. But then the nurses told me after only a couple of weeks that it was time to wean him so he could be placed with a nice Aryan family who would raise him. That's when I decided that I needed to escape."

Gisela looked at her friend, unsure how to respond. She took her hand again. "And you did," she said. "With your son. Which was very brave, and I'm sure it wasn't easy."

"No." Gudrun shook her head. "It wasn't. And I was so scared. When they brought him to me for one of his last feedings, I took Dieter and the bag I had ready under my bed and managed to leave without anyone seeing me or noticing. I was very lucky."

"Yes. And now you are home. With Dieter. And that's all that matters now."

Gudrun nodded, then shook her head. "You can't imagine. I fear every day that they will come looking for me, but I suppose, with how the war is going, they have other priorities. I pray that they have forgotten us. They don't need Dieter. They brought a lot of children from the East. They intend to place them with families."

Gisela put her arm around Gudrun and pulled her close. "You're home, and so is Dieter. I'll help you find a way to feed him," she said with a determination that surprised her.

Gisela had no idea how she could help her friend, but she needed to find a way. Her eyes lingered on little Dieter, sleeping peacefully. She swallowed hard. She had grown very fond of him. His innocent, sweet nature had been a beacon of light in her life since Gudrun had returned. And while she was no mother, she felt strangely responsible for him.

Gisela set the kettle on the iron stove in Gudrun's kitchen, though the flame beneath it was feeble. She had found some firewood in the cellar and kindled a fire, but it was hardly enough for a roaring fire that would be most welcome in the cold, damp kitchen. After their walk with little Dieter, Gisela had gone home and told her mama about Gudrun's predicament, hoping she would have some advice. And she did. Her sister, Gisela's mother, had borne Heinrich toward the end of the Great War. Back then, food had been just as scarce. Now, Gisela stood in the kitchen making the brew her mama had first used for Heinrich and suggested for Dieter. She hoped and prayed that he would take to it.

Gudrun sat on a stool nearby, rocking the hungry, wailing baby, and watching with a mixture of curiosity and doubt as Gisela poured the small amount of milk she had brought into a pot, added a tin cup of water, and a handful of the coarse, gray flour that was all anyone had now.

Dieter gave up crying and whimpered with a high, dry sound that had no weight to it. A cry without force. Gudrun's breasts would soon be completely empty, so they needed to act quickly.

Gisela pulled the shawl tighter around her shoulders and stirred the thin paste. "Just a little longer, *mein Schatz*," she soothed. "I know it's not real food, but it's something. Isn't that right, Gudrun?"

The mixture steamed faintly. When it had thickened as much as it was going to, Gisela poured it into a bottle and pulled a rubber nipple over the bottle neck, securing it with twine. She handed it to Gudrun, who took it with some hesitation. Holding Dieter close, Gudrun whispered into his little ear as she tipped the bottle gently to his lips. He sucked weakly at first, then took in a bit more, then attacked it greedily.

Gisela watched him, relief washing over her. She studied Gudrun's face and could see how a weight had been lifted off her. She even smiled.

"I know this isn't how it was meant to be," Gudrun murmured, brushing her son's fine hair with her lips. "But it will have to do, *mein Schatz*."

Gisela nodded with a smile. "Yes, it will have to. I'm glad he likes it." The only thing left to worry about now was that Dieter's stomach could tolerate the mixture.

———

Within a week, Gudrun's milk dried up completely. Gisela divvied up every little bit of flour she was able to secure with their ration card, giving Gudrun a portion of it for Dieter's meals so Gudrun could use her rations for herself and her mother. Mama didn't mind. It was only the two of them now that had to live off the ration card, and they still had the sack of flour in the attic that they had decided to keep for a rainy day.

Gisela saw Gudrun and Dieter a few times a week, and it was a balm to her soul to spend time with them. Usually, they went for a long walk during one of Dieter's naps. On rainy days, they sat together knitting, or Gisela helped Gudrun wash Dieter's nappies. Gisela enjoyed helping her friend, and Dieter's innocence and his smiles brought so much joy and lightened her spirits. He knew nothing of the chaos around him, nothing of loss and death and destruction. He had tolerated the mixture of cow's milk, water, flour, and, when they had it, a little sugar well, and was thriving despite the lack of his mother's milk.

One chilly day, Gisela was holding Dieter while Gudrun hung his nappies on the line. It would take days for them to dry in this cold, dreary November weather, but at least out here there was a breeze. It would take even longer for them to dry in the damp cold of the house. Gudrun and her mother had run out of firewood days ago. The little that Gudrun scavenged in the woods around them, she kept for cooking. There was none left over for heating.

Gisela pressed Dieter closer to her chest, trying to keep him and herself warm. She watched her friend, whose nose was red from the cold, hang up one of the cloths that served as Dieter's diapers. She had wondered but had never found the courage to ask her about the

SS soldier she had chosen. "Gudrun?" Gisela asked, thinking that now was as good a time as ever.

"Hm?"

"I've been meaning to ask," Gisela said. "For weeks, really. But I didn't know how." Her friend didn't reply, so Gisela went on. "You never told me about Dieter's father."

Gudrun paused and looked at her, puzzled. Then, she understood what Gisela was asking, and her face darkened. Her voice, when it came, was surprisingly calm. "I know," she said.

"I don't mean to pry."

Gisela was suddenly unsure if this had been a good idea. Suddenly, Gudrun appeared very tired, drawn, her eyes more sunken than usual, not from sleep, but from carrying something far too heavy for far too long.

"It wasn't love if that's what you're wondering" she said simply. "They called it service. To the Reich. A sacrifice for the fatherland. A gift to the future. I told you I had my pick, but in the end, I was just a girl with no say in anything." She reached for the next diaper and a clothes pin. "I don't even know his full name." Gudrun paused and looked at Gisela. "I came home," she said, "with a baby and no ring. My mother barely speaks to me. She says it's not the child's fault. She loves him. But I'm just a big disappointment to her."

Dieter stirred in Gisela's arms and let out a soft sigh. "It's not your fault either," Gisela said. "They lied to you. And they wanted to take Dieter from you."

"I think it is my fault," Gudrun replied. "Completely. I chose to leave and enroll in this program. Against my mother's wishes."

They stood in silence for a long moment, then Gudrun came over and gently lifted Dieter from Gisela's arms. "He's warm," she said, surprised.

"He's like a coal tucked into a blanket," Gisela chuckled. She watched Gudrun nuzzle him for a moment. "Why did you name him Dieter?"

"After his father," Gudrun said simply.

Gisela forced a smile. She wanted to ask Gudrun more about him but decided against it. Perhaps with time, her friend would open up. One thing was for sure, however. He was a Nazi, and he had taken advantage of her friend to further the regime's race policies. He hadn't married her, and he apparently didn't care about being a father. Gudrun had made a mistake. But Dieter wasn't a mistake. He had no choice in who his father was.

CHAPTER 16

APRIL 1945

VIENNA, AUSTRIA

They were told to hold the line. What line, Karl wasn't sure anymore. The war had pushed them so far west that they were now defending Vienna. As if they would be able to hold it. He sighed at the rumbling that seemed to have drawn closer in the past hour. Vienna's bones were already being rattled by tanks and artillery, but here, behind the rust-streaked gates of the Seegasse cemetery, time seemed to have slowed. Rain dripped quietly from the canopy of trees, and the only movement was the wind curling between the gravestones.

They had arrived under the cover of darkness, retreating as the Red Army advanced. Some of Karl's men had objected to entering the cemetery grounds. He had to admit that it wasn't much of a position. Just a patch of earth enclosed by cracked walls. Having no choice, the men had eventually followed his orders, finding refuge among the worn, crooked headstones.

Some were almost swallowed by ivy, others half-sunken into the soil, their remnants covered in moss. Here and there, carvings etched in Hebrew were still exposed but had been faded by the wind. Names Karl couldn't read. Symbols he barely recognized. The silence of the night, when the far-off fighting had briefly stopped, had wrapped around him like a blanket. Not comforting, it was too cold for that, but thick and familiar, the kind of silence found only in places where sorrow had soaked into the soil.

Now, in these early morning hours, the rain had started again, at times coming down in sheets that made it hard to see. Large puddles had formed on the walkways. The Soviets were alarmingly close. The fighting was only a few blocks away. Vienna was cracking. Their order was to defend the second district of the Austrian capital with everything they had left, which wasn't much. Anything to prevent the Soviets from taking the city and claiming victory. And they would defend it from this cemetery. Until their last breath.

Since their arrival last night, Karl had been wondering if this was where he would die. In a cemetery. A Jewish cemetery. His blood would desegregate the hollow ground, he thought bitterly. He couldn't die here. No one should have to die here, like this, hiding behind gravestones.

His men, the few that were left of his unit, crouched between the graves, their faces alert, too tired for fear. Karl had found cover behind a low slab, its inscription worn to near nothing. A date remained. 1747. He stared at it longer than he meant to, trying to imagine the man beneath. A father? A husband? How had he died so long ago? He reached down and brushed dirt from another headstone beside him. The Hebrew letters were soft under his glove.

Someone had loved this person once. Had chosen these words. Had stood here and wept.

To his right, a whole row of gravestones was missing, exposing his men from that side. Some had been knocked over and buried with earth as if to preserve them, hide them from destruction. *How ironic*, Karl thought, and dragged his gaze over to the small metal gate near the far wall that had been blown open by previous fighting or other violence, its hinges twisted like paper. Beyond it, the cemetery narrowed into a shaded grove of bare trees filled with smaller, even older stones, some toppled, others buried.

Karl tightened his grip on his rifle. He hadn't fired it in a couple of days. Today, he'd be using it again, perhaps for the last time, defending nothing but the echo of a lost cause.

"Take cover," Karl hissed at his men as a tank came rolling down Seegasse. He threw himself flat on the ground. If they were discovered, the tank would fire, and the last of the gravestones around them would crumble, burying them. Their only chance was to remain hidden, then ambush the tank from behind. Karl knew the Red Army infantry escorting the tank couldn't be too far off.

His soldiers only had one *Panzerfaust* left on them and they had to make it count. They would wait for the tank to pass, then fire at its rear armor.

Karl got ready to give the signal. The tank was beyond them and getting ready to round a corner. He got up and lifted his arm to give the signal, never even hearing the bullet that struck out of nowhere, shattering his elbow and throwing him backward.

The second bullet struck him in the right calf as he tried to pull himself behind a gravestone for cover. Karl felt it shatter the bone. He rolled on his stomach in agony, burying his face in the wet soil to scream. Around him, the screams of his men told him that he wasn't the only one hit. This was it, he realized. Today would be the day of his death. In a cemetery. A hysterical laugh escaped his throat, cut off by the grenade that detonated beside him, spraying dirt and stone as it pitched Karl's world into blackness.

He came to in the back of a Wehrmacht lorry, surrounded by the moaning of other wounded. He was lying on his side. His leg and arm had been rudimentarily splinted and bandaged. The pulsing pain almost took his breath away. But it was nothing compared to his back, which seemed to have been set on fire. The grenade must have hit me, he thought, as he clenched his jaw and gritted his teeth in agony.

He was told that they were retreating, and that he and the other wounded or dying were being taken to the army medical train that would transfer them to the army hospital in Salzburg. Karl looked for his men among the wounded but didn't recognize any of the faces. He tried to breathe through the waves of excruciating pain, but it only lasted a few minutes. Everything went dark again as the lorry rumbled over cobblestones, and a distant train whistle signaled departure.

Karl lit a cigarette and gazed up into the pale blue sky. A pair of doves cooed softly from the eaves of the hospital. It reminded him of peaceful times, which was deceiving. Even Salzburg would be taken soon. As the Soviets closed from the east, American tanks rolled in from the west and north. From what he had overheard, Karl guessed that the Americans were only a week away. He had sworn to himself that he would not be captured, especially not by the Soviets. He didn't want to end up like Erich, who was being worked to death in some labor camp in Siberia.

As he had several times a day for the past week, Karl had limped out of the hospital for a smoke, and to speed up his mobility, get the blood in his limbs flowing, especially in his injured leg. They had mended his arm and leg and tried to remove the splinters that had peppered his back, not entirely successfully. Some of the tiny grenade fragments had buried themselves in his muscles and bones. He had to make his peace with the fact that his body would carry the remnants of war and destruction for the rest of his life.

Here and there, tiny splinters had surfaced, the metal shards pushed out of his wounds by infection. Karl collected them. They served as a reminder that he was still alive. According to his doctors, he would soon he would be well enough to join other recovering soldiers on their daily walk through the city.

They went the same route every day. Two young soldiers lucky enough not to have to be part of the *Volkssturm* accompanied them on their walks through Salzburg. At first, Karl didn't understand why they had to be guarded, but it soon dawned on him. The war was as good as lost, but those fully recovered were still sent to help fight off the Soviets and Americans in a last, disillusioned effort. No one wanted to return to fighting and become cannon fodder. And none of them wanted to end up a prisoner of war either, especially so close to the end. The young guards were there to stop them from deserting.

They took their walks in the morning, right after breakfast. They were not allowed civilian clothes, but had to wear their old, tattered, shot-up trousers and jackets, or the uniforms of those who had died of their injuries or not made it through surgery, if they were in better shape. Once, their uniforms had been a source of pride and triumph; now all they garnered were anxious glances of defeat and hopelessness. Karl longed for home, and he knew that he was going to have to get out of this uniform, and out of Salzburg, if he was ever going to see Wallhausen again. He needed a plan. And soon.

As they rounded a corner to head back toward the military hospital, Karl noticed a black bike parked in front of a bakery. It reminded him of his mother's. He swallowed hard at the thought of Irmtraud. He only had one sister and one brother left now. As far as he knew, Gisela was at home, helping their parents, and Heinrich was still in Northern Italy. With the way things were going, Karl was certain that he too, would soon either end up dead or captured.

Over the next few days, Karl watched for the black bike outside the bakery. It was always there. Every time they walked past it, it seemed to beckon him to jump on and pedal away. It became clear to him that the bike was his ticket home. It would take him weeks, if not months to make it to Wallhausen. Pedaling across a war-torn country, skidding along front lines, trying to avoid friendly, and enemy, fire. The odds of making it home unscathed were slim, but better than finding himself in a prisoner of war camp.

So one morning, as their group rounded a corner near the bakery, Karl took his chance. He slipped into the entrance porch of a house, and when he realized the young, inexperienced guards hadn't noticed, slipped out again and, fighting the urge to run, trying not to attract attention, made his way to the bakery.

Trying to catch his breath, feeling as though his heart might explode, Karl was beyond relieved to see the bike in its usual place. He allowed himself to glance around just once before walking straight up to it with a confidence that said it was his. Then, in one swift movement, Karl grabbed the black bicycle, swung onto the saddle, and pedaled away.

CHAPTER 17

APRIL 1945

WALLHAUSEN, GERMANY

Spring came as if there was no war. Trees and flowers bloomed. Fresh grass stood high. The sun felt peacefully warm while spring storms cleared the air and brought much-needed rain that washed the gloominess and cold of winter away. But the storks did not return. Their nest on top of the town hall remained empty and barren, and the meadows by the river and the old oak had no visits from them.

Gisela wondered what had happened. If they had stayed away in the south of Europe or even Africa, where the effects of the war were less severe. Or had they become casualties and fallen from the war-torn sky? She missed their reassuring presence. It was like a renewed promise each spring when the storks returned, a promise that life would continue no matter what, while everything remained as it used to be. The village was not the same without them.

Gisela and her mother worked tirelessly day in and day out in the garden. Tilling and planting, pruning and seeding. Their supply of food was now almost completely gone, and they had to look ahead and prepare as they always did. There had been no word from Gisela's father, Georg, Karl, or Erich. Only Heinrich had written to them, telling them that he had been wounded in Italy and was recovering in a field lazarette. He did not share what kind of injury, but his letter sounded as if he expected to recover fully. Heinrich said he was hoping to be home soon, because the war would be over. It was all Gisela hoped for, so the men would return. Her father, Erich, Georg, and even Karl.

News came that the Americans were closing in on Wallhausen. They had not yet heard any fighting or bombing. Nevertheless, some of the villagers had fled into the nearby forests in anticipation. Gisela had tried to convince her mother to do the same, but she had refused to leave the house, insisting they had no reason to fear the Americans and that she wanted to welcome them as liberators. So, Gisela stayed with her. But she made sure the doors were locked and the shutters were closed. The workshop had long been boarded up. Gisela had not set foot in it since Georg and Kurt had disappeared. Neither had her mother. The family's carpentry business was a thing of the past.

The Americans finally arrived on a particularly pleasant spring morning. Gisela woke to the sounds of shelling and gunfire. She had slept in her clothes as her mother had instructed her to do, so she was up in a flash. Mama greeted her at the top of the stairs, panic in her eyes. Without a word, they clasped hands and hurried down to the cellar, where they hunkered down between the rickety shelves that held the few remaining jars they had canned the previous summer.

Halfway through the day, with only occasional gunfire erupting, boredom set in. Gisela wished she had grabbed a book to bring with her. Despite the fact that it was a warm spring day with a little bit of sunlight falling through the only window, Gisela was cold. The cellar's damp permeated her very bones. Her mother didn't seem to mind. She leaned against the cellar wall as if asleep, only opening her eyes when the gunfire got too loud, scrutinizing the little window as if she expected to see American troops climbing through it. They were both worried about friends in Wallhausen, especially Gudrun, her mother, and Dieter. With no way to get word to them, all they could hope for was that they were safe.

The gunfire tapered off as darkness fell, and they decided to leave the cellar to prepare a quick meal in the kitchen. When Gisela got up, her body ached, and she was stiff. If her mother felt the same, she didn't let on. Not sure if they had electricity, and not wanting to turn the lights on even if they did, they felt their way up the stairs and into the kitchen. They were sitting at the kitchen table, chewing a piece of the stale bread and the slices of a shriveled old apple they had brought with them from the cellar, when a knock on the front door startled them. Mama put her hand on Gisela's, pressing down as if she were trying to root her in place. The knock came again. They both held their breath. Then they heard a familiar voice. It was Gudrun. Gisela ran to the front door. She unlocked it and pulled her friend inside. Before she closed the door again, she scanned the street, but it lay still and deserted, almost peaceful in the evening air. They went quietly to the kitchen, where Gisela's mother chided Gudrun for being out at night with the Americans so close by. But

Gudrun assured them she had been careful, and not seen a single soul, and that her mother and Dieter were safe at home. She also brought news a neighbor had shared with her in the morning. The bridge had been destroyed.

Gisela understood at once what that meant. She could no longer visit the old oak. As Gudrun described how a remaining anti-aircraft unit had held out valiantly to defend Wallhausen, Gisela thought it sounded more like senseless desperation. Gudrun told them how the Wehrmacht soldiers had fired on the Americans when they started to cross the partially destroyed bridge, resulting in casualties. When Mama frowned and asked how it had all ended, Gudrun lowered her eyes and reported that all of the remaining German soldiers had been killed.

"Are the Americans in Wallhausen now?" Getting up, Gisela's mother brushed the crumbs of their meager meal off the table into her palm and tipped them into her mouth.

"They must be," Gudrun said, her voice hollow with resignation. "I did not see them on my way here, but they defeated our soldiers, so Wallhausen is theirs for the taking.".

"You shouldn't have come. It's too dangerous. Think of your child," Gisela's mother said. Her voice was almost as cold as the damp cellar. Gisela wondered what had got into her.

"I wanted to make sure you knew about the Americans and warn you that they are here. We are now completely at their mercy." The fear in Gudrun's voice was unmistakable.

"I'm glad to hear the fighting is over, "Mama said. "With the Americans here, the war will be over any day. Praise the Lord!" She added, sounding almost jubilant.

"How can you be so happy?" Gudrun no longer sounded fearful. She was dumbfounded. "The Americans are the enemy," she said. "They will punish us. They will take everything from us."

"They are liberating us, child." Mama took Gudrun by the arms. "Don't you see?" She asked. "The war is over. All the fighting is finished. The Americans are bringing peace."

Gudrun shook her head and stepped back, her face unreadable in the darkness.

"Gudrun," Gisela reached out to her friend, but Gudrun flinched away and turned to leave. They heard her walk down the hallway and turn the key, then the soft thud of the front door closing.

"She's been told so many lies," Mama said.

"We all have been," Gisela replied as she sank back onto one of the kitchen chairs.

"Perhaps, we don't have to spend the night in the cellar."

Gisela perked up. "I really don't want to. But I don't want to sleep alone tonight, either."

"Then I will take Irmtraud's side," her mother said quietly.

Gisela swallowed and nodded. Then, remembering that her mother probably couldn't see her in the dark, said, "I'd like that very much, Mama."

Her mother put her hands on Gisela's shoulders and squeezed. "Now," she said, and Gisela could hear the smile in her voice, "it won't be long before the men return home."

The next morning, an American jeep pulled up in front of the house. The driver lifted his helmet off his forehead and looked at their home. Gisela shrank back from behind the curtain. Had he seen her? A satisfied smile played across his face as he admired the beautiful craftsmanship of the half-timbered house her great-grandfather had built. Boasting a balcony with painted woodwork, beautiful green shutters on every window, and gleaming half-timbers, the Fahnrich house, as befitted the home of master craftsmen, was one of the most beautiful in the village. Gisela cursed the fact because it had attracted the attention of this American detachment. What could they want from its hungry inhabitants?

Two more jeeps pulled up behind the first, each carrying at least four soldiers. As the first American driver jumped down and started up the front walk, Gisela saw the dust and smudges of dirt on his face and shuddered. She hurried to find her mother. Two defenseless women against a cohort of enemy soldiers. Gudrun had told her rumors of allied soldiers abusing the local population, taking advantage of them, even torturing or killing them. Still, Gisela knew they had only two choices. They could cooperate with the Americans, or they could make it difficult for them. It would be best to cooperate. She told herself Mama was right. The Americans were here to end this terrible war.

Although she had expected it, the knock, sharp and official, startled her. Radiating calm, mother came out of the kitchen and into the hallway, motioning Gisela to answer the front door. Two

American soldiers stood on the step, helmets in hand, boots caked with road dust. The taller one spoke first, his German careful but serviceable.

"We require lodging. This house will suffice. You may remain. We will share."

He motioned to the interior of the house. Gisela and her mother nodded. There was no alternative, and they had no choice. Gisela stepped aside to let them in. They seemed polite enough, and she reminded herself there was nothing to fear.

The soldiers set their packs by the door, their movements deliberate, almost apologetic. The younger one removed his boots, glancing at Gisela as if seeking approval.

"We will not trouble you," he said in perfect German, his voice low.

All Gisela could do was nod. The house, for so long their refuge, would become a place of uneasy coexistence with these strangers, these foreign men. She wondered how long the arrangement would last.

More American soldiers arrived to stay at their home. They kept to the living room, sleeping in her father's armchair and on the sofa, as well as in her brothers' and her parents' bedrooms. Her mother moved in with Gisela, for which she was grateful. The Americans brought food that they gave to them to prepare meals they all shared, which was a great blessing. While their presence was marked by the scent of foreign tobacco and the low murmur of English at night, their generosity saved Gisela and her mother from starving.

The amount of potatoes, rice, onions, carrots, and flour they brought was more than Gisela had seen in years. Like gentlemen, the soldiers insisted on letting the women eat first and only ate after they were done. There was little conversation between them, except for the two soldiers who had first knocked on their door. They were not there every day, but Gisela was grateful when they were. The younger one, Lieutenant Krueger, who spoke German like a native, offered them wood for cooking. One day, he insisted on making their lunch but struggled with the stove. He had muttered in German under his breath, and Gisela had asked him why he spoke the language so fluently.

He told her that his family had left Germany when Hitler came to power. They settled in America, and when he came of age, he joined the army to help free Germany from the Nazis. He said his parents only spoke German with him and his siblings at home, and that he was grateful now that they had insisted, even though he had wanted to speak only English.

Gisela listened and watched him in silence as he figured out the stove. His *Sauerbraten* turned out to be the best she'd ever had. He didn't say where he had got the meat, and she didn't dare ask. The most scrumptious meal she'd had in years, it reminded her of family dinners and confirmed her belief that things were indeed getting better.

In the evenings, Gisela and her mother retreated to their bedroom for time away from the soldiers, but they listened to their quiet talk, the words indistinct, their tone a hushed chorus of men far from home. Each night after supper, the Americans played cards and drank beer in the living room. They invited Gisela and her mother to join them in a game or two, but they always declined, looking forward to their time alone. The soldiers treated them with respect, but that didn't change the fact that the Americans were strangers, occupiers who had demanded to live in their home. And although Gisela asked Lieutenant Krueger how long they would be staying, she never got an answer to her question.

After the Americans had been in the house for a week, Lieutenant Krueger told Gisela and her mother that they had to assemble with the rest of the villagers in the market square the next morning, when they would be given more information and instructions. Gisela hoped to see Gudrun and Dieter. She had missed them terribly. Gisela hadn't left the house since the Americans had arrived, and Gudrun had not visited. Nor had anyone else in the village. The whole of Wallhausen seemed to be trying to avoid the Americans.

Gisela and her mother arrived at the village square well before the scheduled time. Most of the villagers were already there. Spotting Gudrun, who held little Dieter in her arms, Gisela waved and made her way through the crowd. But when Gudrun saw her coming, her face grew hard. "What is it?" Gisela asked, taken aback.

"I heard you're doing business with the enemy," Gudrun said without looking at her.

Gisela stared at her friend in shock, then recovered quickly, her anger rising. "As you might imagine," she said, "we didn't have much of a choice!"

"There's always a choice."

Gudrun turned to face her, holding onto Dieter's little hand to prevent him from grabbing the few loose strands that had fallen out of her braid.

"There is, isn't there," Gisela said, staring back at Gudrun. She couldn't believe her. Her hate for the Americans reminded Gisela of the Gudrun who had believed the Nazi propaganda and joined the Lebensborn program. Why couldn't she see that the war was lost, and the Nazis would soon be gone? Why was she not happy about that? "I don't understand what has gotten into you," Gisela added with a shake of her head.

"You're collaborating with the Americans who have destroyed and taken over our country like the Tommies and the Bolsheviks have. How could you!"

Gisela couldn't believe what she was hearing. "Hitler and his men have destroyed our fatherland. Sent our men into certain death. Your brother. Mine! What for? Tell me, what for?"

Gisela was almost shouting now. Tears stung her eyes, but she blinked them back. Gudrun just stared at her. So did a few others around them who had witnessed and heard their exchange. Gisela didn't care. Everyone needed to hear and realize that it was their own leader who had turned their fatherland to rubble.

Gisela felt someone tug on her arm. She looked down and saw her mother's hand, trying to pull her away. She let her. There was nothing else she had to say to Gudrun.

Minutes later, an American commander whom Gisela had not yet seen was driven up in a jeep that came to a sudden stop at the steps of the town hall. With the engine still running, he stood up in the passenger seat, raised a sheet of paper, and began to address them in the sharp, foreign cadence of English.

The American officer was a tall, broad man with a square jaw and a faded wedding ring. His uniform was immaculate, his short-cropped hair parted over his right ear. He looked over the assembled faces, some worn and wary, some defiant, most simply exhausted and defeated. Lieutenant Krueger began to translate hesitantly when he paused after a few sentences.

"By order of the United States Army, a curfew will be enforced from eight o'clock in the evening until six in the morning. Anyone found outside during these hours will be detained."

A murmur ran through the crowd. In the faces of her fellow villagers, Gisela could see the mixture of fear and annoyance that crept up in her as well.

"All citizens are to remain in their homes unless given direct permission by American personnel. Any property required by the Army will be requisitioned. You will be notified if you must vacate your dwelling." Gisela felt her mother's hand tighten on her arm. They had been lucky to be able to remain in their home.

"There will be no contact between American soldiers and German civilians outside of official business. No gifts, no visits, no gatherings. This applies to all, regardless of age." Gisela felt relieved that she had declined playing cards with the soldiers.

The American officer's gaze swept the square, pausing on the faces of children, the elderly, and for what seemed like an eternity, on Wallhausen's mayor, who stood stiffly by the steps of the town hall. When he began speaking again, his voice sounded as if it was booming, the foreign words echoing off the facades of the houses lining the square. Gisela caught the word Nazi. Then, Lieutenant Krueger began translating again, his words loud and forceful this time.

"All Nazi organizations are dissolved. No symbols, no meetings, no propaganda. Any violation will be punished severely." Lieutenant Krueger paused, scanning the crowd himself. The sternness in his face belied his age. "Furthermore," he went on, "any knowledge of persons involved with the Nazi Party, or those who have committed crimes under its authority, must be reported to the American authorities at once. Those who conceal such information will be held accountable and will be punished accordingly."

A heavy silence settled over the square. Gisela glanced around her, seeking Gudrun's face in the crowd, but she couldn't find her. They all knew someone who had been a member of the Nazi Party. She knew that Waldemar and her father had refused to join, but Heinrich and Karl had been proud to be members. Worse, Karl was not only a member of the Nazi party, but had called it a privilege and an honor to join the SS. He had been sent to an elite school. The man Karl had become was more arrogant and crueler than the boy who had tormented her growing up. Would she have to report her brothers if they returned home? She shuddered at the thought.

The commander continued, his voice softer now but no less firm. Lieutenant Krueger matched his superior's.

"You will comply with all orders given by the military government. Cooperation will be remembered. Resistance will not be tolerated."

The crowd stared in silence. The commander nodded once, briskly, and then sat back down, and the jeep sped off. The soldiers dispersed, leaving the villagers to stare after them. Gisela watched them go, the directives echoing in her mind, each one a line drawn between what had been and what life would look like now.

The Americans had assured them that no harm would come to them if they followed the directives. They would be under curfew until further notice and asked that any known Nazis needed to be reported to them. While it felt like they were prisoners in their own village, it also sounded very reassuring to Gisela that a new future was dawning and that the war was truly going to be over. Hitler and his men would be gone. How she wished her father were here. He would have welcomed it all. She felt relief wash over her, peppered with a pang of self-righteousness when she thought of Gudrun's accusations.

The following week, the same American officer who had addressed the villagers in the square paid them a visit at home. Gisela was gripped with fear when, unannounced, he entered the kitchen where Gisela and her mother were preparing lunch for the soldiers. She immediately felt more at ease when Lieutenant Krueger appeared behind him. The officer politely shook their hands and, instead of speaking, gave a nod to Lieutenant Krueger, who said, "We need to unlock the doors to the workshop."

"What in the world for?" Her mother stepped forward, wiping hair away from her forehead with the back of her hand. Gisela noticed the tall officer's eyes narrowing.

"We need to see if there's anything useful in there that the army could utilize. We heard you own a telephone."

"That's correct," her mother said. "It's not been used in a long time. I'm not sure if it's still working."

"We will see if it does. We also need to store a few things in the workshop. So, if you could hand over the–"

"I will unlock the doors." Her mother cut him off. "Then you shall have the keys," she added, taking off her apron and heading for the door.

Lieutenant Krueger stepped in front of her. "Please, Frau Fahnrich," he said in a low voice, sounding more apologetic than demanding. "Just give me the keys."

Her mother looked taken aback, but she went out of the kitchen and into the hallway to retrieve the keys from the hallway cabinet that stood under the portrait of her sister. Returning to the kitchen, she handed them to Lieutenant Krueger, who gave them to the officer, who left the kitchen barking incomprehensible commands down the hallway. Two soldiers came running to accompany him out the back.

Lieutenant Krueger started to follow, but Gisela stepped in his way. "What is going on?" She asked. "Is something wrong?"

"Nothing out of the ordinary, I assure you," he said, but he avoided looking at her.

"You're hiding something from us. I can tell," she said, almost whispering.

He looked down the hallway, then after the others. When he was satisfied no one could overhear, he drew closer. "The commander needs your phone," he said. Then added in a whisper, "We also received a report."

"A report?" Gisela's blood ran cold. "What kind of report?"

"That you're harboring a Nazi in your workshop." He said it so quietly that for a moment she thought she had not heard him correctly. Krueger was studying her face. Whatever he read in her eyes changed his expression. His face grew hard, and he took a step back.

Gisela cleared her throat, her mind racing. "We are not hiding any Nazis, I can assure you," she said defiantly, crossing her arms. She hadn't lied. Kurt wasn't a Nazi. He had abhorred the regime, and the war. And he was long gone.

The Lieutenant studied her with furrowed brows, and the hint of disappointment in his eyes told her he was unconvinced, that he still believed the report rather than her. Gisela swallowed hard. As he stepped around her to follow the others to the workshop, he said, "We expect Germany to surrender any day now. The war is over. For good. Your Führer is dead."

Gisela stared after him in a mixture of disbelief, relief, and exhilaration. The war was over. The men could return home. She felt a hand on her arm and whipped around. Her mother was standing behind her, crying. She had shed many tears in the past few years. But these were different. Her face was beaming.

Gisela threw her arms around her, resting her head on her mother's shoulder. "Oh, Mama," a sob caught in her throat. She realized in that moment that, despite all the hardships, she had grown in the last couple of years, and was now much taller than her mama, perhaps even as tall as the woman who had given birth to her and her siblings.

Then she stepped back, remembering the Americans, and the accusation that they were hiding a Nazi. Who had made the claim? Who knew about Kurt other than her father and Georg? Gisela turned and gripped her mother again, this time even more tightly, as she remembered Kurt's conscription card and where she had hidden it. *Gudrun!*

Chapter 18

May 1945

Somewhere in Bavaria

The sun slowly dipped behind the barn, casting the meadow into a golden glow. Karl was resting from his day's labor in the long shadow of a tree, his clothes sweaty and covered in the earthy dust of the fields. The world around him was blooming as if the war had never happened. The farmer who had taken Karl in for a couple of days had given him food and shelter in exchange for helping him plant potato tubers. It had been back-breaking work, but he had never felt more alive.

Every two to three days, he would move on. Biking through a few small towns on his way home, asking local farmers if they needed any help. It was to his advantage that it was still planting and sowing season for some crops. Karl never committed to staying longer than a few days. And he remained in the countryside, avoiding major roads and towns where he might run into the Americans. He had learned from one of the farmers that the war had ended a few days ago. He had never expected to survive, but he had. And now, for the first time in his life, he just wanted to get home as fast as he could.

If only he could hop on a train. Not a passenger train, that was too dangerous. A cargo train would have worked, but they were no longer running. Supply chains had been disrupted. The rail service had all but collapsed. Karl had heard of evacuation trains coming from the East, carrying people who were either fleeing before the Soviets or who had already been expelled by them.

But so far, these were only rumors. Karl was traveling north and hadn't come across any refugees yet, or the Soviets, for which he was grateful. After hearing what had happened to Erich, he needed to avoid them at all costs if he didn't want to end up like his brother-in-law. He planned to get home, hide out for a few months, and then decide what to do with the rest of his life. Perhaps he could learn to become a carpenter. His father had always wanted that, and now he and old Georg could teach him. Then Karl could take over the family business. He would never have thought so before the war, but now it sounded like bliss.

He got up, tried to brush the dirt off his pants, then walked over to the barn where he would spend the night. It was usually their barns that the farmers offered him, not a room in the house. Karl didn't mind at all. He preferred to keep to himself and didn't want to be put in the awkward situation of answering questions about who he was and what he had done during the war. People were highly mistrustful these days. They didn't want a stranger they didn't know anything about in their homes.

The smell and rustling of hay, the light that glowed through the cracks in the wood, the sounds of nature that filtered in, all of this made the barn a refuge for Karl. He stretched out on a pile of hay, the ache in his muscles a dull reminder of the day's labor, closed his eyes, and drifted off to sleep. Sometime later, he was startled awake by a sound that cut through the quiet evening. Karl recognized it at once. It was the low rumble of engines.

He jumped up, nerves humming, and crawled to a gap in the boards. Peering out, Karl saw two American jeeps rolling down the narrow lane toward the farmstead, the dying sunlight glinting off their hoods. He counted the soldiers. Four in the first, three in the second jeep. They had rifles slung across their laps and were scanning the fields as they passed. Karl pressed himself against the barn wall, heart pounding. Were they here for him? What did they want?

The jeeps slowed as they reached the farmhouse. The farmer stepped out, wiping his hands on his trousers, his face calm. One of the soldiers jumped out of the vehicle and approached. He spoke loud enough that Karl could hear him, but he couldn't make out too many of the words. The American's German was clipped and accented by a heavy drawl that made it impossible for Karl to understand the few snippets he did catch. But if the words were obscure, the soldier's tone was unmistakable. It was one of authority and suspicion.

The farmer answered the American haltingly. While Karl couldn't completely understand his replies, he could tell that his current employer was growing increasingly uneasy. Suddenly, the soldier barked an order at two of his men and pointed toward the barn. Karl jumped back, looking for somewhere to hide. Under a mountain of hay? Behind the feeding bin, or the old, discarded cart? He felt himself panic. *Think!* He told himself. *And quick!*

He heard the Americans coming closer, circling the barn. Karl turned and dug himself into the huge pile of hay as quickly as he could. Holding his breath, he listened, willing himself to be invisible as they paused by the door. He could just see out of the hay pile, make out the Americans as they opened the barn door slowly and peered inside, their rifles held at the ready. Then, they turned around and left.

Karl breathed out slowly. His hands had balled into fists. He could hear The Americans climbing back into the jeeps, the engines sputtering to life, the gears grinding as they drove off. As the sounds died, the farm came back to itself. Somewhere close by, a barn owl hooted, greeting the approaching night.

Karl didn't move for a few more moments, just in case the Americans decided to return. He knew he couldn't risk another night at the farm. He had to leave in the morning. The Americans were searching the area. As night settled over the farm and barn, Karl lay in the hollow of a pile of hay, sleep eluding him. He replayed the day in his mind, the farmer's kindness, the planting of potatoes, the simple meals, and the brief illusion of peace. Now he knew there would be no real peace until the occupiers left, and he had returned home.

The barn door creaked open. Karl sat up, muscles tensed. The farmer stepped inside, lantern in hand, his face drawn and anxious. Karl breathed out a sigh of relief and relaxed. He slid down the hay and walked over to the man.

"I assume you saw them?" The farmer whispered. Karl nodded. "Americans are looking for men, German soldiers, anyone who might have fought for the Führer."

Karl wanted to assure the farmer, make up some lie about what he had been up to. Surely, the farmer knew. Most men his age had been soldiers. There was no denying who, or what, he was.

"You must go," the farmer said, his voice urgent. "Now. I can give you some bread and a little water. But you can't stay here any longer."

Karl simply nodded. He understood, but he had hoped he could stay this night, get some rest, and leave early in the morning before the break of dawn. He went back to the hay and gathered his few belongings. When he had them all, he paused, meeting the farmer's eyes. "Thank you," he said quietly. "For everything."

The farmer nodded, the lines on his face deepening. "Be careful," he whispered. "Don't get caught. They'll imprison anyone who fought in the war."

Outside, as Karl mounted his bike to slip into the night, the farmer stepped close to him. "Leave it," he said, taking the handlebars. "Avoid the roads. Don't go through the nearby village. The Americans are staying there. I'd stay in the woods, away from towns and roads."

Karl hesitated. He stared at the bike. It had been his trusty steed for the past few weeks, but it wasn't his. He had stolen it, and it should be easy to give up, but it wasn't. He knew he had no choice. The farmer was right. If he wanted to remain undetected, he had to stay off roads and away from villages. The bike was no use in the forest anyway. He sighed. Now, it would take him many more weeks to get home.

Karl gave the farmer a determined nod and handed him the bike. If nothing else, it was a way of paying the man back for not giving him up to the Americans. He shook the farmer's hand, then turned and slipped into the night. As the barn and the farmhouse receded behind him, Karl moved quickly, making for the forest that lay west of the fields he had worked that day. It would be easy enough to travel through and to hide in. Even shelter would not be difficult. Those things did not concern him, but finding food did. Once more, he would have to take whatever fortune fate put in front of him.

CHAPTER 19

MAY 1945

WALLHAUSEN, GERMANY

The knock didn't startle Gisela. She had expected them. She took a deep breath and opened her bedroom door. In the front hall, she was greeted by an American she had not yet met or seen, and Lieutenant Krueger, whose face was unreadable. He asked her politely to come with him, and she didn't question his request. Gisela knew where they were taking her. She followed them out the back and into the workshop.

The soldier she didn't know took her by the arm and pulled her into her father's office. She didn't protest. The American commander sat in her father's chair, Kurt's conscription card in front of him on the desk. Gudrun had betrayed her. The realization left her numb, the kind of numb that strikes before the pain sets in. She should have burned the card and not hidden it in the book. She had forgotten all about it. Why, oh why, hadn't she burned it? Gisela swallowed hard.

The officer looked her up and down, then held up the conscription card, speaking in a calm, almost grandfatherly tone, which put Gisela somewhat at ease. In contrast, Lieutenant Krueger's voice as he translated was cold and unfriendly. Hearing it, the officer narrowed his eyes and gave his head a discouraging shake, but the Lieutenant was unmoved. Pointing to the conscription card, he asked Gisela, "Do you know this Wehrmacht soldier?"

"I do," Gisela said. There was no need to deny it. She had nothing to hide. Kurt wasn't a Nazi.

"How did you come into the possession of Herr Vogel's conscription card?"

Krueger translated, his voice as cold as before, but it was the soft-spoken officer who had asked the question. Gisela looked at him before she replied. Gudrun's betrayal stung like salt in an open wound, sharp and lingering.

"I found it on my father's desk one day. I assume Herr Vogel gave it to my father," She said and waited for Lt. Krueger to finish translating before adding, "My father hid him in our attic after he had deserted the Wehrmacht."

There was a moment of silence before Lieutenant Krueger translated, haltingly. The commander watched her for a moment before asking his next question. "This man? He was hiding from the Gestapo?"

Gisela nodded. "They came here. They were looking for him," she added. She might have imagined it, but she thought that when he translated, Lt. Krueger's tone became a little softer, friendlier.

"Did you help your father hide the soldier?"

Gisela straightened her shoulders. "I did."

"Where is he now?" Lieutenant Krueger asked of his own accord.

Gisela turned to him. "He disappeared a while ago. He didn't want to get us in trouble with the Gestapo for harboring a deserter." Krueger nodded knowingly before translating her answer.

Gisela noticed the commander's wedding ring on his left hand. Then, he gave an order to Lieutenant Krueger, who took her by the arm and led her out of her father's office and back to the house.

"You must stay in your bedroom for the time being," he said, as they approached the house.

Gisela stopped, wrenching her arm away, and looked at him. "Why am I being made prisoner in my own home?" She asked. "Kurt Vogel was no Nazi," Gisela said, crossing her arms defiantly.

"It's just until we find out who and where Herr Vogel is." Krueger's tone was warm now. She studied his face for a moment and thought she saw a hint of admiration.

***

Confined to her bedroom, the days grew long. The anger and the grief Gisela felt over Gudrun's betrayal were her daily companions. She occupied herself with reading and knitting. Her poor mama had to do all the cooking and cleaning herself. Gisela knew the garden needed tending, but even that was left to her mother while she sat idle, bored, frustrated, and angry.

When someone did finally knock, Gisela looked up, startled. Without waiting for a reply, her mother pushed the door open and walked in, smiling.

"Men have started to come home!" Mama took Gisela's hands and squeezed them. "Your father will be home soon. And your brothers," she said, breathless with excitement. "And Erich won't be long gone now either."

Gisela withdrew her hands. "Erich? He's on the other end of the world," she murmured. "A place of eternal snow."

"He'll return to you," her mother said." Don't give up hope."

"There has been no word from him, Mama. Nothing. He probably–"

"Hush. Don't you say it." Her mother held up her hand.

Gisela walked to the window. It was a cool, overcast summer's day. The swallows flew low, which meant rain was coming. The garden needed it desperately. As she scanned the dry flower beds, anger rose in her again. Anger at Gudrun. The American occupiers who lived in their home. Anger at Erich for leaving her. Anger at being confined unfairly. It was starting to wear on her. All of it. She felt like screaming.

"Lieutenant Krueger has told me that the old men and boys who were called up in the *Volkssturm* shall be released and sent home this week," her mother said. "Your father will be home soon."

Gisela knew her mother was trying to suppress her excitement for her sake. This was welcome news. Gisela didn't want to ruin her mother's joy. Like Mama, she had missed her father terribly. Gisela wondered how he would tolerate American soldiers in his house and supposed they would know soon enough.

Two days later, Lieutenant Krueger told Gisela her house arrest was over. He gave no explanation as to why, but she was grateful, nonetheless. Gisela used her newfound freedom to go see Gudrun. How she had longed to confront her friend over her betrayal. While she had missed their walks and especially little Dieter, Gudrun's treachery had inflicted a wound so deep, Gisela would never be able to forgive her.

Gisela took her old bike and pedaled to Gudrun's house, the anger inside her propelling her forward. Gudrun's mother answered the door and let her in. Gisela waited patiently in the foyer until Gudrun came down the stairs. For a heartbeat, Gisela was disappointed that Dieter was not in Gudrun's arms, but she quickly reminded herself why she had come.

"How have you been?" Gudrun asked as if nothing had happened. "Your mother told me that you've been confined by the Americans?"

Gisela stared at her friend in disbelief but then recovered quickly. "They did. They thought we were harboring a Nazi."

"And were you?" Gudrun asked, her voice low, edged with challenge. The question struck Gisela like a slap. "Were you hiding someone in your attic?" Gudrun crossed her arms, eyes blazing with raw accusation.

Gisela took a step back in a vain attempt to control her anger. "You betrayed me. And my family. To the Americans! How could you?" Gisela growled, shaking her head in disbelief. How did Gudrun suspect they were hiding Kurt? The conscription card alone could not have told her that.

"You were collaborating with the Americans!" Gudrun had almost shouted the words.

"The Americans took over our house. We had no say in it. You had no right! And how would you even know from just finding the conscription card that we were hiding him?" Gisela's hands had balled into fists. She had never felt angrier in her life.

"The drawings in your room. They bore his name. Once I found his conscription card in your book, I put two and two together. The rest was a lucky guess."

Gisela stared at Gudrun, aghast. "I thought you were my friend."

Gudrun studied Gisela's face for a moment. Then she said, "I kept your secret, Gisela. And I forgave you for hiding a deserter. But when you and your family began collaborating with the Americans, betraying our fatherland again, I had no choice." It didn't escape Gisela that Gudrun had spat out the word "deserter."

"By twisting the truth, claiming my family was hiding a Nazi? Why don't you see who the enemy is? Who has left our country in ruins? And to betray me and my family? I'm your friend!" Gisela almost shouted the last few words. Pure, unadulterated rage engulfed her. How could Gudrun betray her like that?

"I was angry with you," Gudrun spat the words again. "For hiding a deserter and then working with the American occupiers. I wanted you to see and understand that they are the true enemy. That you were betraying your own country." Gudrun's fists were clenched now as well. She stepped toward Gisela, her voice lowering. "And I was jealous of you," Gudrun hissed. "You have a husband. A father. And two brothers left. And you're beautiful. You always have been. I have nothing."

Gisela shook her head in disbelief. "You have Dieter! And your mother! And I can't believe you don't see the pain and loss I have suffered. And you try to inflict more on me? I could have been punished with far worse than confinement. How could you, Gudrun. Do you really hate me that much?"

"I don't hate you ..." Gudrun lowered her eyes, and Gisela was surprised to see her shrink with shame. "I'm not proud of what I did," Gudrun whispered. "I understand if you no longer want to be my friend."

"Friends do not betray friends," Gisela said bitterly. She studied Gudrun's face, her stomach in knots.

Gisela waited a moment longer. For an apology. For understanding. But neither came. She turned and left Gudrun's house without another word, vowing to never talk to her ever again. Instead of riding home, Gisela pushed her bike, taking time to clear her head and trying to understand that her longest friendship was in ruins, much like the country.

When Gisela finally got back to the house, she found most of the American soldiers gathered by the front gate, smoking. But instead of their usual carousing, they seemed rather subdued. None of them would look at her. Parking her bike and going in through the back door, Gisela stopped abruptly in the kitchen doorway. Old Georg sat at the kitchen table, eating a bowl of soup.

Seeing her, he jumped up, dropping the soup spoon. Gisela threw her arms around the old man, hugging him fiercely. "You and Father are home!" She shouted. Gisela let go of him. Her face fell when she saw Georg's expression. He lowered his eyes and took a step back, as if he needed to put some distance between himself and her. Gisela shook her head vehemently as the realization sank in. Her father wasn't coming home. She sank onto one of the kitchen chairs and buried her face in her hands. Her father was dead. Sobs rose up rocking her body.

Chapter 20

June 1945

Somewhere in Southern Thuringia

Karl woke and rubbed his eyes. Early morning sunlight broke through the canopy of the beeches he had sheltered under the night before. The forest floor was surprisingly comfortable to sleep on. Overall, he was proud of himself for how easily he had adapted to surviving on the run. The forest provided everything he needed. Foraging, finding water, and securing shelter were daily challenges, but he had managed to endure so far. Occasionally, he had to do without water for a day or so, but he always eventually found a stream or spring where he could drink and wash.

He knew he was losing weight and constantly kept his eyes on the ground, searching for anything edible. So far, he had survived on beech nuts, acorns, and forest berries, as well as the early season mushrooms his father had taught him to recognize as edible. Sometimes he resorted to nettles and dandelions, eating them raw or mashing them into a paste he added water to in an effort to make soup.

Karl was not lost, exactly. He knew he was traveling in the general direction of Wallhausen and that he had covered a significant distance since leaving the farm. But he was not entirely sure of where he was, either. The best he could do was to continue, hoping he would eventually stumble across familiar landscape, the red earth and towering forests, the open water meadows and rivers of his youth that would mean he was close to Wallhausen, and home.

Karl had just settled for the night after a particularly long day. He'd found a glade, ringed by pines. A mossy hollow beneath the drooping limbs of a fir made an excellent bed. The hush of the forest was broken only by the distant hoot of an owl. He had just drifted off to sleep when he was jerked awake by the sharp crack of a branch snapping.

His heart hammered. He held his breath, listening. Perhaps a deer, or a sounder of wild boars? Or had it been human? He heard another sound, closer this time. Relief washed over him as he recognized the shuffle of hooves and the low grunt of animals. He peered into the darkness. Not twenty meters away, a group of shadows moved, low to the ground, rooting through the forest floor. Karl remained still as they snorted and pawed. A sounder of wild boars was nothing to trifle with. He had heard stories about them growing up. Horrific tales of people getting killed and even eaten. A wild boar sow defending her piglets was to be avoided at all costs. He sighed in relief as the animals wandered off. Karl allowed himself to drift into sleep again as the sounds of their foraging faded into the night.

The next thing he knew, Karl was startled awake by a hand clamped over his mouth. He thrashed until a hoarse whisper cut through the panic. "Don't shout. I'm not going to hurt you."

The hand withdrew. In the gray light of dawn, Karl saw a gaunt face. The man's eyes were sunken and wild. He wore the remnants of a German uniform, the insignia torn away. His hands were trembling with hunger. "Please," he rasped, "do you have anything to eat? Anything? I haven't eaten in days."

Karl scrambled away from the stranger, shaking his head.

The man watched him for a moment, then asked, "Do you know in which direction I can find the Americans?" He looked around the glade, as if searching for clues on where to head.

"Why would you want to find them?" Karl got up, brushing bits of moss and pine needles off his clothes.

"They'll feed you," the man said, his voice raw. "That's better than being caught by the Soviets. They shoot men like us, or worse. I need to find the Americans," he said again, his voice plaintive now. "I want to be captured by them, not the Russians."

Karl nodded, although he didn't agree. He'd rather not be captured by anyone. "Well," he said, turning to go. "I'm heading home. Good luck finding the Americans."

"Wait, where are you going?" The man reached out and tried to grab his arm.

"I told you," Karl said briskly, taking a step back. "I'm on my way home." The man was giving him the creeps. I'm leaving now. Good luck," he added, and started walking.

He had almost reached the edge of the glade when a distant shout echoed through the trees. The voice was harsh, guttural, and unmistakably Russian. The stranger darted to Karl's side, his eyes widening in terror. "The Bolsheviks," he whispered, his voice shaking. "A patrol."

Karl's mind raced. If the Soviets found them, there would be no mercy. They had to run.

He motioned for the other man to follow. They crouched and slipped into the undergrowth. They had to move like deer, Karl thought, silent and fast. Behind them, the shouts grew louder.

Karl ducked under a bank of low branches. The other man stumbled after him. They could hear crashing boots. The Soviets were close, their voices louder and more distinct. Then a shot rang out, splintering a tree trunk inches from Karl's head. He dove behind a fallen log, dragging the stranger with him.

Karl's mind was racing. They had no weapons. They had nothing to defend themselves against the Soviet patrol that was now fanning out around them. He met the other man's gaze. His eyes swam with fear, and with something that frightened Karl even more, defeat. Karl looked away, afraid it was contagious. He could not fall into the hands of the Soviets. If he were captured, it would mean starvation, death, or worse, the gulags in Siberia.

Suddenly, without warning, the man jumped up and ran back in the direction they had come. The patrol pursued him, firing several shots. The bullets seemed to miss, or at least there was no screaming, or the sound of a body falling. Karl realized this was his chance.

Staying low, he crept through the fern and underbrush, hoping the Soviets had not noticed that there were two of them.

When no shots were fired, and no one ran in his direction, he pushed on, moving faster now, crawling on his belly through the dense brush, branches cutting his hands and face. After a few minutes, he paused, listening. But there was nothing; once more, he was engulfed in silence. Had he escaped? Karl had no idea and decided he couldn't dwell on it. He needed to press on, get as far away from the Soviets as possible. Finally, what seemed like hours later, he collapsed under a canopy of beeches at the edge of the forest.

As Karl lay looking up at the leaves, thinking he had not even noticed when the forest changed from conifers to hardwoods, he heard a familiar sound that reminded him of home. Every morning of his childhood and youth, he had woken to the hiss and whistle that told him what time it was. Now, as the chugging of a train drew closer, he felt almost giddy.

Getting to his feet, Karl scanned his surroundings. The forest behind him lay as quiet as the fields and meadows in front of him. There was not a soul around, nor any houses, roads, or villages. Spotting the train tracks beyond a line of poplars, Karl stared at shimmering iron rails. In the distance, he could see the train coming. As it grew closer, he saw that it was a short freight with battered wagons, their iron sides streaked with grime. At least half of their doors were wide open.

Karl didn't think. He bolted toward the tracks. Wallhausen was just a village, but its train station was a major stop between East and

West and North and South. If he was lucky, this train was heading in the right direction.

He ran as fast as he could, his lungs burning and his sides hurting. He had to make it. He cut through the field, stumbled, and almost lost his shoe, but pushed on, reaching the line of poplars. The locomotive had already passed. A wagon's open door loomed just ahead. Karl reached out, fingers grasping for the cold metal handle. His hand slipped. The train threatened to pull away. Karl lunged, catching the edge of the box car with both hands, the force nearly wrenching his arms from their sockets. His feet skidded, knees scraping raw, but he held on, the muscles in his arms burning. With a final surge, he hauled himself up, his feet scrambling to find a hold. Finally, he clung to the doorframe, chest heaving. Then, with all the strength he had left, he pulled himself up and in and collapsed onto the floor.

Karl lay on his back for a moment, listening to the clack of the wheels and his own heavy breathing. Then he turned and scanned the space around him. The wagon was dim and empty; the floor littered with straw and the remnants of old cargo. Eventually, he sat up and looked out. The landscape drifted by. Fields, meadows, forests. When houses and villages began to appear, he retreated into the dimness of the wagon. Safely out of sight, Karl leaned against the wall of the box car and let the rhythm of the train lull him into sleep.

CHAPTER 21

JULY 1945

WALLHAUSEN, GERMANY

Gisela stretched her aching back and wiped her forehead with the back of her hand. The air shimmered from the heat, and she longed for a cool bath. She looked at the flower bed, and at the weeds she still had to pull, and knew her bath would have to wait until evening.

An American jeep pulled up, sending dust swirling. It hadn't rained in days, but the humidity told her a storm and much needed rain would arrive soon enough. A soldier, Gisela didn't recognize, jumped out of the vehicle and leaped up the front steps two at a time. She wondered what message he brought, then dismissed the thought. The Americans brought news daily. She crouched back down and began to pull weeds again. Another hour, and she would be done.

By the time Gisela had finished in the garden, more jeeps and even a lorry had pulled up to the house. She knew something was going on, so she cleaned up her tools and headed inside.

The house felt like a beehive. It was bustling with soldiers, all of them packing and running back and forth. Gisela went looking for Lieutenant Krueger and found him in the living room.

"What is going on?" She asked, taking in the room, which was littered with half-filled boxes.

"We are leaving, Fräulein Fahnrich," he said. He seemed preoccupied.

"Frau Schmidt. As I told you weeks ago," Gisela snapped, trying and failing to hide her annoyance. Still, this was good news. The Americans were finally leaving their home.

"Have you found other accommodations in the village?" She asked, attempting to sound as if she was merely interested, instead of delighted at the prospect of having them gone.

He looked at her, frowning. "No," he said. "We are leaving the village. You haven't heard?"

"Heard what?" Gisela shook her head in confusion.

"We are leaving Wallhausen. The Soviets will be here soon. They are taking over."

Gisela stared at him. "But why?"

Lieutenant Krueger shrugged, returning his attention to the papers he had been packing. "Above my pay grade," he said. "I don't make these kinds of decisions. All I know is, we swapped villages with them. Wallhausen for another farther upstream."

Gisela couldn't believe what she was hearing. They were people with lives. Not just pieces to be swapped.

"You can't just leave us to the Soviets!"

As bad as the Americans might be, the Soviets were a hundred times worse. Stories of their hateful revenge against any German frightened even the stoutest men. Neither did she want to be governed by communists. She swallowed hard as her thoughts turned to Erich, laboring in a Soviet gulag in Siberia.

Lieutenant Krueger was watching her. "They promised us that they will treat you fairly."

"You're a fool if you believe that," Gisela said bitterly.

Lt. Krueger frowned. He opened his mouth as if he was going to say something, then apparently changed his mind and returned his attention to his packing. Gisela watched him for a moment, realizing that he had never truly cared about them. He had a job to do. He wanted to rid Germany of Nazis. That's all that mattered to him.

***

By noon the next day, the Americans were gone. Gisela stood by the window, staring out into the rain that had begun falling during the night and had turned the dusty roads into a muddy, puddled mess. In the garden below her window, flowers, heavy with rain, bent low, their soaked heads drooping. She watched the wind drive the rain sideways, whipping the nearby linden trees. Their fruits tore free and spun through the rain, sailing down to the muddy ground below.

Behind her, the house was eerily quiet. It felt empty and too big. When Gisela was a child, she had always thought the house wasn't big enough for her large family and had complained about having to share a room with her sister. That was one of her many regrets now.

Something she couldn't take back. Something she would never have again.

It was just her and her mother now. They hadn't heard from Heinrich or Karl. She had stopped waiting for a letter from Erich. There hadn't been any. She didn't want to know why. If she had no other news, it meant he was still alive, somewhere. And that gave her comfort. She preferred not knowing. She had gotten used to not knowing.

The reality of her father's death had sunk in after Georg's return. The old man had barely been able to tell them how he had been shot, early on in the *Volkssturm*. He had provided no details. For her part, Gisela knew her father's death had left a hole in her heart that would never close.

For a couple of days after they had learned of her father's death, Gisela had found her mother sitting in his big armchair in the living room, staring out the window as he had done in his final weeks at home. It had frightened her. Gisela had feared her mother would fall silent like her father had. But she didn't. When, about a week after his return, Old Georg had asked to come back to work, Gisela's mother had welcomed him and had begun to spend time in the workshop's office herself. Mama saw no reason not to continue the business. They had to rebuild and live off something. With Georg here to help, perhaps they could make a living again. They were grateful for him, not just his labor, but his presence as well. They shared their meals with him. And having a man check on them daily and be close by was a comfort while they waited for the Soviets to arrive in Wallhausen.

Now, looking out the window through the sheets of rain, Gisela spotted a figure approaching the house. She took a step back, her heart starting to race. The figure leaped up the stairs, then there was a sharp, impatient knock on the door. Gisela heard her mother open the kitchen door and come down the hallway. She flew out of her room and stepped into her mother's path. "We don't know who it is. We are not expecting anyone. We can't just open the door, now that the Soviets are coming!" she said.

"Perhaps we can see who it is from the living room window," her mother suggested, already opening the door. They went in, and her mother looked while Gisela held her breath behind her.

"No one is there anymore." Her mother shrugged.

Gisela looked as well. Her mother was right. The person had vanished. Had she imagined it? But someone had knocked on the door. Her mother had heard it, too. They both jumped at the sound of the back door creaking open. Someone was coming down the hallway. Old Georg? He wouldn't be coming for supper for another couple of hours. Gisela reached for her mother's hand. She shrieked as the living room door opened, then raised her hands to cover her mouth, unable to believe what she was seeing. It wasn't until her mother ran and threw her arms around him that Gisela understood. One of her brothers had come home.

Gisela watched Karl eat faster than she had ever seen anyone eat, ever. He looked haggard, all skin and bones. He clearly had been starving.

She put a hand on his arm. "Don't eat too fast. It will make you sick. Slow down." He nodded but didn't slow down.

Gisela couldn't remember a time when she had given Karl advice, and he had quietly accepted it. But the man sitting at the kitchen table, spooning soup, did not seem the same person. He was subdued. His good looks were gone. The beautiful blonde head of hair was a matted gray mess. His eyes and cheeks were hollow, and a scruffy beard covered half his face. Gisela had always thought Karl had a hard time growing a beard because he had always been clean-shaven.

Karl told them how he got injured and about his journey home. He told them he would have to leave again and go into hiding, because the Soviets would surely come looking for Nazis, and after all, he had been in the SS. But Gisela's mother wouldn't hear of it. Georg suggested hiding him in the workshop attic, leaving out the fact that they had hidden someone there before. Karl protested, but they finally convinced him.

Gisela assembled some provisions, found pillows and blankets, and took Karl up to the attic. He followed silently up the stairs, helped her arrange the broken pieces of furniture into a suitable hideout, and thanked her. As she turned to leave, he reached for her hand. Gisela looked at him in surprise. "I need you to do one more thing for me."

She nodded. "Of course. Anything."

"Get a sharp knife from the kitchen and bring it to me," he said, looking at her intently.

"What for?" Gisela frowned.

"I need you to remove a SS tattoo from the underside of my arm."

Gisela took a step back. "I... I can't do that."

"If you don't, the Soviets will shoot me when they find me."

"You'll need to ask someone else. I can't–"

"Who? Mama? Old Georg?"

They stood for a moment, staring at each other in the dusty light of the attic. Karl had never been her favorite brother, and he had not cared greatly for her. But that had been 'before'. Now, they were simply 'family'.

"I will get the knife," Gisela said, finally. "But I'm not sure I can do it, Karl."

He smiled at her, and there was actually warmth in it. "None of us is sure of what we can do, Gisela," he said. "Until we do it." Trying to ignore the queasy feeling in her stomach, Gisela returned to the house and found a potato peeling knife that she knew was very sharp. She had peeled countless potatoes with it, but now it felt foreign to her. It no longer felt like a kitchen utensil.

She walked back to the workshop slowly, counting the steps to the attic as she climbed them. "You can do this, Gisela," Karl said as she came through the door. "I know you can." He smiled and winked. "Just think of all the times you wanted to get back at me, and how often you dreamed of hurting me."

Gisela stared at him, then a laugh escaped her. It grew into a roar. She hadn't laughed like this in years, and it was Karl, of all people, who had made her laugh.

Karl gave her an encouraging nod and started to unbutton his shirt. He took it off and flung it aside. It was so dirty, Gisela knew she'd have to burn it. Then he sat down on the attic floor and lifted his left arm so she could see the B that had been tattooed just below his armpit.

"What does it stand for?" She asked. She had expected the SS symbol.

"My blood group," Karl said. "Members of the SS were tattooed in case we got injured and needed a blood transfusion."

"You never told me what you did in the SS," Gisela said suddenly.

As soon as she spoke the words, she regretted them. Karl's face grew dark and hard, reminding her of how cruel he used to be when they were children.

"I will tell you sometime," he said." All of it. But not now. Now, we need to hurry and get this taken care of." Gisela nodded as he pointed to the knife. "Try to scrape it off first. If that doesn't work, you'll have to cut it out."

Gisela lifted the knife, then lowered it, delaying. "Shouldn't I get some iodine and bandages from the house? You'll bleed."

"You can bandage me up later. Let's get to it first," Karl said through gritted teeth. Raising his arm, he closed his eyes. "Do it," he said. "Now."

Gisela moved in close and put the blade to his skin. She swallowed hard. *Just like peeling potatoes*, she told herself.

⁕

It was two days later when Gisela heard from a neighbor that the Soviets were in the meadows by the old oak. The terror in the woman's eyes sent chills down Gisela's spine. She had barely stopped speaking before Gisela spun around and ran for home. Karl, Georg, and her mother listened to the news in silence. Then, they went to the workshop. When Karl was safely back in the attic with as many supplies as they could gather, Gisela and her mother watched George fit a lock to the attic door. As soon as he was finished, and Karl was locked in, they went back to the house to close and lock all the shutters. Then Georg went home, and Gisela and her mother locked the doors behind him. Then, they waited.

They could see from the small, unshuttered side window in Mama's bedroom. Below, the street lay deserted. From time to time, they heard military machinery. Once or twice, Gisela was sure she heard someone scream. Then the first soldiers appeared, rifles drawn.

As the Americans had been, the Soviets were drawn to their house. Once again, Gisela cursed her great-grandfather's craftsmanship. There was a sharp rap on the door.

"Don't answer," Gisela hissed. "Maybe they'll leave." But they didn't. They fanned out and surrounded the house.

The stories about Soviet occupiers were bone-chilling. All of Wallhausen had been so relieved when they had learned it was the Americans who would occupy their village and the surrounding areas. But now they had left, leaving them to the Soviets. There was another loud, impatient knock on the back door. Then, a shot was fired, and Gisela and her mother heard the unmistakable sound of wood splintering.

Gisela had already locked the bedroom door. She and her mother stood, frozen, listening to the sound of boots on the stairs. Men were talking. The language was utterly foreign. Harsh and guttural, Russian sounded like the growl of beasts. Gisela felt sweat break out across her chest, cold and terrible. Unable to stop staring at the door, she edged closer to her mother.

The Russians didn't knock or wait for them to unlock the door. They kicked it in. Gisela held her breath, clinging to her mother. The two soldiers who appeared in the doorway holding rifles stared at them for a moment, then barked something they couldn't understand and motioned at them to get out of the room. Gisela and her mother were so paralyzed with fear that they couldn't move. Gisela screamed when one of the men took her by the arm, dragged her away from her mother, and pushed her out of the room. On the stairs, she felt a rifle at her back. They were herded into the living room where a Red Army commander was waiting for them.

The man looked them up and down before speaking in halting, broken German. "We will take house," he said, gruffly. "You will leave. For safety," he added, looking at Gisela. "Go. Pack."

Gisela and her mother backed out. In the hallway, they skirted soldiers who once again occupied their house. This time, though, Gisela wanted to leave. The Soviet officer was right. It was safer. In her bedroom, she took a big basket, grabbed Erich's letters, a book, a couple of summer dresses, some undergarments, her cardigan, and a brush while her mother watched. Then they went upstairs and did the same for Mama. "Where will we go?" Gisela whispered. "And what about Karl? He is locked in the attic!" She felt panic, rising like cold water, threatening to engulf her completely.

"Hush, not now," her mother hissed. "They might hear and understand."

She pushed Gisela out of the room. They went downstairs and were heading for the front door when one of the soldiers stepped in their way. He looked Gisela up and down. Then, as she raised the basket in front of her, as if she could fend him off with it, he stepped forward and reached for a strand of her hair, pulling it out of her braid, fingering it as he mumbled something in his strange language. Without warning, he grabbed her arm. The basket dropped, and Mama screamed.

Coming out of the living room, the commander took in the scene in front of him. He barked an order, and the soldier raised his hands and stepped away from Gisela, although his eyes still followed her.

"Leave!" The commander shouted. "Now! Go!"

Grabbing the basket, stuffing the clothes, books, and letters back into it, Gisela's mother stood, grabbed Gisela's hand, and pulled her out the front door. They dashed past a group of Russian soldiers who had gathered in the front of their house. Glancing over their shoulders, the women turned into the street, walking as fast as they could, their eyes downcast. They tried to ignore the cat calls and a couple of the soldiers who briefly followed them until they were whistled back like dogs by their commander.

"Where are we going?" Gisela asked as they turned down an alley and finally out of sight. Her mother didn't answer but rushed along. They slid through small alleys and back yards, trying to stay off the major streets and out of sight. "Mama? Where?" Gisela panted, trying to catch her breath.

"To our friends, where else?"

Gisela skidded to a halt, holding her side, staring at her mother. "To Gudrun's? We can't. She betrayed me. Us. She is no longer my friend, Mama!"

"That may be. But her mother is my friend. They will take us in," Mama said, stubborn, her face set.

Gisela stared at her. There had to be someone else.

"What about cousin, Elise?" Gisela asked, following her mother, who had begun walking again. But even as she said it, she knew what the answer would be.

"She has a big family and a small house. We can't burden her. Gudrun and her mother have room and will appreciate the company."

Gisela doubted very much whether Gudrun would appreciate her company. But her mother was right. They had little choice.

"I don't like this. I don't like this at all. I don't trust her, Mama," Gisela mumbled.

Her mother stopped and turned around. "Stop being such a child! Do you think this is a time to fuss over friendships?"

Gisela stared at her; Mama was never sharp.

"Grow up, Gisela," her mother said more gently. "We have to do what we have to do. And there is Karl to think of. I will get word to Georg. He'll be able to get inside the workshop, warn Karl, and hide him somewhere safe. Now, we need to get off the streets. So, let's hurry along."

Gisela muttered under her breath but followed her mother to the end of the alley. They scanned the street. No one was in sight. They ran across, and a few minutes later, knocked on Gudrun's door, looking over their shoulders while waiting to be let in.

Gisela and her mother watched Gudrun peer at them through the window. Then the door opened, and Gudrun pulled them inside. She shut it quickly behind them, throwing the locks.

"The Soviets have sequestered our house," Gisela's mother said, trying to catch her breath.

"Of course, you must stay here," Gudrun said. "My mother will insist you do." As she reached to take the basket from Mama, Gisela eyed her former friend carefully. The welcome seemed genuine enough.

"Where are Dieter and your mother?" Gisela looked around the empty hall, suddenly terrified. Had Gudrun sent the baby away? With the Soviets everywhere? Would she do that?

"They are upstairs," Gudrun said. "And they are well. We have been so worried. No one knows what is happening. They will be so happy to see you," she added, smiling directly at Gisela. "You can have my brother's bedroom, right next to mine."

"Thank you," Gisela still could not bring herself to look at her friend, but then she felt a hand on her arm.

"I'm glad you came," Gudrun whispered. But all Gisela could offer was a nod as she followed Mama up the stairs.

Kneeling in front of Dieter, Gisela put one wooden block on top of another. The little boy waved his fists and toppled them in an instant. Gisela laughed and kissed his forehead. "Then let's do that again. You seem to like it."

Gudrun appeared in the doorway to the living room. "He loves you," she said, smiling as she leaned against the frame and folded her arms.

"He loves blocks," Gisela replied, busying herself with building another tower for Dieter.

"Will you ever forgive me for what I did?" Gudrun asked suddenly. Her smile had vanished. Tears swam in her eyes.

Gisela swallowed hard. "You have never apologized for what you did. Or shown remorse. How can I ever trust you again?" She knew she sounded harsh, unforgiving. But Gudrun had wounded her deeply.

"I am so incredibly sorry, Gisela." Gudrun stepped into the room, her hands hanging at her sides now. "If I could take it back, I would." She wiped at her cheek. "I understand if you can't forgive me or ever trust me again. I don't deserve your forgiveness. I don't. I know that," Gudrun said as she lowered herself down to the old Persian rug to sit down next to Gisela. Dieter took a block and held it out to his mother. She took it and managed a small smile.

"He does love you so," Gisela said, watching Dieter hand Gudrun another block. While she appreciated Gudrun's apology, she needed time. She had always found it easy to forgive, but with Gudrun, it was different.

She was about to say something, to make a comment about Dieter, or something to break the silence between them, when there was a commotion in the street. Gisela turned to Gudrun, who sat frozen, her eyes fixed on the window, listening intently.

"Are our mothers back yet?" Gisela murmured, trying to keep the fear out of her voice.

Gudrun shook her head slowly, her eyes flitting from the window to the hallway and the front door. Food was running short, and their mothers had left that morning to go to a farm on the outskirts of Wallhausen they had heard, that was selling vegetables, eggs, and milk. Gisela had offered, but Mama had pointed out that at their age, she and Gudrun's mama were less likely to draw unwelcome attention from the Soviets. Given their previous experience, that was certainly true. And although she didn't say so, Gisela knew her mother would also try to get in touch with Georg and see what she could find out about Karl.

The noise was closer now. Someone, several someones, were on the front steps. Without speaking, Gisela and Gudrun both stood up, putting themselves in front of the baby. Then they screamed as the front door burst open. Three Soviet soldiers rushed into the hall, and Dieter began to wail.

Rifles dangled casually off their right shoulders. The men stopped in the hall, getting their bearings. Then they looked into the living room, and what Gisela saw in their eyes made her blood run cold. Gudrun grabbed Gisela's hand. Together, they stepped backward as the soldiers came toward them. The men were smiling now. One was missing a tooth. Dieter was screaming.

"Run!" Gudrun yelled, "Run!" She dove for her son, tripping over the blocks, but the soldiers were faster.

Two of them grabbed Gudrun and dragged her into the hallway and up the stairs. Gisela could hear her, fighting, kicking the banisters, screaming her son's name. And she wanted to run, too. She wanted to grab Dieter off the floor. To grasp the fire iron and swing it at this man who stood, staring at her, smirking, licking his lips. But she was paralyzed. Frozen. Then he reached down and began to loosen his belt. Gisela screamed. But he was faster than she was.

Before she knew what was happening, he had grabbed her by the hair and pulled her down the hallway. Gisela could hear Gudrun screaming upstairs and fists pounding. The screams subsided to whimpers as the soldier threw her out the back door. Gisela landed on her side, hitting her head so badly her vision blurred. She caught a glimpse of the pond where she and Gudrun had spent so much of their childhoods playing. Then the kicks started.

The first one caught her in the stomach. Gisela doubled up, hugging her head, trying to protect it and her face. The next kicks landed on her shoulders, then her legs. Then he leaned down, grabbed her, and threw her on her back. Gisela fought. She scratched and bit, and heard a sound, like an animal growling that she realized was coming from her. His fist struck her right cheek, and for a moment, she thought she would pass out. Then he climbed on top of her, and she felt herself choking. Until suddenly, his weight lifted, and he was gone.

Gisela opened her eyes. As she struggled to sit up, she saw Karl beating the soldier. Hitting him over and over again. "Hide!" Karl yelled. "In the shed!"

"Dieter," Gisela murmured. She could no longer hear crying.

"Now!" Karl shouted.

The man who attacked her was on the ground. He appeared to be dead. Gisela stumbled to her feet and staggered toward the garden shed where she and Gudrun had played as children. Slamming the door behind her, she peered through the wooden slats in time to see Karl give one final kick to the Russian soldier's head before he turned and ran back into the house.

Leaning against the door, Gisela tried to catch her breath. Her whole body was trembling. She listened intently. As far as she could tell, the house lay still. There was no noise. For a moment, she considered leaving the shed, but the thought made her lose her breath. Her cheek was throbbing. She put a hand to it and winced at the pain. All at once, voices erupted from the house. Gisela's heart stopped when she realized they were Russian. The back door banged open, and she stuffed her hands in her mouth to stop from screaming.

The two Russian soldiers who had dragged Gudrun upstairs staggered through the door, dragging a bloodied Karl between them. At the sight of their comrade, they cursed and dropped Karl, one of them stomping on his head as he hit the ground. Gisela felt her knees give way. She heard a shot ring out, and when she looked back through the slats, saw one of the soldiers holstering his sidearm while the other hefted the man who had attacked her over his shoulder. They gave Karl one final kick, then turned toward the house.

The silence that followed was interrupted only by Gisela's sobs. Karl lay where he had fallen, blood seeping from the bullet wound in his head. *Karl!* She screamed silently. She didn't want to hide any longer. Gisela burst out of the shed. Running toward Karl's body and then sank down next to him. His eyes were open. As she reached out to close them, Gisela heard a faint whimpering coming from the house.

Her hand froze midair. The whimpering coming from the house tugged at her, but how could she leave Karl like this? He had come for her and saved her from those animals. And now he was dead. Karl had given his life for her, just as Waldemar would have. He had loved her after all.

Gisela stood up slowly, her hand still outstretched, unable to wipe the tears that coursed down her cheeks. She backed away, her foot catching, so she stumbled and flinched at the horrible animal sounding wail that she realized was her own. Bile rose, choking her. Gisela turned and vomited into a bush. Then, she heard the whimpering again and turned toward the house.

Inside, Dieter sat where he had been left, unharmed, blocks scattered around him. Gisela picked him up. She held his tiny body against her own and said a prayer as she made herself step into the hallway and begin climbing the stairs. The upstairs hallway was completely quiet. Ahead of her, Gisela saw the door to Gudrun's room, smashed open, hanging from its hinges. Gisela spotted her friend's body on the floor, next to her bed. She turned into the little room opposite Gudrun's that was Dieter's nursery and placed the baby in his crib. He protested with a wail as she hastened back to Gudrun.

Her friend was still breathing. Gisela pulled the comforter off the bed and covered her trembling body. Gudrun's dress had been ripped to shreds, and her face was so badly beaten that she was barely recognizable. Sinking to the floor, Gisela lifted Gudrun's head into her lap. Gudrun whimpered and grabbed her hand. She mouthed a few words, but Gisela couldn't make them out. Wincing in pain, Gudrun tried to clear her throat. She tried again. Her voice was louder now but sounded foreign and hoarse. "Dieter," Gudrun managed. "Take care–" Her face contorted in pain. "Take care of him."

"Of course I will," Gisela whispered.

She held her friend's hand until it went limp. How she wished she had told Gudrun that she had accepted her apology. That she forgave her. That they were friends. Forever and always. Gisela threw back her head and wailed, her own cries mixing with Dieter's, sharp and raw.

Gisela did not know how long it was before she finally let go of Gudrun. Laying her friend's head down gently, she wiped the hair from her forehead and stroked her cheek. Then Gisela dried her face with her sleeve and went to Dieter's room. He stared at her with big, wide eyes, his face streaked with tears, his cheeks flushed pink. She lifted him out of his crib and rocked him gently, her lips grazing his forehead. Dieter was her responsibility now. She had promised Gudrun as she lay dying. She would protect him for the rest of her life, not matter what it cost her.

Chapter 22

October 1949

Wallhausen, East Germany

Holding Dieter's hand, Gisela entered the office that had once been her father's and was now her mother's. As soon as the little boy saw his grandmother, he flew into her arms. Mama tousled his wispy, blond hair. "And what have you been doing all morning?" she asked.

Dieter looked at her, his face beaming, but he didn't speak. At five, almost six, the fact that he was not yet speaking was of great concern to Gisela. Dieter was an intelligent child who felt deeply. When she read to him, he would nod in acknowledgement, laugh, or even cry at particularly sad sections of a story. He just didn't utter a word. Ever.

Gisela looked around the small room. It was a tidy space now. How her mother managed to keep wood shavings out was nothing short of a miracle. Mama sat behind the desk confidently, as if she had always belonged there. A ledger lay open in front of her. And a letter, Gisela noticed.

"More orders coming in," her mother said, returning her attention to the ledger. "We will need to hire another carpenter soon and even offer a couple of apprenticeships. People are rebuilding. The only problem is the supply of wood."

"Yes, the Russians have taken everything," Gisela replied bitterly.

"This new government is the problem, I fear." Her mother dropped her voice to a near whisper. "The GDR won't have the same comforts as West Germany," she added with a sigh.

A few days ago, their new country, the German Democratic Republic, had been announced and proclaimed in East Berlin. Gisela didn't like the prospect of living under communism, but Wallhausen was their home. Their family had lived here for generations and generations.

"I thought we needed a master carpenter to employ apprentices. Georg is a journeyman."

"Well, that's where I come in," her mother said.

"What do you mean?" Gisela asked. She took a pen from Dieter, who had managed to get ink all over his little hands.

"Georg has been teaching me. I'm working on my masterpiece. If it passes, I will be a master carpenter, and then I can hire apprentices and keep the business. The local government has already threatened to take it over if we can't find a viable solution to keep going and contribute to the welfare of the state," her mother added, her last words rife with sarcasm.

"You're making furniture, Mama?" Gisela was taken aback by this new development.

"I am, indeed," her mother said. "And it turns out, I'm not half bad at it."

Gisela was astounded. Her quiet mother had not only turned into a businesswoman, but she would soon also be a master carpenter. "May I see your piece?"

For a moment, her mother hesitated. Then she got up from her chair. "Alright, let me show you."

She was leaving the room when Gisela's eyes fell again on the letter on the desk. "Who is this from?" she asked.

Her mother paused, her eyes beaming. "I will share it over dinner."

Gisela nodded, pleased that her mother had a secret, whatever it was. She took Dieter's hand, pulling him with her as they followed Mama into the workshop. "But Mama," she asked, "don't you need to be a carpenter first, to be able to become a master carpenter?"

"Oh, I have been one for fifteen years," her mother said. "Your father insisted."

Gisela shook her head. How could she not have known this? She should have. After all, the house was filled with her mama's beautiful creations. The trays with the ornately carved handles, the angel on her nightstand, and the intricate Christmas ornaments. Her mother had been working in wood for years.

The desk she showed Gisela was beautiful, carved and detailed around the drawers and top. "You've made this?" Gisela asked. "It is beautiful."

"It's not finished yet," her mother said dismissively.

"Look, Dieter, your grandma built this desk," Gisela said proudly. Dieter went over to the desk. He ran his little hand across it and turned to his grandmother with a wide smile.

"With Georg's help," Mama said bashfully.

Georg had heard them and came over. "Don't believe your mother. I showed her a few tricks. This is all hers," he said, no less proudly than Gisela.

"Enough of this!" Mama clapped her hands, obviously embarrassed at the praise. "It's supper time, and Dieter must be starving."

"Everything is ready. The table is set," Gisela said and headed out of the workshop. When Dieter didn't come with her, she looked at him with raised eyebrows.

"Dieter can help me straighten things up a little, then we'll wash up." Old Georg smiled at the little boy. "We'll be there right away." Old Georg called after her. Gisela waved in agreement as she made for the door.

"I'll lock up," her mother called.

Gisela gave her a wave as well. Her mother was full of surprises today, and she felt incredibly proud of her. It was women who had stepped in to rebuild after the war when so many men had been lost.

***

At supper, her mother, Georg, and, of course, Dieter, were high-spirited. Gisela eyed the letter on the kitchen counter and wondered if it was the reason for her mother's cheerfulness. Heaven knew they all needed anything they could find to help them forget the horrific war years.

When the table was finally cleared and the dishes were washed, the women joined Georg and Dieter at the table again. The old man was perusing the newspaper, as her father had always done. Dieter was whittling a piece of wood. Gisela reminded him that he shouldn't forget to feed the animals before going to bed, even though she knew he never did. The animals were his world.

At last, her mother took the letter out of the envelope, unfolded it, and flattened it on the table.

"It's from your brother, Heinrich." Gisela looked up. Dieter stopped whittling, and Georg put down the newspaper.

"He writes to say that he'll be released by the Americans and come home next month." She turned to Gisela, beaming. "Your brother is coming home!"

Her mother pushed the letter across the table toward her. Gisela wanted to be happy. She was glad Heinrich had survived. The brother she knew the least. She wanted to be grateful. But all these years, she had hoped for news about Erich, and none had come. She knew she needed to accept that he was gone, but as long as she didn't accept it, it wasn't real.

Her mother stroked her arm as if she knew what she was thinking. Gisela got up and put her arm around Mama's shoulder. "That is the best news," she said, kissing her cheek.

"The best news indeed. We can use the extra help in the workshop," Old Georg said. Heinrich had learned the trade, and Gisela knew his return would not only finally put a man back in the house but also provide some much-needed help running the business. Things were finally looking up for them. She nodded at Dieter. Without delay, he rose from his chair and headed out back to feed the pets they had taken in. Dieter adored all animals and was happiest when he got to spend time with them. She touched his shoulder as he passed her.

As she turned to leave the kitchen, her mother caught her by the arm. "Perhaps," she said gently, "it is time to let go, Gisela."

Gisela pulled the white cloth off the ancient Opel in a big swoop. A layer of dust that had sat on top swirled all around her in the dying sun. She coughed, then had to sneeze. It had taken her until now to convince her mother to let her uncover her father's car. Erich had taught her to drive all those years ago. She told herself it was just like riding a bicycle, something you never really forget how to do. It was a shame that the car had just stood there all these years, unused, out of commission. It had refused to start when the Americans tried to requisition it. The Soviets hadn't moved it either but had removed all four tires and taken them with them. She would have to find some on the black market, get the car repaired, and secure some fuel before she would be able to drive it. First, she decided to start with a thorough cleaning.

Gisela felt almost giddy at the thought of riding in a car again. It had been so long. She opened the driver's side door and slid in. The seats were covered in dirt, leaves, and debris. She put her hands on the wheel and closed her eyes. Erich sat beside her and Karl was in the backseat, pulling her hair. They were laughing at Karl's jokes, and Erich shot her one of his radiant smiles. She sighed.

"It looks good on you," a voice behind her said.

It sounded both familiar and strange. The dialect was not from this region, but she knew it. She had heard it before. Gisela opened her eyes and stared at her hands on the wheel. The worn leather pressed against her palms told her she was awake and here. And that the voice she was hearing was real.

"Gisela?" Her mind had just taken her back a few years, but who she heard now couldn't be here with her, in the flesh. "It's me," Erich said.

She jerked around, and her hands flew to her mouth. It was true. He was here. In the flesh. Erich. Skin and bones. Pale, sunken eyes. Graying hair and equally graying stubble on his chin.

Gisela scrambled out of the car and flew into his arms. He held her tight for a few minutes, then stood back and looked at her. "I'm home," he breathed, his eyes tender and swimming with tears.

"You're home," she echoed and pressed her head against his chest again. She wouldn't let go of him. Not for a very long time.

She didn't know how long they stood there in the dying light of the day.

"It will be wonderful weather tomorrow," he said suddenly. "Look at the sky. It's on fire."

Letting go of him, Gisela let go of him and followed his gaze. He was right. The sky was doused in a bright orange and red. A sky like that would mean the best weather the next day. She felt him studying her and smiled shyly.

"We have so much to catch up on, Frau Schmidt," her husband said with a smile, then took her face between his palms and gently kissed her on the lips.

In the weeks that followed, Gisela found that Erich had changed. He was different. Quieter and subdued. Less cocky and confident. Careful, and at times, distant. During the war, they had never had the opportunity to spend much time together. And with the years of separation, he had become a stranger.

Gisela tried to bridge the distance between them by reading to Erich every night, as she once had. These were their quiet moments. They weren't conversing. They had long ago caught up and shared their experiences from the war with each other. Between them was the silent agreement not to let the past overshadow the present. They never wanted to speak of the war and everything they had lived through, ever again. So, in quietude, Gisela read to Erich to bring them closer. To comfort them. To grieve together. To forget and forgive. To heal. To love again.

One night, Erich took the book from her and closed it. She looked at him in surprise, and the broad smile that greeted her reminded her of the young Erich. He pulled another book from behind his back and handed it to her. It was a poetry collection by Rilke. The hardbound volume looked brand new. Gisela traced the shiny gold lettering with her fingers.

"It's for you," Erich said softly, with a twinkle in his eye. Gisela mouthed a thank you and kissed him, pressing the book against her chest. It was the first gift since his return. Knowing how much he treasured the poet, this book would find a permanent place on her nightstand.

Erich gently pulled it from her and opened it. Gisela let him read to her for a change. She had grown fond of the new, quiet, reserved Erich, and secretly admitted to herself that she preferred him over the young, cocky pilot he'd once been.

Erich had not only been a stranger to her when he returned, but also a complete stranger to Dieter. For weeks, the boy was afraid of this new man in the house, eyeing him from a distance, never drawing close, and rejecting any of Erich's attempts to get into his good graces. But once Erich had physically recovered and Dieter had understood that the stranger loved his mother and would stay around, he slowly warmed up to him.

Two months after Erich's return, right before Christmas, she found the two of them in the workshop. The light was low inside from the overcast sky and the tall frost-blurred windows. Erich was sitting on a tall stool, sleeves rolled up, his shoulders no longer quite as straight as when she had met him. Dieter stood opposite, small hands resting on the wood, eyes fixed on the plane Erich worked in slow, deliberate strokes. Shavings curled away in soft ribbons. Without looking up, Erich slid one of the curls across the bench toward the boy. Dieter picked it up, smiling faintly, and wound it around his little index finger.

"Have you ever used one of these?" Erich asked him.

Dieter nodded and pointed to Old Georg and his grandmother, who were standing deep in conversation by her office. Erich set the tool down, then nudged it toward Dieter. "Here," he said. "Show me. Light hands." The little boy stepped forward, his glance flicking between Erich and the plane. Dieter worked the first pass along the grain. Gisela saw the boy's mouth twitch with pride. She lingered in the doorway a little longer, unseen, watching Erich and Dieter for a few more moments. They were not yet father and son, but they were not strangers anymore either.

Eventually, she walked over to them. "So, what are you two building?" She asked.

Both looked up at her, but only one answered. "Dieter and I are building an aeroplane."

Dieter stretched out his arms and pretended to fly. Pursing his lips, he made a sound like an engine.

Gisela couldn't help but laugh and tousled his blond hair. Erich winked at her, then encouraged Dieter to continue. She kissed Dieter on the head and smiled at Erich, whose eyes shone with quiet pride, as if the three of them had always belonged together.

Epilogue

May 1955

The old oak barely provided enough shade. Its thinned-out branches and sparse leaves belied the once thick canopy in which Erich's parachute had gotten stuck so many years ago. Gisela watched Dieter play chase with the dog, a yellow mutt, that they had adopted a year ago. Dieter had begged for a dog since he was five years old. She had tried to pacify him with rabbits, a bird, a hamster, and a cat. He had loved them all and taken good care of them. Eventually, they had finally given in.

Gisela chuckled as Dieter and the dog rolled around in the grass together. She wiggled her back to find the best spot to rest it against the rough bark of the old oak and closed her eyes for a moment, letting the warm sunlight rest on her face. An occasional shadow caressed her cheek as the wind stirred the few branches and leaves above. The ground smelled of earth and fresh grass. May truly was the most beautiful month of the year. The month she had met Erich.

Gisela felt a pair of warm lips graze her own and smiled.

"It's time to go, Fräulein Fahnrich," Erich teased and took her hand to pull her up.

She opened her eyes, looking into the tanned face of her husband, and slapped his arm playfully. "It's Frau Schmidt," she protested, rolling her eyes dramatically.

Erich's hair had thinned and was now completely gray as if he were an old man, but he was still as handsome as back in 1942 when she had met him for the first time. The years of separation and his ordeal in Siberia had marked him for life, but his cheeks were no longer hollow, and his body no longer that of a starved man.

Gisela let Erich pull her up and lead her over to her father's Opel, parked not far from them in the high grass. Erich called Dieter to come.

"Coming, Papa!" he called back, the dog chasing after him, and together they climbed into the back.

The day Dieter called Erich *Papa* for the first time was etched into Gisela's memory. They had been washing the old Opel together, and when Erich had asked Dieter to pay special attention to the wheel caps, he had answered, "Yes, Papa."

Those had been the first two words Dieter had ever spoken. Gisela and Erich had just gazed at each other in awe. Then Erich had handed the little boy a bigger sponge and replied with "Thank you, son."

Dieter had spoken in complete sentences from that day on, like any other boy his age. It had been the moment when Gisela's world had finally felt complete.

Thinking back on it, she climbed behind the wheel as Erich settled himself in the passenger seat. She loved driving, and he let her. He leaned back and closed his eyes.

"A migraine again?" She asked.

He nodded. Erich had been suffering from migraines daily since his return. In recent months, they had increased in severity. She had urged him to go see a doctor, but he had refused. What could she do? Sometimes she wondered if it would have been better for Erich's recovery if he had returned to his family in Bavaria. Perhaps the climate and better healthcare there would have improved his health. Now, he was condemned to live under the communist regime with her. She knew how big a sacrifice that was. He had made it for her. She couldn't have left her mother and her life, and he had understood that. Wallhausen was her home and always would be.

Different regimes had come and gone, but she had endured. And Erich had returned after all. So many others were only names and photographs now, but here, by her side, was the sum of her fortune. A husband, a son, and the quiet mercy of an ordinary, perfectly beautiful May afternoon.

A Note from the Author

Dear Reader,

Thank you so much for reading *Sky on Fire*. I hope you liked it. Readers like you are everything to authors, and I would really appreciate it if you would take the time to leave an honest review on Amazon—just scan the QR code below. Reader reviews matter a lot. Other readers will appreciate hearing your opinion on the book—and of course, your feedback is very useful to me as I embark on my next books.

Warmest Regards,

C. K.

About the Author

C. K. McAdam writes historical fiction. She holds a Ph.D. in Interdisciplinary Humanities and teaches college. Together with her family, she resides in Texas but hails originally from Germany where she grew up. In her free time, she loves to travel, hike, read historical fiction, play pickleball, spend time with her family, and go on walks with her corgi Merlin.

Subscribe to the author's newsletter by visiting **www.mcadambooks.com** for more info, giveaways, news, and updates.

Connect with the author on social media and don't hesitate to leave reviews. Every author appreciates them very much.

amazon.com/author/ckmcadam

instagram.com/ckmcadam

facebook.com/ckmcadam

twitter.com/CK_McAdam

ALSO BY
C. K. McADAM

The Seamstress of Auschwitz
The Poet's Daughter

www.ingramcontent.com/pod-product-compliance
Lightning Source LLC
Chambersburg PA
CBHW061234310726
48971CB00007B/2068